TO DESECRATE A FESTIVAL

Aana was on her way to the kitchen to check on her teakettle when the front door burst open. In came the dancer.

"What are you doing?!" She aimed her cane at him like a sword. "Who are you?!" she demanded.

Cold eyes glared at her through the thin slits of the make-shift mask.

"Your family will hear of this!" she threatened, backing into the kitchen. "I'll . . . " The rest was cut short by a blow that successfully made it past the extended cane and impacted her chest. Air left her lungs in a heavy grunt and she careened off the stove before hitting the wall and collapsing to the floor like a broken doll.

Lying on her side, fighting to remain conscious, she watched the hi-tops approach. She was dizzy, her limbs numb. Through the impending haze, she saw that the man was holding a four-foot flensing knife—the same kind used to remove the outer skin from a bowhead whale. As he held it next to his masked face, she realized with an unsettling clarity that the *tuungak* had heard and granted her wish: she was going to die on the eve of *Nalukataq*.

Just not in the way she had expected.

Other Inupiat Eskimo Mysteries by
Christopher Lane
from Avon Books

ELEMENTS OF A KILL
SEASON OF DEATH
A SHROUD OF MIDNIGHT SUN

CHRISTOPHER LANE

SILENT AS THE HUNTER

AN INUPIAT ESKIMO MYSTERY

AVON BOOKS
An Imprint of HarperCollins*Publishers*

This is a work of fiction. Names, characters, places, and incidents are products of the author's imagination or are used fictitiously and are not to be construed as real. Any resemblance to actual events, locales, organizations, or persons, living or dead, is entirely coincidental.

AVON BOOKS
An *Imprint of* HarperCollins*Publishers*
10 East 53rd Street
New York, New York 10022-5299

Copyright © 2001 by Christopher Lane
ISBN: 0-380-81625-3
www.avonbooks.com

First Avon Books paperback printing: January 2001

Avon Trademark Reg. U.S. Pat. Off. and in Other Countries, Marca Registrada, Hecho en U.S.A.
HarperCollins ® is a trademark of HarperCollins Publishers Inc.

Printed in the U.S.A.

10   9   8   7   6   5   4   3   2   1

➤➤ AUTHOR'S NOTE ⮜⮜

WITH THE RELEASE of this, the fourth installment of the Inupiat Eskimo Mystery series, I feel it necessary to reiterate two points. First, I am not a Native Alaskan (seven years in Anchorage does not a Native make) and have never resided above the Arctic Circle. In order to portray the noble people of the far north, I have relied on research. Second, I have allowed my imagination to run free in terms of settings and characterization. Translation: the events, places, individuals, and groups portrayed here are largely (in some cases totally) fictional. They are not meant to reflect reality, but to propel the plot forward.

Having issued that disclaimer/confession, let me just add that it is my sincere hope that as you read this novel you will be not only caught up in the mystery, but intrigued by the mystique of the Inupiat (The Real People) as well as motivated to learn more about them and the unique land they inhabit.

Christopher A. Lane

Christopher Lane
2000

UNNUAQ

(NIGHT)

In the darkness and
silence of night,
the tuungak speak.
Their terrible voices are
a cold, whispering wind.

GRANDFATHER ATTLA

➤➤ ONE ◄◄

WHEN SHE HEARD the commotion, the hoots, the hollering and shouting, her leathery face curled into a smile. It wasn't the neighborhood kids arguing over a game of ball, she could tell, or that no-good Ronnie who lived on the next block beating the hell out of his wife again. No, these were the happy, boisterous sounds of festival.

Doddering to the window, she lifted the edge of the curtain and peered out. Yes. There they were: shadows twirling and bouncing like overwrought wraiths in the glow of evening light, members of the umiak crews come to announce the end of the whaling season, the coming of Nalukataq.

This would be her ninety-seventh celebration, she realized, watching the crew work its way up the row of houses. She was old, tired, her body and mind progressively failing her. Her end was near and she sometimes wished it would hurry up and get here. Yet the sight of the men cavorting, faces hidden behind wooden masks, ignited within her a spark of childlike excitement. She felt giddy, young . . . alive. If every day was Nalukataq, she mused, waving a frail hand at the approaching dancers, she might never die.

Anticipating their arrival, she took her cane from beside the stove and started for the front door. She was entering the Arctic entryway, a small foyer that served to keep winter's cold air and the summer dust out of the house, when the first series of knocks came. Three heavy thumps. Chuckling at the thrill this produced, she called raspily, "Coming!" There was a second knock, and as she hurried to answer it, breath now labored, bad hip aching from the effort, she decided that if she passed on at this moment, expired en route to greet the whalers, it would be as a happy woman. What better time to exit this world than on the eve of the whale festival, so full of hope and enthusiasm?

Upon reaching the door, she pulled it open and pretended to be startled by and a little afraid of the figure occupying the porch. The man was dressed in fur-fringed mukluk boots with long, dangling tassels, a pair of nondescript black pants, and a white shirt with a zigzag pattern along the bottom cuff. The blouse wasn't as elaborate as the ones she had sewed for her late husband half a century before, she thought to herself, but it was adequate. At least the man wasn't wearing threadbare jeans and a T-shirt with a sports company slogan on it, like some of the young folks did nowadays. His mask, she noticed, was authentic, probably handed down from a father or grandfather. Fashioned of wood, it had a round, almost domed face with thin slits for eyes and a thin smiling mouth. A black band ran across the nose, signifying status. The wearer was either the head of a crew, or the second in charge.

Fanning out from the sides of the face were wing-like appendages with jagged edges that bore hand-drawn whales.

"Nalukataq!" the dancer shouted.

She nodded back, laughing as the man performed an awkward jig and nearly fell off the porch.

"Tomorrow we celebrate the whale!"

"AgviQ," she agreed.

"Uh?"

"AgviQ," she repeated, a little disappointed. "The bowhead."

"Ah . . . yes, ma'am." The man made a clumsy circle, hopped off the step, and ran to catch up with his friends.

She watched him go, then closed the door and began shuffling back to the kitchen. A whaler that didn't know the Inupiaq word for the very beast he hunted for months each year? It was shameful, but unfortunately, not that surprising. Nowadays young people seemed to have little respect for the old ways. Despite being taught Inupiaq in school, many of them acted wholly uninterested in their heritage. This frightened her. If the traditions and language weren't carried on, The People would lose their way. Lose themselves.

Which was another reason not to give herself over to the grave just yet, she thought with a hint of amusement. The youngsters had to be taught the history of The People and trained in the ways of the Elders in order to be adequately prepared for the challenges of living in a white man's world. That foundation was essential to their survival. Once it was laid, they could act like naluaqmiut if they wanted to, sit on their

behinds and watch television, play basketball instead
of practicing seal hops and high kicks, shop at the grocery store rather than look to the Land for their provi-
sion. But at least they would know who they were,
where they came from, that they were Inupiat: The
Real People.

Working at the Cultural Center once a week was her
way of helping to keep the Inupiat identity alive.
Spending her Friday afternoons in the center was a
small, but necessary investment in future generations.
Though most of her time there was taken up with busy
work—filing, pasting newspaper articles into scrap-
books, dusting various displays—every so often she
was afforded the opportunity to share her experiences
and knowledge with children. Today, for instance, she
had led a second grade class from the elementary
school on a tour of the museum, concluding with a sto-
rytelling time. With dozens of fresh, innocent faces
looking up at her, she had recounted folktales about
Bear Woman, Caribou Man, Kajortoq the White Fox,
and the ever-mischievous Raven. Remarkably, the
youngsters had listened with rapt interest, laughing at
the antics of the characters, blinking at her with wide
eyes as the stories took unexpected turns, nodding their
heads at the moral lessons.

There was still hope, she told herself as she laid
aside her cane in favor of a teapot. She filled the pot
and set it on the wood stove before checking the flame.
Low. Nearly gone. What a fitting portrait of the Eskimos of the remote north. The fire of The People continued to smolder in the hearts of some. But it was
dying and might be extinguished altogether if not care-

fully tended and stoked. Adding a small log to the stove, she watched as tongues of fire leapt up and began consuming it. Children. They were the ones who would keep the flame alive.

She closed the stove, and was about to go to the pantry cabinet for tea, when there was a knock at the door. Three heavy thumps. Probably the whaling crew making another pass through the neighborhood, she guessed, sharing the news of festival a second time. And who could blame them? Nalukataq, no matter the year or the quality of the season, was cause for joy.

Retrieving her cane, she hobbled toward the door, pain radiating through her hip with every step. Either the weather was about to change or the tuungak were telling her that danger was near. Or she had overdone it at the Cultural Center. Though she was as ardent in her belief of the ruling spirits and their ability to influence daily life as anyone in Barrow, the third explanation made the most sense. Being around the kids had been fun and satisfying, yet had left her depleted. It had taken most of her strength to give the tour and relate the tales. In return, she had received grins, hugs, a feeling of accomplishment, and a lingering fatigue. Not a bad deal.

The knock came again. "Coming!" She was panting by the time she reached the door. Taking hold of the knob, she pulled it open and found herself standing face to face with another dancer. This one was taller, his shirt made of denim without design or beadwork. He was wearing jeans with oil stains on the knees. On his feet were a pair of ratty hi-tops. His mask was cardboard, poorly cut, the whale images crudely drawn in black crayon. The seven-year-olds who had visited the museum that afternoon could have managed more fitting creations.

Despite the man's pitiful attire, she forced a smile. When he didn't speak or dance, but simply stood there stupidly, one hand behind his back, she prodded, "Have you come to announce the celebration of the whale?"

He twisted his head from side to side, either looking for something or answering in the negative. She couldn't tell which.

Losing patience, she asked, "Is this your first festival?"

He twisted his head again, seemingly checking the road, which was now empty and quiet.

"What's the matter with you? Can you speak? Are you drunk?"

As if in answer to her questions, the man abruptly tried to push his way into the house.

She reacted by swinging her cane at him, striking him in the leg. This caused him to swear softly and draw back to the porch. "I didn't invite you inside!" she admonished. "Now go on! Dry out!" She slammed the door. "Today's young people . . ." she muttered in disgust. To desecrate a festival with such inappropriate behavior. . . .

She walked stiffly through the entryway and was on her way to the kitchen to check on her teakettle when the front door burst open. In came the dancer.

"What are you doing?!" She aimed her cane at him like a sword. "Who are you?!" she demanded.

Cold eyes glared at her through the thin slits of the makeshift mask.

"Your family will hear of this!" she threatened, backing into the kitchen. "I'll . . ." The rest was cut short by a blow that successfully made it past the extended cane and impacted her chest. Air left her lungs in a heavy grunt and she careened off the stove before hitting the wall and collapsing to the floor like a broken doll.

Lying on her side, fighting to remain conscious, she watched the hi-tops approach. She wanted to get up, to get away, to shout for help, but couldn't move or utter a sound. Something inside was broken. She was dizzy, her limbs numb. Through the impending haze, she saw that the man was holding a four-foot flensing knife, the same kind used to remove the outer skin from a bowhead whale. As he held it next to his masked face, she realized with an unsettling clarity that the tuungak had heard and granted her wish: she was going to die on the eve of Nalukataq. Just not in the way she had expected.

UVLAAQ

(MORNING)

At dawn the tuungak hide
their faces but not their eyes.
They are always watchful.
Always watchful.

GRANDFATHER ATTLA

➤➤ TWO ◄◄

TAUT, SLENDER BICEPS flexing, relaxing, flexing in perpetuity. Fists drawing oblong circles in the air, forearms falling from chest to side, reaching back up again. Knees rising with the smooth efficiency of alternating pistons.

Each stride was a study in grace, each breath a perfect duplicate of the last, lungs and feet working to create a peaceful, almost meditative rhythm that somehow matched the morning: sun perched on the horizon like a jewel, ice floes transformed into a thousand hills of gold, open shallows of the Chukchi Sea glaring fiercely, sandpipers congregated on the shoreline, flittering in and out of tangled heaps of driftwood on desperately thin legs. Overhead, the sky was a portent of good fortune. Ablaze in colors, it was marred only by a small pink-crowned cloud that floated like a lazy hand, fingers reaching to point down at the sleeping community.

As he ran up the thin spit of land toward the Point, mind serenely detached from the effort of his body, Justin was reminded of the song that would be sung that afternoon at the festival. Without voice, without breaking form or stride, he silently recited the words.

> *Great AgviQ, most elusive, AgviQ*
> *Hiding in the sikuqqat, hiding from our umiak*
> *Until the time of blessing, when anuiaq is come*
> *And the nauliguan from hunter's hand is thrown*
>
> *Quyanaqpak, quyanaqpak*
> *For parka, maktak, niqipiaq*
> *May your kila know our happiness*
> *O, AgviQ, know our happiness*

His placid smile grew and he unconsciously quickened his pace, excited by the prospect of dancing, eating, singing, games . . . The length of the celebration was variable, determined by the number of whales taken that season. In good years, it lasted up to a week. This year, however, had not been very good, therefore Nalukataq would be only one day. But that didn't bother Justin. No matter how brief, this festival would be one to remember. Not only would he be drumming for his school's dance team, but he would be competing in the five-kilometer foot race. It was just for fun and he would win his division easily, even if forced to run backwards with his feet tied together. Still, it would afford him another opportunity to impress Julie Foxglove.

Julie's face superimposed itself across his vision— perfect eyes, perfect cheeks, perfect lips—and Justin misstepped, slipped, and nearly turned his ankle in a rut. *Concentrate!* he told himself. This was no time to lose focus. The state meet was just two weeks away. Which was why he was training like a mad man, putting in nearly 80 miles of road work a week, and would abstain from some of today's games. The blanket toss in particular was infamous for injuring participants. State was his big chance. His only chance. If he did well, took one of the top three spots, he just might be able to snag a track scholarship to an Outside college— Washington, Oregon, maybe even Southern Cal.

This line of thought caused him to accelerate further. Now he was moving close to top speed, doing what his coach referred to as a fartlek: a run that interspersed fast and slow sections at regular intervals. He had to force himself to slow down. Tomorrow was fartlek day. Today was his long run. He would go out on the Point and back, logging 20-plus miles. It was supposed to be a relaxed run in which he paid attention to his form and further built up his endurance.

Pushing images of the festival and Julie and the fun run and Julie and the state meet and Julie out of his head, he gazed up the road and could just make out the Department of Wildlife facility poking out of a thin mist that had settled over the northern end of the peninsula, blurring the marriage of land and sea. Off to his right was the suburb of Browerville. Like the rest of Barrow, it was quiet and still: streets deserted, houses shuttered, windows dark, many covered with aluminum foil to keep out the midnight sun.

That was the great thing about running, he told himself for the hundredth time. The solitude. When you got up and took off at five in the morning, you had things to yourself. No traffic, no people. Just the ever present spring light and a deep, expansive calm: his own breath, the tapping of his shoes on the gravel, a gentle whisper of wind as his body parted the air.

He could tell that the endorphins were kicking in, coursing through his bloodstream. He felt feather light, his youthful legs indefatigable. It was almost as though he were floating . . . gliding . . . flying toward the top of the world.

A row of houses materialized in the distance. Straining, he could just make out the third from the corner: single-story, wood in need of paint, rusty metal chair sitting in the middle of the yard. It was his aunt's home. Aana, he called her, for she was actually his great aunt. She was old—how old, no one was quite sure—and seldom ventured from her home anymore, except to work in the museum. And to attend the festivals. Justin was sure she would be at Nalukataq to hear him drum and to watch him race.

Leaving the road, he followed a trail that dissected a field of waist-high grass. Every time he ran to the Point, he made this little detour to offer his respect to Aana. Though he never stopped for longer than a minute or two and always politely declined her offer of refreshments, she seemed to appreciate the gesture. And no matter how early he arrived, he always found her up, usually fussing over her backyard garden. Since the passing of Uncle, she had become rather nocturnal, active at night, napping periodically throughout the day.

Reaching the street, Justin decided to sprint the remaining quarter of a mile. So what if it didn't jive with his training schedule? Today was special. Today was Nalukataq. He was so energized he could hardly

stand it. Knees jumping, legs stretching, arms swinging, he did his best impression of Michael Johnson.

Sweat was running down from his hair, stinging his
eyes, by the time he reached Aana's driveway and
broke the imaginary finish line tape, chest pushed forward to emulate Johnson winning another 400-meter
dash. Panting, thighs burning, his smile swelled as he
trotted in a recovery circle. He was a machine. A running machine. Forget finishing in the top three spots at
state. He would take first, the gold medal. A full-ride
to USC would be forthcoming. By next fall, he would
be wearing gold and maroon, doing his workouts in
Trojan Stadium. The USC fight song echoed in his
head.

He raised his hands in victory, acknowledging the
cheers of the invisible crowd and was about to head
around back to see if Aana was brooding over her cabbages when he noticed movement at the corner of his
vision. Whirling, he saw a blur of white whisking over
the rooftops. It swooped toward him and abruptly lit on
Aana's mailbox. A snowy owl. About the size of a
hawk, but fuller in body and white as ice.

"Hoo!"

Justin watched it primp, beak working over its feathers. He couldn't remember encountering an owl after
sunup. And such a brash one! Perched just six feet
from him, it acted as though it had either never seen a
human being, or was intimately familiar with and
therefore unconcerned with the species. Some tanik
tourist must have made the mistake of feeding it
scraps, Justin surmised. Now it was hanging around in
broad daylight expecting to be fed.

His fascination with the bird quickly wore off,

replaced by a sense of duty and a tinge of fear. According to tradition, snowy owls were a sign of both new life and impending death. They were a portent of heaven.

Though Justin wasn't certain he really believed that, he knew that Aana did. Already frail, the woman spoke often of preparing for her trip to qilak, the afterworld. Seeing an owl in front of her house would alarm her and might possibly convince her that death was coming to claim her.

"Get away!" Justin yelled, waving his arms. "Go visit someone else!"

The large bird flapped its wings, but didn't take off.

"Shoo!"

The bird hooted back at him, its gaze alert and intense.

Justin glanced around, looking for something to throw at it. If the owl wouldn't leave of its own accord, he would drive it away with force. He was kneeling to gather a handful of gravel from the driveway when the bird suddenly lifted off.

"Lucky for you!" he muttered, letting the pebbles drop. He rose and was heading for the backyard when the bird landed on the roof above Aana's porch.

"Hoot!" It actually seemed to be taunting him now.

"Why, you . . . !" He balled up a fist, took a step forward, and then forgot about the bird as his eyes drifted from the roof to the front door. He blinked at it and for a long moment, couldn't decide what he was seeing. The face of the yellow home was bleached to a pale cream by the low sun. Two windows acted as wide-set eyes. The awning over the porch formed a square nose. And a rectangle of darkness created the illusion of a mouth—an open mouth. The door was standing wide open.

Something's wrong. Justin shivered. The admonition raced through his mind again, accompanied by a host of horrible images: Aana falling . . . dragging herself to the door . . . opening it . . . passing out before she could call for help . . . The nightmarish scene shifted and in his mind's eye Justin saw an intruder breaking in, assaulting Aana, stealing what few valuables she had . . .

There were any number of reasonable explanations, he told himself, trying to quell the rising sense of panic. Maybe she had simply forgotten to close the door. Or maybe she had failed to get it latched. Something along those lines. He would go in and find her fixing breakfast, oblivious to the fact that her door was standing open.

As Justin approached the house, the owl began hopping along the eve, making chattering noises that almost sounded like derisive laughter.

"Shut up!" he told it.

He ascended the porch and peered inside. "Aana?" Nothing. Even the imbecilic bird was quiet for the moment. "Aana?" He rapped his knuckles against the door. "It's your nephew, Justin."

The owl hooted and chirped.

Stepping across the threshold, Justin leaned through the entryway and examined the small living area. It was undisturbed: trinkets on the shelves, pictures propped up on the old wooden chest that served as a table. He moved further in. "Aana?"

Outside, the bird was growing more agitated, talons ticking on the ceiling like a shower of hail.

"Aana?" He moved further in, glancing at the kitchen. The tabletop was free of dishes. A kettle sat on the wood stove. Turning his attention to the hall, he listened for sounds of movement. "Aana?" Was she sleeping? Occupied in the toilet? He took a step toward the bedroom, then hesitated, uncomfortable with the idea of barging into his aunt's private living space. The best thing, he decided, was to check out back first. He would probably find her in the garden, on hands and knees, attending to her vegetables.

En route to the back door, he traversed the kitchen. As he was passing the stove, it hit him: kettle on the burner. He stopped and stared. Aana never set her kettle on the burner unless she was making tea. He lifted the teapot by the handle. It was empty, the bottom smoky black. Was her memory finally starting to go? he wondered. She had apparently gone off and left the pot to boil dry. He looked in the stove and found that the fire was out. Good thing. Otherwise, she might have burned the house down. Except . . . why was the fire out? She would need it to cook breakfast.

Puzzled and a little worried by this, he was closing the stove when he noticed something on the floor, under the table: a small square of wood. He knelt and picked it up. It was a tile bearing the carved face of a frowning woman. One of Aana's charms. The female. Justin glanced up at the wall and saw its counterpart, the male, a charm fashioned of lighter wood, smiling down on him. He stood and tried to affix the frowning charm to a nail protruding from the plaster next to the male, but failed as the tile snapped in half. He set the two pieces on the table, carefully uniting them to recreate the sad woman's face. Aana would be disappointed.

The charms had been given to her by her father, Justin's great-great-grandfather, who had once used them in his umiak to ward off evil.

Justin instinctively bowed his head in reverence to his ancestor and to the charm, which was now ruined and would no longer be effective in bringing good luck. As he did, he realized that the linoleum in the rear hall was covered with a thin swipe of mud. This wouldn't have been remarkable except for the fact that Aana was a fastidious housekeeper. Despite a bad hip and persistent arthritis in her hands and shoulders, she kept an immaculate home. If someone tracked mud across the floor, she would have admonished them verbally and then immediately mopped up the mess—or made the perpetrator do it.

Edging around the table, he saw that the smear led away toward the back door. *Something's wrong*! He bent down and ran a finger through the mud. Not mud, he realized in horror. Dried blood. "Aana . . . ?"

He went to the door, pulled it open, and was about to push through the screen when he spotted a colorful swatch of fabric caught in the jam. It was ragged, about the size of a child's sock. He recognized the pattern. It was from Aana's favorite atikluk dress, the one she liked to wear for festivals.

"Oh, God! Aana?" He hurried onto the back porch, letting the screen slap shut behind him. "Aana?" Leaping into the yard, he raced for the garden: cabbages the size of basketballs, overzealous squash vines . . . no Aana.

He called her name two more times, half expecting her to emerge from behind a rhubarb bush and ask him to stay for breakfast. Staring down at the swatch of fabric, he tried not to panic. Where was she? What had happened? What should he do?

Tell someone. He had to tell someone. He glanced at the back door. He could call 911. No. Aana didn't have a phone. And besides, what would he tell them? He didn't need an ambulance. He needed . . . help. The police?

At this, his body seized control. He ran around to the front of the house, jumped the crooked picket fence that bordered the side yard, and started up the street at a pace that would have made a world class sprinter envious. He ran across the field, up the trail, along the road. He ran without conscious effort or fatigue, without emotion, without noticing that his legs and lungs were screaming at him to stop.

Run! an inner voice demanded. And he simply obeyed it. Rushing through the empty streets of Barrow, he dashed through the blanket toss area, cut beneath the fun run banner, zigzagged recklessly through the silent tents where Eskimo ice cream would be served that afternoon. With his endurance finally beginning to wane, he entered a neighborhood, rounded a set of corners and spied his destination: a modest, two-story home with a Blazer parked out front.

Calling forth every reserve in his being, he gritted his teeth against the pain that was flowing through his chest, focused on the name stenciled next to the doorpost, and ran toward the letters A-T-T-L-A as though they represented an Olympic gold medal.

"Ray! Wake up!"

He opened his eyes and found that he was hugging

his knees to his chest, sheets and blankets tangled around him like shackles. He shivered before realizing that he wasn't chilled anymore, wasn't in the water, wasn't drowning.

"Are you okay?"

Still dazed, he glanced over at Margaret and tried to catch his breath. It had all seemed so real.

"Another nightmare?"

He didn't answer.

"The same one? Where you fall through the ice out on the floes?"

She knew him too well. He nodded, sighed, and wiped perspiration from his neck.

"I think you should talk to someone." She began unraveling the covers. "A counselor or . . ."

"I'm fine."

"If you were fine, you wouldn't dream about it every night."

"Not every night."

"Most nights." Smoothing the sheets, she pulled them up around his chin, then snuggled in close, an arm and a leg slung over him. "I worry about you because I love you." When he didn't respond, she added, "It's natural to be disturbed by a traumatizing experience like that."

He shook his head. "It just doesn't make sense."

"What doesn't?"

"I'm a cop. I've had dozens of 'traumatic experiences.' I've been shot at, chased, beaten up . . . remember the caribou trip? I nearly drowned a couple of times."

"You never told me . . ."

"I almost froze to death up on the Slope." He sighed

again. "I've been to the whaling camps out on the floes since I was a kid. I was never that scared."

"Think about it though. Now you've got four people at home to provide for, take care of, love . . . That's a lot of responsibility. A lot of stress."

"You make it sound like part of some midlife crisis."

"No. You're too young for that."

He frowned at the ceiling. "Maybe not."

She slid over on top of him and rubbed her nose back and forth against his.

"What are you doing?"

"We're Eskimos," she laughed. "I'm giving you an Eskimo kiss."

He rolled his eyes. "Somebody made that up for the taniks because it sounded exotic. I've never in my life seen an Eskimo, much less an Inupiat, kiss like that."

"Well, now you have." She laughed again and gave him a real kiss. "Better?"

He knew that she was trying to cajole him into a better mood, and despite his best efforts, it was working. "Yeah," he muttered.

"Today's festival. I order you to have a good time."

"Oh, so you're my boss?" He grabbed her by the shoulders and rolled her over so that he was on top.

Looking up at him, she said matter-of-factly, "You bet I am. And you like it that way."

He laughed at her.

"So listen up, buster. This is the first time you've had Nalukataq off since we've been married. The kids want us to take them to the blanket toss."

"The blanket toss? They're too young. Especially Freddie."

"I wish you wouldn't call him that."

"It's better than Alfred. Every time I say that, I think of your father."

"That's the point. Naming your first male child after the maternal grandfather is a way of showing respect. If you don't like Alfred, try Al."

"Al . . ." He shook his head. "Sounds like an auto mechanic."

She sighed. "Anyway . . . He'll be fine on the mini blanket. So will Keera. They're really gentle with the little guys."

Ray grunted, unconvinced.

"My point is, you need to relax, try to forget about that thing out on the pack." She pulled his face down and kissed him. "Have some fun." She gave him a longer, more passionate kiss, and her hands began to stroke his back.

"*This* is fun," he admitted.

"I knew you'd see it my way."

He was in the process of removing her top when something clunked behind him. He twisted his head and flinched when he saw a figure standing next to the bed.

"Raymond! Some-body at door!"

He swore softly. "Grandfather, what are you doing in here?!"

"Ray . . ." Margaret cautioned, pulling the covers up.

"Some-body at door," the old man repeated grumpily.

"Then why don't you answer it?"

"Dis not my house."

"It is now. You live here, right?"

"Not dressed," the old man sniffed.

"Do I look dressed?" Ray asked incredulously.

"Get door," Grandfather grumbled, walking away. "Udderwise, I can't get no sleep."

Ray sat up. "That man . . ."

". . . Deserves your respect," Margaret quickly inserted.

"He's been here for a year."

"Nine months."

"Whatever." He slipped out of bed and began pulling on a pair of jeans. "I've warned him I don't know how many times about wandering into our bedroom like that."

"You have to be patient with him, Ray. He's getting old."

"Old, my eye. He's been playing that old business to the hilt, pretending to be half-senile since I was a teenager. He knows what's going on." He stood and zipped his pants. "We've gotta get a lock for our door." He plucked a T-shirt from the dresser. "What time is it, anyway?"

Margaret turned over and squinted at the clock. "Five-something."

"Geez . . . who in the world . . . ? It better not be Lewis. Or what'shisname from up the street."

"Harold."

"Yeah, Harold. I told him the last time he showed up drunk, banging on the door, that I'd arrest him if it happened again."

"He locked himself out of his house. And it was forty-below."

"That's what he gets for drinking." Ray padded into the hall. "Should have taken him to the station anyway, just for smelling like booze. Barrow is dry for a reason, you know."

"Ray . . ." Margaret called after him. "Good mood, remember? Hurry back and we'll pick up where we left off."

"Mmm-hmm," he mumbled. With his luck, she would be fast asleep when he returned. As he approached the stairs, he heard the knocking. Whoever was out there was enthusiastic about gaining entry. Probably Harold. Or maybe Billy Bob, playing a prank, getting even for having to work Nalukataq. Thank goodness they didn't have a doorbell, otherwise the idiot would have woken the . . .

"Who is it, Daddy?"

He turned and saw Keera emerging from her bed-room, a stuffed Pooh under her arm.

"I don't know, honey. Go back to bed."

"But I'm hungry. Can we have pancakes?"

"Not until later. Much later."

"Pam-cakes?" a shrill voice chimed. And here came Freddie, aka Alfred, toddling out of his bedroom, car-rying a Tigger.

"How'd you get out of your crib?"

"Pam-cakes," he repeated, rubbing his eyes.

Ray scooped him up in his arms and started down the stairs. Keera trailed after them. "Pancakes, huh?"

"Yah!" both kids shouted.

At the door, Ray looked through the peephole. All he could make out was a fist pounding on the door. "Who's there?"

"Uncle Ray?!"

"Who's Uncle Ray?" Keera wanted to know.

"I am. And whichever nephew this turns out to be had better have a good reason for . . ." He opened the door and Justin Clearwater nearly fell inside. He was sweaty, out of breath, eyes wide in terror.

"Justin? What's the matter?"

"It's . . . Aana," he panted, bending in half.

"Aana Clearwater?"

The boy nodded without looking up from the ground.

"What happened?"

"I don't . . . know . . . something . . . something . . . bad."

➤ THREE ◄

"WHAT'S WRONG? Is she sick?"

Justin shook his head, huffing at the ground.

"Hurt? Did you call 911?"

"It wouldn't help. She's . . . She's . . . I don't know."

"Take it easy." Ray set Freddie down and opened the door wider. "Why don't you come in and we'll . . ."

"We have to go! Right now!"

"Where?"

"To Aana's house! You have to see it!"

"Okay. Let me get my keys. Come in for a second."

Justin took a step backwards. "I don't want to. We need to hurry! You have to come!"

"Wait in the Blazer then. It's open. I'll be right out."

Justin nodded and staggered toward the driveway.

"What's wrong with Aana?" Keera asked.

"Aa-na!" Freddie chimed.

Ray closed the door and frowned at them. "I don't know. I guess we'll find out."

"You mean me and Freddie get to go?"

"It's Freddie and I. And no. You two need to stay here with Mommy."

"And Ataata," Keera pointed out.

"At-aa!" Freddie shrieked.

"Right. Mommy and Grandfather."

Ray led them back up the stairs and they ran into the bedroom. Keera jumped into the bed and Freddie climbed up, pulling off half the spread in the process.

"What are you two doing up?" Margaret asked.

"We get to stay with you and Ataata!" Keera said excitedly.

"At-aa!" Freddie squealed.

"What?" She raised up and looked at Ray. "Who was at the door?"

"Justin," Ray answered. He collected his keys and wallet, his holster and badge from the dresser. "He thinks something might have happened to Aana."

"Aana Clearwater?"

Ray nodded.

"What?"

"I don't know. But Justin's pretty upset, so . . . I told him I'd go out there with him and have a look." He bent down and kissed her on the forehead. "How about a raincheck on . . . *you know*."

She nodded, obviously concerned about Aana.

He hugged the kids.

"Can you make pancakes first?" Keera asked.

"I'll make some when I get back."

"Promise?"

"Promise."

"Be careful," Margaret said. She cautioned him like this every time he left for work.

"I will," he answered, as always.

"I love you."

"Love you too."

It was a ritual parting they had adopted to compensate for the uncertainties that were a part of his job. Police work, even in the sleepy town of Barrow, Alaska, was risky, unpredictable work. There was always a chance that he wouldn't be coming home once he walked out the door. They had mutually decided that if the unthinkable ever happened, they wanted their last communication to be a meaningful one.

Ray found Justin in the Blazer, perspiration glistening on his face, neck, and arms. He was shivering and looked pale. Ray pulled a polar fleece jacket out of the back. "Here, put this on." He started the car and waited until they were out of the neighborhood before asking, "So what's going on?"

Justin wiped his face with the sleeve of the jacket. "I don't know, Uncle Ray." He paused, then explained, "I was running. Today's my long run and I was headed for the Point. I stopped off at Aana's, like I always do on long runs. And . . . I don't know. There was an owl on the mailbox."

Ray glanced over, wondering if perhaps Justin was in shock or suffering from hypothermia. One of the first signs of the latter was groggy thinking.

"An owl?"

"A snowy owl. I tried to get it to leave . . . but it wouldn't, and . . . then I noticed the door was open and . . . I went inside and . . ." He shook his head.

"And . . . ?" Ray prodded.

"And there was . . . there was blood."

"Blood?" Ray felt himself tense a little and he instinctively pressed down on the accelerator.

"On the floor. Dried blood. And a piece of fabric caught in the back door. From Aana's festival dress."

"There was no . . . ?" Ray paused, reluctant to use the word *body*. "You didn't see Aana anywhere?"

Justin shook his head. "Just blood and the piece of her dress."

Ray's mind ran through a dozen scenarios, including one in which the old woman cut herself with a kitchen knife and staggered out the door looking for help.

"Did you check the garden?" He knew that the garden was what kept her going. She spent hours tending to it and was famous for the crop she brought in.

"Yeah. But . . ." He was still shaking, despite the jacket, and his teeth had begun to chatter.

Ray flicked on the heater and urged the Blazer down the Point road with a heavy foot. They reached the cut-off into Browerville a minute later and Ray barely slowed for the turn. They skid wide, the back end fish-tailing and he had to twist the wheel hard to regain control and keep from going into the ditch. He made a right onto Aana's street and came to a halt in front of the house.

"Stay here," he told Justin.

Hopping out, he unbuttoned the cover on his holster. Chances were, Aana was at a neighbors, having her finger bandaged and lamenting the fact that she had been careless while slicing vegetables at the sink. Or out in the shed, preparing to hang caribou meat on her drying rack. Had Justin checked the shed? The blood could have been from the meat. There were a thousand explanations that did not involve tragedy or foul play. But as Ray approached the house, he stuffed his hand inside his jacket and gripped the butt of his gun. His training told him to be ready for anything, that was how you stayed alive and enjoyed a long career as a cop. Experience told him to trust his instincts. And right now, his instincts were telling him that something was wrong. He could feel it.

When it came to police business, he didn't put much stock in the tuungak. The spirits and their supposed activities and influence upon man were part of the old ways, creations of the Elders meant to entertain, teach, and also keep people in line. With the threat of punishment from unseen entities always looming, you tended to watch your step in terms of behavior. But the bit about the owl had disturbed him nonetheless. As a kid, he had been entranced and a little frightened by Grandfather's stories about the power various animals exerted and their ability to foretell the future. As an adult, he dismissed the stories as lore and myth, yet a hint of that fascination and fear remained.

He stopped on the porch and examined the door. It was shut. Justin had said it was standing open. Apparently he had shut it on his way out. Except . . . the poor kid had been nearly hysterical. Ray made a mental note to ask about that and to clarify exactly where the boy had been and what he had done—if and when this turned into something other than an inability to locate a rather eccentric and decidedly old aunt. Surely she would turn up.

The knob was in good shape and gleamed as though it had just been polished. The lock was intact. There were no scratches or marks to indicate that it had been tampered with. He paused to withdraw a pair of leather gloves from his jacket pocket. Pulling them on, he carefully tried the knob, hoping not to smudge any fingerprints that might be there. The knob clicked and turned.

Pushing the door open, he called, "Aana!" Silence. "Aana!" He waited a second, glanced at the doorjamb, which, like the lock, was in fine shape, and stepped inside.

The living room was in order: Native artwork standing on the shelves, knitted pillows arranged nicely on the sofa. The carpet was freshly swept. Ray could see the indentations from the wheels of the vacuum.

He continued into the hall and went to the bedrooms. One was set up as a sewing and craft room. A wide table held an old sewing machine and several photo albums. On the other wall, fabric and yarn had been stacked into wooden cubbies.

Ray went on to the other bedroom. "Aana . . . ?" he called from the door. Even as a policeman and a concerned relative, he felt a little awkward about going into her bedroom. What if Justin was wrong and she was sleeping? Or worse, cleaning herself up?

"Aana?" The house was quiet, and Ray's gut told him that it was empty. Still, he paused, listening for the telltale signs of occupation. When none came, he stepped into the bedroom. The bed was made, the pillows fluffed, the bathroom dark and empty. Thankfully.

Relieved at this, Ray opened the closet with a gloved hand: clothes, another photo album, shoe boxes. No corpse. Which is what he had been thinking about and dreading ever since Justin had shown up at his door, huffing and puffing. While Aana was amazingly spry and quick-minded for her age, Ray knew that her time was coming. One of these days he would receive a call to come out and arrange a body transport.

Hopefully not today, he thought as he closed the closet and returned to the hall. In the kitchen he looked around, looked under the table. No blood. No mud. No dirt. It was immaculate, as always. Aana allowed for nothing short of perfect neatness.

He felt the wood stove. Cool to the touch. The teapot was sitting by the sink, and the counter free of debris, as was the table. Both had been cleared and wiped.

Ray started into the back hall, thinking to himself that if he didn't find the swatch of Aana's dress in the door, he would start wondering about Justin. Was the kid running too much, too far, too hard? Was it affecting his mind? Wasn't it true that ultra-long distance runners sometimes had hallucinations?

He got to the door and scowled at the hinges. Unless the swatch was microscopic, Justin had been mistaken. He covered his hand again with his sleeve and pulled the door open. He checked the other side, the jamb, the lock, looked out at the path leading to the garden. All seemed to be in order.

Two questions arose as he closed the door and went back down the hall to the kitchen. First, where was Aana? Second, what was up with Justin? The former needed to be addressed. Any time an old lady wasn't where she was supposed to be, you needed to be concerned and find out why. The latter . . . Ray had known Justin since he was born. He'd always been a good kid, always stayed out of trouble. He was at that risky age now, the time when young people experimented with drugs and sex and alcohol. But Justin was an athlete. He lived to run and, as far as Ray knew, wouldn't even think of polluting his body with chemicals or exposing himself to a STDs or premature fatherhood. So why the story? Was he looking for attention? Had he fallen while running, hit his head, gone crazy?

Ray went through the living room and the Arctic room, closed the front door and was going down the steps when he noticed the watering can. It was dull metal and had been there as long as he could remember. For decoration, he assumed. Sometimes there were flowers protruding from it, or dried things that looked like stalks of wheat. The watering cans Aana used for her garden were green plastic and she kept them around back.

Ray blinked at the watering can. There were no flowers or dried stalks in it. But there was a rolled up piece of paper. He reached over and pulled it out. Pressing it flat, he saw that it was a handwritten note:

Clara,

My sister in Wainwright has taken ill and I am going out to stay with her. I should be back in a few days, God willing. Please water the garden and help yourself to the rhubarb pie in the ice box.
Thanks so much.

Aana Clearwater

Case closed, Ray thought with a smile. The missing aunt had been located. Justin's fears, though well intentioned, had been unfounded.

"What's that?"

He looked up at Justin.

"A note. It says Aana went to visit her sister in Wainwright."

"Really?" Justin held out his hand and Ray gave him the note. His eyes narrowed as he read it.

"Something wrong?"

"Well . . . yeah." Justin tapped the note. "For starters, Aana's sister in Wainwright is Aana Nelly Clearwater."

"So?"

"So Aana Nelly died last spring."

"She did?" Ray took the note back and examined it. "Maybe she meant a different sister."

"She doesn't have another sister," Justin informed. "And then there's the thing about the pie."

Ray reread that part: help yourself to the rhubarb pie in the ice box. "What about it?"

"Aana doesn't make pies. Clara does. Aana grows the rhubarb and Clara makes pies out of it."

"I remember that now." Ray shook his head, angry at himself for being so accepting and ready to take the note at face value, while simultaneously disappointed that the note had failed to explain Aana's disappearance.

"Then there's the signature."

Ray looked at it: Aana Clearwater. "Right. She wouldn't sign Aana in a note to Clara. Clara is her friend and knows her by . . ."

"Hillary."

"Geez . . ." Ray rubbed his eyes. Maybe it was the fact that it was still before six on a holiday or that he was anxious to get back to his family and prepare for festival. Whatever the reason, he was being terribly unobservant. "Good catch, Justin."

"What did you think about the blood and the dress?"

Ray started to tell him that there hadn't been any blood or dress swatch and that he had forgotten to look for the charm. Instead, he put the note back into the watering can and took Justin by the arm.

"Show me."

⋙ FOUR ⋘

RAY REACHED FOR the doorknob, but stopped before opening it. "When you left here earlier, did you close the door?"

"Uh . . . no, I just . . . I ran. I was afraid something had happened."

Ray opened the door. "Maybe Clara shut it."

"I doubt it."

"Why?"

"She's not an early riser like Aana."

"Is that right?"

Justin nodded. Ray liked him. He was a good kid, a smart kid, with an eye for detail, which came in handy if you were in law enforcement.

"Don't touch anything," Ray instructed as they moved into the living area. "Where was the blood?" Ray asked.

Justin led him to the kitchen. "Right there." He pointed at the tile under the table.

Ray squatted and ran a gloved finger over it. Smooth, clean, nary a speck of dust.

"It was there," Justin insisted.

"I believe you," Ray said. And he wasn't just saying that. He really did believe the kid. Why would he make up a story like that?

"And the charm . . ." Justin looked at the table, then to the cabinet. "I left it right here."

"What charm?"

"One of her charms fell off the wall." He turned to the remaining charm, the male face. "I picked it up and it broke. So I just laid it on the table."

Ray glanced at the wall where the male charm was grinning at them, then at the tabletop. It was as clear and clean as the floor. No placemats, no napkins, nothing.

"The piece of dress was down here," Justin went to the back door. "Right in here." He pointed at the middle hinge.

Ray nodded, frowning.

"I saw it."

"I know." Ray pulled the back door open and stepped out onto the porch. The morning was pristine, sunny and clear. Perfect for festival. He glanced down at the porch. It had been recently swept. He stepped into the yard and went to the garden. It was flourishing, as always, plants growing to tremendous sizes, the rows neat and free of weeds. The dirt in between each had been neatly raked. He looked beyond the garden, at the shed.

"Did you check the shed?"

Justin shook his head.

Ray made his way through the garden, gingerly pushing through the enthusiastic branches. As he was about to emerge from the far end, he noticed a muddy spot. He paused and bent over it. The rake had been dragged through it, but thanks to the mud, part of a boot print remained.

"Does Aana have anyone help her with the garden nowadays? A handyman or anything?"

"Not that I know of."

"Watch your step here," Ray told him. "Don't walk on that track." He rose and noticed that a branch from a rhubarb bush had been snapped off and hung limply next to the boot print.

At the shed, he found the door padlocked. "Know the combination?"

"No."

Ray went around to the side window. It was milky, almost opaque.

"You know, Uncle Ray," Justin said. "Maybe I over-reacted. I mean, the blood's gone so . . . Maybe Aana cleaned it up. Maybe she just cut herself in the garden or . . . or maybe it was just mud and . . ."

Ray cupped his hand, trying to see inside the shed. The sun was at just the wrong angle, glaring off the glass.

"What we should probably do is check next door at Clara's."

"You said Clara was a late sleeper." Ray rubbed the glass, but the layer of dust and cobwebs was on the inside.

"She is. But if Aana cut herself and went over there . . . then came back and cleaned up the kitchen . . . or Clara did . . . then . . . then they went back next door for coffee?"

"Maybe." Ray tried to pry his fingers into the side of the window. It appeared to be unlatched, but was stuck. It probably hadn't been opened since the shed was erected some thirty years back. "Can you give me a hand?"

Justin went over and they both pulled. Suddenly it slid back and hit the opposite end of the sill with a thud and a pop. "Oops." Justin made a face at the jagged crack in the glass. "Aana's gonna kill us, Uncle Ray."

Ray stared inside. "I don't think so." He moved Justin away with an arm.

"What?"

"Go back to the porch."

"Why?"

"Just do it."

Justin shrugged. "Okay." He started into the garden, then stopped. "What are you gonna do?"

Ray waved him away. "Go!"

"I'm going."

Ray waited until he saw Justin hop onto the porch before sticking his head through the window. There between a plastic watering can and a collection of shovels and hoes was an overturned wheelbarrow. Ray had seen that much through the glass. What he hadn't seen was the blood. At least he thought it was blood. A pool of something that looked almost purple in the early morning light was seeping out from under the rim of the upturned wheelbarrow.

"Did you find something?" Justin called from the porch.

Ignoring him, Ray pulled himself up and awkwardly tried to squeeze through the window. It was a tight space, almost too narrow for his hips. He twisted and managed to scrape through, smacking the back of his head against the sill in the process. When his feet had found the floor, he brushed himself off and looked around. The shed reeked of manure. There was an old plywood cabinet on one side bearing a pair of gardening gloves, a trowel, a sack of what appeared to be fertilizer, and several empty pots. On the other side was an old snow machine, more tools and shovels.

Ray bent down and examined the floor next to the door. It was clean. No dirt, no mud, no seeds, nothing. Next to the door was a broom. He eyed the broom before going to the wheelbarrow.

As he approached, he could tell that the liquid was blood. No other substance had that thick, sticky, glossy appearance. It had formed a design that resembled North America, a main body with four red/purple arms reaching out crookedly from the corners, and the surface had dried to a thin crust. Like a lake freezing over, Ray thought.

He paused for a moment, hoping that he had discovered an animal, a fox perhaps, that had gotten trapped in the shed. Maybe it had tried to chew its way out and injured itself, or been injured already and come here to find a place to hide and die. Part of him wanted to believe that. But the rest knew a fox would have a tough time slinking into a locked shed and slipping under an overturned wheelbarrow.

He shook his head and a fragment of a prayer that Margaret had tried to teach him floated through his mind: *Deliver us from evil.* It could have been anything—an animal, part of a caribou carcass, a chunk of whale blubber—but something told him that what he was about to uncover was not "anything." It was evil.

What was it Justin had said about the owl? One had come and perched on Aana's roof? According to Grandfather and the old ones, that was an omen. It meant that someone was about to go to the afterworld. That someone was about to die.

Ray shivered and told himself to quit being silly. He took a breath, let it out, took hold of the handles and lifted the wheelbarrow. And there she was, just as he had expected: balled up in a fetal position, head tucked down, knees tucked up, arms clutching legs, gray hair obscuring her face. He felt her neck out of habit. There was no pulse, but he hadn't expected one. She had already set out for qilak.

He took the trowel from the cabinet, crouched down and lifted her hair, just to make sure that the woman lying motionless in Aana's shed, in Aana's backyard, next to Aana's garden, wearing Aana's favorite festival dress was in fact, Aana. Her features were empty and the glow that had been her life was gone. But, yes, it was her.

He looked for the source of the blood but couldn't see it. Had she been stabbed? He used the trowel to push her hair away from her neck. It wasn't cut. Her back didn't have any noticeable wounds. He rolled the body slightly. The blood had soaked the dress along the shoulder, torso . . . It seemed to come from either the leg that was against the floor or the hand gripping it. He couldn't tell which and returned her to her initial position.

Rising, he decided to wait until he had backup to do any further investigating. There wasn't a coroner, per se, in Barrow. But when necessary, they called in a doctor from the hospital, usually Melissa Bradshaw. She was young, bright, and had arrived in Barrow the previous fall. Ray had worked a few cases with

Melissa and found her to be very competent. He had also found her to be rather charming.

Ray went to the door and tried to open it before remembering about the padlock. He turned back and looked at the body. Someone had killed Aana, covered her up with the wheelbarrow, and locked her in. She probably wouldn't have been found for a day or two, maybe longer given that it was festival and things were hectic, if it hadn't been for Justin. And the open door. And the blood on the floor. And the dress swatch.

None of that made sense. Why hide a body but announce the crime with sloppy cover-up work? Unless Justin had shown up right after the event and before the assailant had time to clean things up. Maybe the murderer had been out in the shed, disposing of the body when Justin had appeared, curious and worried about Aana. Except . . . why not close the front door?

Ray made a mental list of things he needed to check: where Aana had been on Friday, if she'd been seen last evening by the neighbors, what time Justin had come by this morning, what time the victim had . . . what time *Aana* had passed on. Melissa could probably tell him. Unless she was off for festival.

Ray realized that, according to tradition, he shouldn't go to festival today. He'd been in contact with a dead body. That in itself was taboo. If he went to festival now, he would displease the tuungak and bring bad luck to the whalers. Or so the Elders said. It had been an off season this year. Could next year be worse?

All of that was moot, of course, given that he had just stumbled onto a murder. The chance that he would get anywhere near festival now was slim to none.

He went to the window and considered climbing out. No. This was a crime scene and needed to be preserved as such. Besides, the back of his head still smarted from climbing through the narrow sill. He stuck his head out the window and squinted into the sun. "Justin?"

"Yes, sir."

"Would you call my office, please?"

Justin raised his eyebrows. "Your what?"

"The police. Call the police."

"Why?"

"Just do it."

"Okay . . . but . . ."

"But what?"

"Aana doesn't have a phone."

"Go next door, then. Find a phone, call the police. Ask for the captain. Tell him where I am and that I need backup with a fingerprint kit, camera . . . bolt cutters . . ."

"Bolt cutters?"

"Yeah. And I need a silent ambulance."

"A what?"

"An ambulance—no siren."

Justin's face paled.

"I know," Ray consoled. "This will be hard for all of us. But I need your help. Are you okay?"

"Yes, sir," he answered unevenly.

"Good. Have the captain call in Melissa Bradshaw—Dr. Bradshaw. Got all that?"

"Yes, sir."

"Oh, and call my wife. Tell her I'm going to be tied up for a while." Ray put his hand to his brow and saw Justin nod.

"You . . . you found her, didn't you, Uncle Ray?"

"Yeah," Ray sighed.

"Is she . . . ?"

"She's dead, Justin."

"Should I . . . ?"

"Just make those calls, like I asked. Okay?"

"Yes, sir."

When Justin had disappeared into the house, Ray glanced back at the body and realized that the smell of manure was now competing with another smell: the stench of death.

⊷ FIVE ⊷

TWENTY-SEVEN MINUTES PASSED before the back door swung open again and Justin came out onto the porch. He was followed by a man in jeans and a hat, carrying a suitcase. Squinting into the sun, Ray could tell that the hat was of the cowboy variety and knew it had to be Billy Bob, a member of the Barrow Police Department by way of Texas. As he watched the two of them come down the steps and into the garden, Ray wished he had specified that Lewis be sent. Billy Bob was a good cop, but didn't understand the ways of The People. He wouldn't appreciate the delicacy of handling a murder case on a festival day. Beyond that, he had a weak stomach and would probably loose his breakfast at the sight of Aana lying there in a small lake of blood.

"Well, now . . ." the cowboy said as they pushed through the garden. He was smiling, buck teeth hanging out, and obviously had no idea why Ray had called for backup.

"Watch that muddy spot!" Ray cautioned.

"Oh, these boots ain't new," he said, planting a heel in the mud. "These here's my kicking around boots."

48

"Stop!" Ray ordered.

Billy Bob stopped.

"Crime scene."

"Huh?"

"This is a crime scene."

Billy Bob's face fell. "It is? Why didn't ya say so?"

"Isn't that a fingerprint kit you've got there?"

"Yeah."

"That's so we can dust this place. There's been a murder."

"A murder?"

Ray grit his teeth together and mentally removed the "good cop" status he had given Billy Bob. Sometimes he could be a dope.

"I got a call at home from the captain and he said to get the kit and hot-foot it down here to Browerville. He didn't say nothin' about no murder."

"Well, I'm saying it. Be careful. Try not to track up the mud."

Billy Bob moved slowly, with wide eyes.

"Did you bring the bolt cutters?"

"They're in the car."

"I'll go get them," Justin volunteered.

"Thanks." Ray waited until Billy Bob was at the door. "Dust the lock and the handle."

He nodded, set down the case and got out the kit. As he worked, Ray asked, "Have you got evidence bags?"

"You betcha."

"What about the ambulance?"

"Uh . . . don't know about that. I do know that they had it at the festival grounds yesterday, all done up with streamers and balloons to lead the runners in today's big race. So it might be a few minutes, gettin' here."

"I guess there's no hurry," Ray muttered. "How about Melissa . . . Dr. Bradshaw?"

"Nope. Don't know about that, either."

Justin came back with the bolt cutters. This time he was followed by a woman. When they came out of the garden, she spotted Ray in the window of the shed. "I hope you've got a good reason for waking people at the crack of dawn. I had night shift and didn't get to bed until about an hour ago."

"Sorry." He watched her pause at the mud, look down, then tell Justin to step around it. No wonder he liked this woman. Not only was she attractive, but she paid careful attention to details.

Coming to the window, she asked, "Body?"

He nodded.

"Who is it?" She poked her head in.

"Aana Clearwater."

"Ah . . . geez . . . what happened?"

Ray shrugged.

"Can I get in there for a better look?"

He liked that about her too. She was eager. What he didn't like was the fact that whenever she was around, he felt the need to impress her. Neither did he like the subtle sense of guilt that flickered in his heart, reminding him that he was married and that appreciating this woman was tantamount to betraying Margaret. Nothing was going on or would go on. They were just friends.

"Billy Bob's going to cut the lock as soon as he lifts the prints."

Melissa looked over at Billy Bob and said hello. The cowboy responded with, "Mornin', ma'am."

She handed her bag through the window to Ray. "Help me in."

Ray set the bag down, took her hands and began pulling her up. He steadied her waist as she slid through and she came to rest so close to Ray that they were touching hips and arms. "That was fun," she said grinning. Before Ray could decide if she was just joking or actually flirting with him, she went over to the body. "Well . . ." Donning a pair of surgical gloves, she felt the neck for a pulse, then began circling it. "Can't tell where the blood came from."

"I couldn't either."

She stooped down and Ray watched as her pants tightened around her derriere. "You shoot pictures yet?"

"Uh . . . no." He called to Justin and had him retrieve the camera from Billy Bob. Melissa waited, crouching, pursing her lips at the body. As Ray began to snap off shots, she asked, "When did you find her?"

"About a half hour ago."

"No sign of a puncture wound." She continued moving around the body, pulling back whenever Ray was ready to take a picture. "A few minor laccrations and contusions on the face. Could suggest a struggle." Lifting Aana's hair with a pen, she observed, "Neck looks okay. No bruising to suggest that she was strangled." She retracted her arm as Ray took another picture, then lifted the hair again. "Here we go."

"What is it?"

"Contusion just above the right temple." She examined it. "From a blunt object." She looked around the shed.

"Maybe she fell and hit her head," Ray suggested. "She's fallen before. Last year she fell and broke her hip."

"Or maybe the other way around."

"What?"

"When you get old, your bones get brittle and break more easily. Chances are, when she fell and broke her hip, she actually broke her hip first, then collapsed."

Ray snapped another half dozen shots from varying angles. "I think I'm done." He turned around and clicked off a series that would record the interior of the shed and its contents, then handed the camera out the window to Justin. When he returned to the body, Melissa handed him a pair of the latex gloves.

While he was putting them on, she got out a miniature tape recorder and activated it. After dictating the date and time, she said, "Victim is female, approximately . . . ninety?" She looked at Ray for confirmation, but he shrugged. "Found lying on her left side, holding knees to chest. Contusion to left temple . . . minor abrasions to face . . ." She clicked it off. "Help me roll her."

They gently turned the tiny woman to her right side. It was an easy job as Aana's body was already stiff and seemed reluctant to give up the fetal position. Her clothing was soaked with blood, the skin of her arm sticky with it.

"Oh, man . . ." Ray pointed at the gap in Aana's left hand. Her ring finger was missing.

Melissa nodded and switched on the recorder again. "Ring finger of the left hand has been severed." She looked around, as though it might have been misplaced and left on the floor. "Body is rigid suggesting the first stages of rigor mortis . . . which would put the t-o-d at . . . let's see . . . about . . . eight hours ago."

Ray glanced at his watch and considered this. Eight hours ago put the time-of-death at 10 P.M.

"What's this?" Melissa used her pen to slide something out of the pool of blood. It was a face carved in ivory.

"The charm," Ray said. It was stained red now and the frowning woman appeared sinister.

"What charm?"

"The one that Justin broke."

Melissa picked it up and turned it over in her gloved hand. "Doesn't look broken to me."

Ray went to the window and had Justin fetch an evidence bag. He put the charm into it before stuffing the bag into his jacket pocket. "Billy Bob, you about done?"

"Gettin' there," a Texas accent called back.

"We need the kit in here."

"Gimme two more minutes."

Ray went back to the body and looked at Melissa expectantly, hoping she could tell him something useful. She wasn't using her recorder and had stopped jabbing and poking and prodding. She was just crouching there, staring.

"What is it?"

She sighed at him. "There isn't enough blood."

Ray looked at the pool and cringed. It seemed like quite enough to him.

"So . . . either the finger was severed after her heart stopped, or . . ."

"Or?"

"It was severed in another location and then the body was transported here. Or maybe both."

Ray thought about Justin's description of the kitchen: blood on the floor, a dress swatch in the door hinge. "Okay . . ."

"Either way, the loss of the digit wasn't the cause of death."

"What was?"

"The blow to the temple." Melissa was looking at Aana's hand. "Why take an old woman's finger?"

Ray tried to come up with an answer, but couldn't. In a motion picture he had seen a collection agent take a man's finger for failure to pay a debt. But that was the movies and no one would strong-arm an old woman. Would they? "Maybe we're getting ahead of ourselves."

"What do you mean?"

"Isn't it possible that the finger was severed accidentally—that she got it caught in a piece of machinery, or—I don't know . . . lost it somehow? Then she fainted from shock and hit her head on the way down? Or . . . maybe got pulled down and . . ."

Melissa was shaking her head. "Not enough blood."

"Right . . ." Besides, he thought, even if the explanation proved to be true, how would Aana cover herself with a wheelbarrow. No matter how he looked at this, it seemed to shout: murder.

"And it would be very tough to lose an inside finger without so much as scratching the others," Melissa continued. "It's not easy to cut through bone. I mean, it would take a sharp instrument in the hands of someone who wanted that particular finger."

Ray trembled slightly as shivers danced up and down his back.

"I'll expedite the autopsy and see if I can come up with something more solid for you."

"Thanks."

"That's assuming you can get permission from the closest relative."

"That shouldn't be a problem." What will be a problem, Ray thought, was explaining this travesty to that closest relative. So far, it seemed pointless and random.

Ray's mind began trying to organize the pertinent information into some sort of logical whole: an attacker breaks into Aana's house . . . no, wait . . . the door wasn't forced. She let him in? Then he clubs her or hits her with his fist. Next he cuts off her finger. Talk about sadistic. Imagine the pain. Then the sicko drags her to the shed and covers her with a wheelbarrow. It was like something on the national news—a horrific crime carried out in L.A. or New York. Not Barrow.

There was a noise at the door, a clunk, and it swung open. Light streamed in. Ray looked up and saw Billy Bob holding the bolt cutters, a big smile of accomplishment on his face. Beside him was a small man wearing a Chicago Bulls T-shirt under his police jacket. Ray recognized Lewis Fletcher.

"What you got?"

Before Ray could answer him, another shadowy figure appeared, this one short, overweight, wearing a tie and a heavy frown.

"Hey, captain," Ray called gravely.

The captain stepped into the shed and looked down at the body. Lewis came in behind him, but stopped short.

"Aiiya!" Lewis took a step backward, grimacing. "Auk!"

"There's blood all right," Ray sighed.

The captain blew air at the body. "Tell me that's not who I think it is." When Ray didn't say anything, the captain asked, "PiyaqqugniQ?"

"No. It couldn't have been an accident, sir." Ray quickly filled him in, offering up the half dozen or so bona fide facts they had gleaned thus far.

"So what you're saying is . . . homicide?"

"I'm afraid so, sir."

The captain rubbed his face and swore. "Of all the days . . . why during festival?"

➤➤ SIX ➤➤

"EVIL SUANNAN," Lewis muttered, sounding spooked. "Much bad luck."

"Have you notified next of kin?" the captain asked.

"No, sir."

"Let me do it."

"Yes, sir."

"What happened?" Billy Bob, who had yet to set foot inside the shed, leaned forward and gawked at the body. His eyes grew wide, his face went pale, and he hurried out.

The captain sighed, "Aana . . ." He swore softly. "Who the hell would do this to an old woman?"

They were silent for a moment.

"She was one of the last of her generation."

Ray nodded. Aana was a contemporary of Grandfather's. Her husband had been an umialik—a whaling captain. After his passing, she had gone on as a keeper of the old ways.

"Did you know she was my sixth grade teacher?"

"No, sir."

"And at the museum . . . the kids loved her. She

taught them to respect and value their heritage." The
captain sighed again and deflated a little. "She'll be
missed."

"Evil suannan," Lewis muttered again from beyond
the door. "Bad luck."

The captain whispered part of an Inupiaq prayer:

> *Receive our dear one*
> *O, Watcher of the Land*
> *In your arms*
> *Carry her to her rest*
> *To the house of sivulliQ*
> *Her new home: qilak*

"A-men," Lewis grunted.

The captain shook his head sadly and left the shed.
The others followed. Outside, Billy Bob was doubled
over, breathing hard.

Ray was about to tell him to go back to the station
and down some Pepto-Bismol or something when a
figure appeared on Aana's back porch: Native, even
shorter than the captain, more overweight, with a skull
that was hairless, except for low, bushy eyebrows.

"Perfect . . ." the captain muttered at the ground. He
cursed, then brightened artificially and turned toward
the porch. "Mayor Hodish."

The round ball of a man leapt off the porch and wad-
dled through the garden as though he were late for a
meeting. Ray hurried over to keep the boot print from
being further ground into the mud.

"Mayor . . ." Ray greeted obsequiously. He didn't
like Hodish and didn't know anyone who did. The man
was an ill-tempered control-freak who had only three

goals: power, money, and the elevation of the Inupiat tradition to something of a state religion. In Ray's mind, the man was a menace and never should have been elected to office.

Hodish didn't slow, speak, or even give Ray a courtesy glance. He simply strode directly up to the captain, short arms swinging, and demanded, "Well . . . ?"

"It's a . . . uh . . . a homicide, sir," the captain informed reluctantly.

Hodish huffed. "You gotta be kidding me."

"No, sir."

"We haven't had a murder in eons. Why does it have to be now? Why on festival of all days?" He turned and swore at the sky. "This is going to be a publicity nightmare."

Another reason not to like the man, Ray thought. He had yet to ask who the victim was. His only concern was how it might affect his public image.

"Do you know how many tourists are in town for Nalukataq? Do you?"

The captain shook his head and when the mayor turned his angry gaze on Ray, he shook his head too.

"Record numbers. Three times as many as last year. Three times! We've got news crews from Anchorage, Fairbanks, Juneau, reporters from Outside. There's even a documentary film team from the Discovery Channel shooting a piece on whaling."

"Da guy from A-B-C iz here too," Lewis added. "I saw him. Gonna do something down at da blanket toss."

"Yeah, like report a murder." The mayor ran a beefy hand over his chubby face. "Why now? Why me?"

"Sir, I'm sure that . . ." the captain started to say.

"Let me tell you what I'm sure of," Hodish interrupted. "I'm sure that unless we handle this in just the right way, we're screwed."

Ray noticed the use of *we*, implying that the mayor was a member of the police force and would actually be involved in the investigation. Which was not true.

"And what is the *right* way?" the captain asked. Ray could tell from the look on his face, a mixture of contempt and outrage at the man's lack of respect for the dead, that the captain was about to lose his patience.

Hodish held up a fat finger. "Quickly." Another thick finger flicked up. "Quietly."

"We weren't planning to shout it from the rooftops," the captain said, giving voice to what Ray was thinking. "Or drag our heels, *sir.*"

The mayor was oblivious to this bit of insubordination. He stepped to the shed and glanced inside. "Aiyaa!" He turned away in disgust. "I can see it now, headline news across the Lower 48: Murder in Barrow." He huffed again. "What a nightmare."

"Sir, we'll handle it as diplomatically as possible," the captain said. "Of course, we'll have to close the airport, alert the council . . ."

"You're not listening, captain," Hodish interrupted. "It has to be quiet. You can't close the airport or alert the elders."

"But sir . . ."

"Any suspects?"

"Not yet. We just arrived on the scene."

Ray nodded as Hodish glared around, as though looking for confirmation.

"A nightmare . . ." He shot a glance back at the shed,

as if all of this were an *inconvenience* and Aana's fault to boot. "You've got twelve hours."

"Sir, you can't be serious. To investigate fully, we need . . ."

"I'm totally serious. You've got twelve hours from right now." He checked his watch. "If you don't have someone in custody by six P.M. heads will roll." He cut his eyes at the captain, implying he'd be the first to go.

Ray finally spoke up. *"Sir,"* he said, barely able to get the word out, "a homicide investigation can run days, weeks, months . . ."

"This one won't."

"Depending on how it lays out, it could . . ."

"I don't want *could*. Festival ends tonight."

"It ends at sunup tomorrow," Ray corrected.

"The tanik won't hang around that long. They'll be leaving tonight," Hodish said forcefully. "If one of them did it, I want to know before they scatter to the winds."

Ray clamped his mouth shut, determined not to lay into him. There was no way it could be done that quickly unless the perp waltzed into headquarters and confessed. They wouldn't even be done documenting evidence or looking for witnesses by 6 P.M.

"Do whatever it takes. Deputize more men. Skip your donut breaks. I don't care. Just clean this up." A finger rose again, this time aimed at the captain. "Quickly." The companion flipped up. "Quietly. I don't want any of the media to pick up on this. Got it?"

Somehow, the captain managed to say, "Yes, sir."

"Ki! Get with it! I'll be in touch." He stomped back through the garden and disappeared into Aana's house.

Or, what had once been Aana's house. Despite Hodish's complete lack of sympathy, she was dead. The victim of a heinous crime. A crime they were supposed to "clean up" quickly and quietly so that Hodish didn't look bad. The jerk.

"How did he get to be mayor?" Melissa muttered.

"I didn't vote for him," the captain said.

"Me neither," Lewis said.

Ray shook his head, agreeing.

"He gave out nice T-shirts," Billy Bob said. They all gave him the evil eye.

The ambulance pulled up and parked with two wheels in the sideyard. The captain waved the driver and his assistant over.

"You ready to have her loaded out?" he asked Ray and Melissa.

They both consented and the ambulance team, clad in plastic gloves and face shields, went to work, carrying a stretcher into the shed.

"Okay . . ." the captain sighed. "We all see the mayor's point, right? We need to do this quick and quietly." He didn't sound convinced or enthusiastic. "But I also want it done right."

Heads nodded.

"Melissa, obviously you've got the autopsy. We need the results ASAP."

"Will do." She smiled at Ray with tight lips and then stepped into the shed to assist the ambulance team.

"I'll have Betty field calls. No matter how covertly we handle this, it'll leak and people will want to know what happened." He paused, then looked at Lewis. "You're in charge of evidence."

"Aiiya . . ." Lewis groaned.

"Do it by the book: document each bag, write it up, take everything back to the evidence locker." The captain ran a hand over his face, then addressed Ray and Billy Bob. "You two work the site. I want it dusted, printed, photographed . . ."

"We already done that, sir," Billy Bob said.

"The house too. Everything. I want pictures. I want hair. I want blood. I want you to knock on doors and see if the neighbors know anything." He stopped when the ambulance men came out of the shed bearing the body. Aana looked small and shriveled, her face almost unrecognizable. All of the joy, energy, and passion that had comprised her life had departed, leaving only a pathetic, empty outer shell.

As they were loading her into the ambulance, the captain said wearily, "Let's get on it."

Ray could tell that the case had hit the captain hard. His normal management strategy was to yell and cajole and treat them like errant children. If they screwed up, he breathed fire. If they were in trouble, he was the father who could handle anything. But right now, he seemed shaken.

Ray watched him leave, then helped Lewis collect the evidence bags that Billy Bob had filled. "We'll give you a call when we finish up here."

Lewis nodded, clearly nonplussed about his assignment as a glorified errand boy. "How come you guys get to work da site?"

"Just lucky, I guess," Ray said with heavy sarcasm. Working the site would be dull and laborious and would require hours and hours spent searching meticulously for things that probably weren't there. By the time they finished, the festival events would be over, his family would be disappointed, and unless some earth-shattering break presented itself—a bloody, fingerprint laden weapon hidden in the closet—there would be no way they would even come close to apprehending a suspect by Mayor Hodish's ridiculous, arbitrary deadline.

When everyone was gone, Ray asked Billy Bob, "You want the neighbors or the house?"

The cowboy considered this carefully. "Probably be best if I took the house."

Ray frowned. The house was easy compared to knocking on doors and trying to get information from people without giving out any. "Why's that?"

" 'Cause they's yer folk. I think they'd open up more to you."

Yer folk? Ray thought. It sounded a little bigoted. But for once, Billy Bob was right. They were his folk. He'd grown up with many of them, knew just about all of them. They trusted him as a police officer and a friend. Billy Bob, on the other hand, was relatively new and decidedly white.

"Okay."

"What about me?" Justin asked.

Ray looked over at the boy. "Why don't you go home?"

"I don't want to. I want to help."

Ray started to tell him no, but changed his mind. Though he looked fine, Justin had to be grieving. They all were. Lending a hand with the case might enable him to work through some of it, bringing a modicum of closure to the terrible tragedy.

"All right. You're with me."

➤➤ SEVEN ◂◂

"GET THIS FOOTPRINT before you work the house," Ray told Billy Bob. He knelt down and examined the mud. The indentation had a grid pattern, like something left by a work boot.

"You think the killer made it?" Billy Bob asked.

Ray shrugged. "No idea." He was still reeling from the fact that an old woman had been murdered. In Barrow. Tiny, sleepy Barrow. Not just murdered—savagely executed.

He took an extra evidence bag out of the kit and left Billy Bob to the task of casting the print. With Justin trailing after him, Ray walked around the house to the front door. The note was still in the watering can. He plucked it out and scanned the text again before locking the note into the bag. He stuffed it into a jacket pocket and glanced up and down the street. "Eeny, meeny, miney, mo . . ."

"It would go faster if we split up, Uncle Ray."

"No. Let's stick together." He didn't want to hurt the kid's feelings, but he was just that: a kid. He had no experience in police matters and might miss something important. Letting him tag along was enough of a favor—and a risk.

"Let's start next door." Ray eyed his watch as they walked to the house next to Aana's. It was pretty early to be doing a door-to-door. But the arrival of the ambulance and all of the hubbub with the mayor and the captain and the police officers had probably roused some of the closest neighbors from bed. Besides, it was festival and the activities started at 7:30 with a pancake feed.

As they approached the first door, Ray saw eyes looking out at them from between the curtains. He stepped onto the porch and knocked.

The door jerked open and Clara Brown grinned at them. She was a tiny woman, even smaller than Aana, with a face shaped like a moon and an infectious smile. "Aarigaa! Ray-mond At-tla!" She doddered out and gave Ray a hug. Then she noticed Justin and her eyes lit up. She readjusted herself in a series of tiny steps and hugged him too.

"Have you come to tell of Nalukataq? Hmmm . . . where your masks? Hmmm . . ." Her voice and hunched manner reminded Ray of Yoda from the "Star Wars" movies.

"How are you, Clara?" Ray asked in a raised tone that he hoped compensated for her poor hearing.

"Aarigaa!" she chimed. "How is anyone not good on festival?" She laughed.

"Uh . . . we were wondering if you happened to see Aana . . . uh, Hillary, last night?"

"Celery?"

"Hillary," Ray repeated more loudly.

"Hillary?" She looked past them, at Aana's house. "She is my friend."

"I know that. But have you seen her recently? Did you see her yesterday evening?"

She blinked at them and then her eyes widened. "Yesterday the dancers came." She nodded, bending her upper body toward the ground, like she was bowing.

"Of course. But did you see our aunt last evening?"

Clara's face shrank into a frown. "Was she dancing?"

"No. I just wondered if . . ."

"Agnaq not spose to dance for agviQ."

"I know women aren't supposed to . . ."

"It taboo—of-fend da tunngak."

"Yes. But . . ."

"Bad suannan."

"I understand. But . . ."

"No mat-ter what young ones say." She looked at Justin. "Don't let agnaq dance da whale dance," she told him.

"No, ma'am."

"It not right. They not chase whale. They not visit camps. If they do . . ." She shook her head. "Akkusaa-gruk, girl leave village and go to camps." She shook her head again, gravely. "No agviQ. Next year, no agviQ. Year after . . ."

"I've heard that story," Ray said. He wasn't just humoring her. His grandfather had related it many times, emphasizing that allowing women or dogs in the whaling camps was anathema.

"It mistake to anger tuungak."

"Yes, ma'am."

"You go festival?"

Ray nodded. He wasn't about to say no, that he had to work a case or explain that Aana was dead. There would be time for that later.

"So you didn't see anything ... uh ... strange or ... out of the ordinary last night? You didn't hear anything ... shouting ... uh ... yelling?"

"Dancers come, invite to Nalukataq. Make loud noise. But then gone."

"And you didn't hear anything after that?"

"I go to bed. Uvlupak festival! I didn't want miss it!"

"Okay. Well, thank you."

"Happy Nalukataq!"

"And to you, Clara."

They walked to the street.

"That was no help," Justin said.

"Unfortunately, that's probably what we'll get from a lot of the neighbors. Most of them are elderly and the chances of anyone hearing or seeing anything are slim. But ... We have to check."

They slowly worked their way up the line of homes, crossed the street and worked back down the block. Everyone had been thrilled to welcome the whalers, they learned. But no one had noticed any disturbance other than the raucous dancers.

When they were standing directly across the street from Aana's, Ray checked his watch again. It had taken an hour just to do the street.

"I need to make a call," Ray said. "Why don't you go in and see how Billy Bob's doing? Remember, don't touch anything."

"I won't."

Ray went to the car and used the radio to patch a call

home. The line rang three times before a gruff voice answered, "Who dis?"

"Grandfather, this is Ray. I need to speak to Margaret."

"Ray-mond. I got dream for you."

"Great. Tell me when I get home. Can you put Margaret on, please."

"You gotta be care-ful."

"I know. Can you get Margaret for me?" Grandfather had always been different—a keeper of the old ways, a believer in the tunngak, a man who sometimes saw into the unseen world—but in the past couple of years, his mind had started to betray him. He was getting senile, forgetful, sometimes downright weird. About once every couple of weeks, he would wander off and be found at a bus stop or in a café, unaware of his surroundings. Which is why he had come to live with them. He was no longer safe on his own. Ray suspected Alzheimer's but thus far the tests had been negative.

"I close my eyes, I seed dem."

Ray sighed, trying to be patient. The best strategy was to humor the old guy. "Who did you see?"

"Da tuungak. Day send UkpIk."

"UkpIk?" It was the Inupiaq word for the snowy owl. Ray was reminded of Justin's mention of the owl. It was a coincidence, he knew, but that didn't stop a shiver from going up and down his back.

"He come take some-body."

"Okay. Thanks for the warning. Can you put . . ."

"Dat not all. In dreamworld, I see anaun chase dancers. He chase off agviQ. Bad hunting many season."

"Oh, yeah . . . ?" This was getting laborious. Some

man had chased off the dancers and, in theory, chased off the bowhead whales. What an informative dream . . .

"All start when make sad agnaq half."

Sad woman half? Ray thought of the frowning charm that Justin had broken and that had subsequently been discovered in mended form, under Aana.

"You check who bodder her."

"Bother who?"

"Dis impo-tant, Ray-mond."

"I understand," he lied. In truth, it made no sense whatsoever.

"Check who bodder."

"I will. Now, can you? Grandfather? Grandfather?"

There was a clunk and a moment later, Margaret said, "What's going on?"

"Good question." He explained briefly about Aana.

"That's horrible. Poor Aana . . ."

"But don't go spreading that around. We're supposed to keep it quiet in hopes of . . . I don't know what. Catching the killer before he can get out of town, I suppose. It's the mayor's idea."

"That is so sad."

"Yeah." Ray waited a beat. "Anyway, don't expect me home anytime soon."

"Ray, the kids wanted to go to festival."

"I know. I guess you'll have to take them."

There was silence for a moment. "Well . . . be careful."

"I will."

"And Ray?"

"Yeah?"

"Nail this guy, okay? For Aana?"

"I'll try."

He hung up the radio and sat there for a minute, thinking. Grandfather's words echoed in his mind: *check who bodder her.* The old man was crazy and couldn't know what had happened to Aana. But . . . it was good advice. Maybe Aana had a beef with a neighbor or something. Though it would have had to be some beef to result in murder. He picked up the radio again and called Betty at the office.

"Dispatch."

"Hey, Betty. It's Ray."

"Ray . . . I heard about Aana. That's . . . it's just . . ."

"I know. Listen, I need some computer help."

"Name it."

"Could you see if Aana filed any complaints recently?"

"What sort of complaints?"

"I don't know . . . dispute with a neighbor, vandalism, somebody playing their stereo too loud . . ."

"Got it. Anything else?"

"No. That's it."

"Okay. I'll call you back in ten."

"Thanks."

Ray hung up the radio, got out of the Blazer, and went inside the house. He found Justin watching Billy Bob take samples from the kitchen floor. The cowboy was prostrate, lightly scraping the linoleum under the table with a utility knife.

"You take any complaints from Aana in the last couple of months?" Ray asked.

"Any what?"

"Complaints. You know . . . dog barking all night or somebody having a party that was keeping her awake . . ."

"Not that I recall."

"Yeah. Me either. I think I'd know if she was having a problem with someone." As this statement hung in the air, Ray realized that he obviously didn't know about a problem she'd had with someone. The woman was now dead.

"You do a search yet?" he asked.

"Naw. I been too busy taking samples and dusting for prints."

Ray got two fresh pairs of surgical gloves out of the evidence kit and led Justin down the hallway.

"I'll take the bedroom," he told him, handing him a set of gloves. "You take the sewing room."

"What are we looking for?" Justin asked.

"That's the sixty-four thousand dollar question."

"Sixty-four thousand?"

"It was a game show."

Justin blinked at him. He was too young even to remember the revival of the show. That made Ray feel ancient.

"Just look for anything out of the ordinary. Don't disturb things. Don't touch. Just look. If you see something, call me. Don't touch. Got it?"

"Yes, sir. But then, why do I need gloves?"

"Because it's natural to handle things. I've done it myself before and blown evidence."

The boy pulled the gloves on and stepped into the room. He looked around suspiciously, as though the perpetrator might leap out from behind a stack of fabric.

Ray watched him, amused and also thinking that the

captain would have a fit if he found out that he had let a fourteen-year-old do an evidence search at a murder scene. But the captain wasn't here. And Justin was his nephew and had found the body. Besides all of that, Ray doubted there was any evidence to be had.

This crime was strange and didn't fit the pattern of a burglary. The only sign of a struggle had been in the kitchen. And that had apparently been cleaned up. Nothing seemed to have been stolen. In Ray's mind, the attack had come swiftly, while Aana was fixing tea—which would explain the dry kettle on the dead stove—and been over in a matter of seconds. The motive had been . . . what? A finger? Mikilgaq: her ring finger?

"Did Aana wear rings?" he asked Justin.

"A wedding ring," the boy answered from the other room.

"What kind?"

"Ivory. It had a whale on it."

"A whale?"

"Yeah. She was very proud of it and liked to tell the story of how Uncle won it in a bet when he was just sixteen. His umialik told him that it would guide him to his bride."

Ray hadn't heard this before. "And did it?"

"He didn't believe the old man and he kept the ring for a while. Kind of forgot about it. Then he found it in his things one day when he was twenty. He took it to Nalukataq and tried to sell it. It was beautiful, but no one wanted it. Until a young lady came along. She had to have it, but didn't have the money. As he looked at her, he knew that he had to have her. It was love at first sight."

"And that was Aana?"

"Yep. They got married a week later. She got the ring and he got her."

Ray smiled. He could almost hear Aana telling the tale and laughing wickedly at that punchline.

"Was it valuable?"

"To her it was priceless."

Ray nodded and went on to the bedroom. It was interesting information, but . . . you wouldn't kill a woman for her wedding ring. Not an antique ivory ring like that. It would be worth something, but would be almost impossible to sell and very easy to trace. Only a collector would . . .

Ray lost his train of thought when he entered the bedroom and found the closet doors next to the bed standing open. He tried to remember if he had left them open. He didn't think so.

"Billy Bob . . . !"

"Yeah?"

"Did you come in the bedroom?"

"Nope."

"Is somethin' wrong?"

"I don't know."

"You need me in there?"

"Not yet."

"Give me holler if you do."

Ray glanced into the closet: clothes hanging on the pole, sweaters up on a shelf, shoe boxes down below. Nothing out of the ordinary. He checked one of the shoe boxes and found it full of old photographs. There was Uncle and Aana standing on the beach, a seal-skin boat behind them. They looked young and happy.

He closed the box and checked the bathroom. It was

clean and the cabinet held the usual supplies: tooth-paste, toothbrush, lotions, a few over-the-counter med-icines. Not much in the way of makeup. But Aana had never been big on painting her face.

He went back into the bedroom and checked the nightstand. There were a couple of books in the drawer, a flashlight. He looked under the bed and found a shallow box containing Uncle's old caribou parka. Next to it was another shoe box. He opened it, expecting photographs, but found papers instead. Flip-ping through them, he saw bills, receipts, old letters. He was about to replace the box when an envelope caught his eye. The return address was: Barrow Coun-cil of Elders.

Ray removed the envelope and slid out the letter. It read:

Dear Mrs. Clearwater,

The Council has received your grievance against Ronald Pilchuck and will take the matter up at its next meeting. We appreciate your concern and will contact you when a decision about possible charges or arbitration is reached.

Quyanaqpak for your patience.

Edward Muqta

➤➤ EIGHT ◂◂

"YOU FIND SOMETHING?"

Ray looked up at Justin but didn't answer. He read the letter again before asking, "Did Aana have some sort of . . . problem with Ronnie Pilchuck?"

"Ronnie?" Justin shrugged. "I know she didn't like him much, but . . ."

Ray folded the letter and put it back into the envelope. After pocketing it, he asked, "You find anything?"

Justin shook his head. "Just sewing and knitting stuff: yarn, fabric, spools of thread . . ."

"Okay." He ushered Justin back down the hall and into the kitchen. Billy Bob was standing at the counter, loading up the evidence kit.

"I'm about done, Ray."

"You print the doors?"

"Yep. Front and back. Got the floor too. Problem is, things are pretty darn clean. I'm bettin' the only prints on the knobs'll be ours."

"Somebody wiped this place down," Ray surmised. His beeper sounded and he glanced at the number. "I'll be right back."

He went to the car, wishing the department still had the budget for cell phones. Beepers were useful, but you had to find a phone or a radio to contact whoever it was that wanted to talk to you. Cell phones were far more convenient and with the drop in cell phone prices, it only made sense. He had made this argument more than once to the captain and been told that until a new mayor was elected, there was no chance. Hodish was not only demanding, but a spendthrift and had chopped their funding to the bone. According to the mayor, cell phones were *naluaqmiu ikayuqti:* the white man's crutch.

Ray radioed into the office and Betty answered.

"I've got good news and bad news."

"Give me the bad first."

"Okay . . ." She cleared her throat. "No record of Aana filing anything in the past two years."

"What's the good news?"

"Well, it seems that somebody out in Browerville has made six complaints in the past eight months about one of the residents."

"Let me guess," Ray said, truly guessing, "Ronnie Pilchuck."

"Exactly."

"I recall going out there on three occasions," Ray said. "Two drunk and disorderly and one domestic dispute. Who took the other calls?"

There was a pause. "I'm not sure. I'll have to do a little more checking."

"Pull Ronnie's record, too."

"Okay."

"Who made the calls?"

"They were anonymous. And since they weren't to

911, the phone company wouldn't give me the number of origin. Just the area."

"We could get a court order."

"We could. But right now, we don't have one."

"Anonymous complaints . . . from a neighbor who was afraid Ronnie would retaliate?"

"I would be. Ronnie is one mean SOB."

"Yeah." Ray recalled trying to subdue Ronnie and having him fly into a drunken rage that left Ray with a black eye and Billy Bob with a broken rib. He was the resident black sheep and seemed to spend as much time in jail as he did at home. Part of the reason for that was that he was out of work and drawing all manner of public assistance. That left him with too much time and, apparently, too much money. Where he got his booze, Ray had no idea. Fairbanks, he assumed.

"Thanks, Betty."

"You bet."

"Oh, hang on. There's one other thing. Could you call over to the Council and find out if there are any outstanding grievances against Ronnie?"

"I think I can do that right here, on the computer. Sit tight for a sec." There was a clunk, and then Ray heard Betty typing at her keyboard. "Here we go . . ." More typing. "Okay, yes. There are three. A couple for possession of alcohol. One for spousal abuse. And . . . last month Ronnie was accused of . . . huh? That's interesting . . ."

"What?"

"Someone filed a grievance stating that he has been committing adultery."

"Adultery?"

"That's what it says."

"And the Council is taking that seriously?"

"Looks like it. You know, his wife left him recently."

"How recently?"

"Oh, a couple weeks ago. She up and moved to Kotzebue. And I don't blame her one bit. I don't know about the adultery part, but I'm pretty sure he was beating her."

Ray considered this. Despite the myths about Eskimos engaging in wife swapping and bigamy, The People believed in fidelity and were committed to the institution of marriage. There were laws on the books reflecting this.

"Who filed the grievance?" he asked.

"Doesn't say. The name has been withheld."

"Great . . ."

"Probably need a court order for that too."

"Yeah. Okay. Well, thanks. I'll check back later."

"Happy festival."

"Same to you," Ray muttered without conviction.

He hung up the radio and stared out the windshield of the Blazer. If Aana had been the one making phone complaints . . . if she'd contacted the Council . . . and Ronnie had somehow found out . . . and blamed her for having his wife leave him . . . was he crazy enough to kill her . . . ?

There were several problems with this. First, Aana didn't have a phone. She would have had to go to someone else's house. Clara's? He would have to ask about that. And why call anonymously? She had a relative on the police force who could make sure Ronnie didn't retaliate. Of course, Aana was an independent woman. Very strong and willful. Maybe she didn't want special treatment. And she was a keeper of the old ways. According to the letter Ray had discovered, she had chosen to pursue the matter through traditional channels, by contacting the Council rather than the department. That made sense. Like Grandfather, Aana saw the Council as the supreme authority, above the mayor and the Borough government and all other law enforcement agencies. Given all of that, one question still remained. What would possess Ronnie, or anyone else for that matter, to sever her finger? Ray could imagine Ronnie going berserk and harming her. But taking her mikilgaq? That was sick. Why would he do that? The only way to find out, Ray decided, was to have a talk with old Ronnie.

He got out of the Blazer just as Billy Bob and Justin were emerging from the house.

"You need back in?" Billy Bob called from the door.

"Not right now."

Billy Bob set the kit down and draped yellow tape over the door. Ray started to stop him. The tape would alert the neighbors to the crime and cause rumors to fly, bursting Hodish's bubble of secrecy. But they had to preserve the scene. And spin control was not their problem. It was the mayor's.

When Billy Bob and Justin got to the curb, Ray said, "We need to go see Ronnie Pilchuck."

Billy Bob winced. "Why?"

"Because he may be a suspect."

"*May* be?" Justin said.

"Innocent until proven guilty," Ray said, thinking to himself that Ronnie was a slimebag capable of just about anything. It would be no surprise to anyone if he turned out to be a murderer.

"Let me run this back to the office," Billy Bob said.

"No. We need to go now. It's just right over there," Ray said, pointing across the side street. "Put the kit in your car. And get your gun."

"Don't worry none about that. I remember the last time we paid a visit on Ronnie." Billy Bob rubbed his ribs. "I'll make sure to have my revolver and my pepper spray and my awareness."

"Your what?"

"My awareness. That's what my karate instructor is always talking about."

"Oh, that's right. You're taking karate."

"Darn right. Next time somebody goes to mess with me . . ." He made several quick motions that were apparently supposed to be intimidating, but looked more like a chicken flapping its wings. Billy Bob was too skinny and gangly to evoke fear. "They'll be sorry."

"I'll bet."

"I'm telling you, Ray, you should take lessons too."

"Why's that?" They had been through this before, but Ray found it amusing to listen to Billy Bob's sales pitch.

"Gives you confidence, fer one thing." He raised his head proudly. "And you never know when it'll come in handy." Billy Bob made a chopping motion with his hand, accompanied by a Bruce Lee-like howl.

"I'll think about it."

"You do that, partner."

Ray waited with Justin as the cowboy ninja put the evidence kit in the car and strapped on his service revolver.

"You think Ronnie did it, Uncle Ray?" Justin asked him.

Ray shrugged. "That's why we need to talk to him."

"I never liked him."

Neither did I, Ray thought. Ronnie was a loser. He was mean and Barrow would have been better off without him. But as a policeman, Ray was supposed to remain impartial and not allow his personal feelings to enter into the equation.

When Billy Bob came back over to them, Ray told Justin, "You stay here."

"I wanna go with you!"

"No." Ray shook his head. "Absolutely not."

"But I . . ."

"You're not going with us."

"Uncle Ray . . ." Justin whined.

"You can't go," Billy Bob said, " 'cause we need somebody to stay here and watch the house. Right Ray?"

Ray caught the cowboy's wink. "Right. We have to preserve the crime scene. You need to stay here and make sure nobody tries to go inside. We'd post a man, but we're shorthanded."

Justin sagged, but agreed. "Tell me what you find out."

"We'll come straight back and fill you in," Ray said. He and Billy Bob started across the street. "Nice work. Where'd you learn to handle kids?"

"Growing up, I was always having to negotiate with brothers and sisters and cousins. After a while, you figure out that ever-body wants something out of a deal. The trick is makin' 'em feel like they got it."

"I see," Ray said, not entirely convinced.

They crossed the next street and walked up to the second house. It was a single-story home, like Aana's, that hadn't been kept up. The paint had faded and peeled, grass was growing on the roof, and the roof of the carport had actually collapsed. Parked in the yard were two ATVs and three snow machines, all of which had seen better days. At the curb was a relatively new, but dented Jeep Cherokee.

"Now how does someone who is down on their luck afford all these ve-hicles?" Billy Bob asked.

Ray shook his head. The truth was, Ronnie was not down on his luck. He was simply unemployed—by choice, as far as Ray could tell. There was a time when not having a job meant the possibility of starvation. But that had given way to unemployment checks and state fund checks and workman's comp checks and handouts from the Native corporations . . . Ronnie probably made more than Ray did. The condition of his home was simply a matter of neglect. The man was a slob and a slacker who knew how to bilk the system.

As they walked up to the door, the screen of which had been torn and was standing open, Ray turned and could see Justin standing in Aana's yard. The kid was watching them. Ray waved and then muttered to Billy Bob, "Maybe we should have called for backup."

"Backup? You don't think the two of us can handle Ronnie?"

"Well, last time we barely did."

"Last time I wasn't a martial artist."

"Touché."

"Huh?"

"Be careful. He may be armed."

"You want me to take the back?"

"No. Let's stay together. If he runs . . . he runs. We'll catch up to him eventually. But if he decides to fight, I want somebody by my side who is an expert at self-defense." Ray meant this as a joke, to lighten things up.

But Billy Bob looked at him soberly. "Okay."

"Okay." Ray withdrew his revolver and reached to knock on the door. As he did, he saw that it wasn't quite latched. "Barrow Police!" he called. When there was no answer, he pushed it open and peered inside. The place was a mess: pizza boxes on the floor, a beer keg in the corner, paper cups and tequila bottles on the coffee table.

"Barrow Police!" Ray waited a second, then stepped inside the mud room. Billy Bob followed him, gun raised at the ceiling.

"Whew!" the cowboy said. "This place stinks to high heaven."

Ray made a face, trying not to be overcome by the stench. The air was heavy with the smell of warm beer, cigarettes, and urine. Ray made his way through the small living area, to the kitchen. It was littered with more empty bottles and another aluminum keg. Ray wondered how Ronnie managed to get so much contraband liquor into a dry town. Apparently it hadn't been difficult. He glanced in the sink and saw a broken glass and a trail of vomit.

"Looks like they had *some* party," the cowboy observed.

"Yeah." Ray waved to Billy Bob and they started down the hall. The floor plan was the same as Aana's house, but with the walls nicked and caked with grime and the carpet stained and torn, it seemed like a different world.

The first bedroom door was open. Inside, four small

kids were sleeping on the floor in bedrolls. Their faces were dirty and the room smelled like soiled diapers.

"Time to call social services," Billy Bob whispered. "Poor thangs."

Ray gestured and they both got ready to enter the other bedroom. Ray hesitated, wondering if he should announce their entry. No. They had already done that. And they had probable cause to hit the bedroom. Not only was Ronnie a murder suspect, but he had broken numerous liquor laws. Besides, knocking or yelling would only alert him to their presence and give him a chance to either flee or take up a weapon.

Ray reached for the knob, twisted it quietly, then quickly thrust it open. He and Billy Bob rushed inside. This room smelled like marijuana. There was a bag of something that looked like dope on the closest nightstand, along with a bong pipe. In the bed were three lumps. As Ray approached them, gun raised, he saw the knife leaning against the wall in the corner. A flensing knife that whalers used to peel the skin from a bowhead. He could tell from across the room that the blade was bloody. Next to the knife was a cardboard mask, like the ones the whalers wore when they went around doing the festival dance. There was also a pair of boots sitting there, work boots with hard rubber soles like those that had made the print in Aana's backyard.

Ray walked around to the other side of the bed before noticing the glass sitting on the far nightstand. It was half full of water and had something floating in it. He gagged and failed to suppress a retch when he realized what it was: a human finger.

➤➤ NINE ◀◀

"WHY, YOU SICK BASTARD!" Ray took hold of the blankets and yanked them back to expose three naked bodies: a blonde woman, a redhead, and Ronnie. The women shrieked and began to gather the sheet to cover themselves. Ronnie rolled to his back and looked up groggily, his mouth hanging open. He was a skinny guy with long, greasy black hair and a goatee.

Ray jabbed the gun at him. "You're under arrest! Twitch and I blow your gray matter all over the room!"

Ronnie squinted at the barrel of the gun.

"Take it easy, Ray . . ." Billy Bob cautioned.

"Easy, my eye." He pulled the redhead out by the arm. "Get dressed!" He waved the gun at the blonde. "You too!"

Both of them frantically gathered clothing from the floor and began hopping into it.

"Cuff him!" Ray told Billy Bob.

Billy Bob rolled Ronnie to his stomach and drew his arms back. Ronnie put up no resistance. After the cuffs were in place, he asked sleepily, "What am I being arrested for?"

"Possession of controlled substances," Ray said. "Possession of alcohol."

Ronnie swore sadly.

Ray wrenched him to his feet before adding, "Oh, and murder one."

"Murder?" one of the women shrieked.

The other cursed and began to cry.

"I didn't kill anyone!"

Ray laughed angrily. "Yeah, right. That's why the murder weapon is sitting over there, next to a pair of boots that I'm willing to bet matches the print left at the scene."

"I didn't do anything!" Ronnie argued.

"Nice finger you got there," Ray said, nodding at the glass of water.

Billy Bob let out a groan and turned away.

The blonde leaned down to examine the glass as she was buttoning her shirt. "Oh, my God!" She went running for the bathroom.

"A finger?" Ronnie said, craning his head.

"We better read him his rights," Billy Bob suggested.

"Screw the rights!" Ray said. "I say we drag his sorry butt outside and pistol whip him until he confesses."

"Ray . . . !" Billy Bob cautioned.

"Confess to what?!" Ronnie asked. "I didn't do anything."

"Outside!" Ray ordered.

"Cool down, Ray," Billy Bob told him.

"You cool down!" Ray shot back. He could tell he was out of control. He'd seldom if ever been this angry. But then, he'd seldom found an elderly relative's dead body stuffed under a wheelbarrow in a shed, minus one finger, and seldom found the finger floating in a glass of water next to a man's bed.

Ray took a breath and tried to compose himself. He knew that if Ronnie so much as batted his eyelashes, he would go berserk and hurt the man. Any excuse . . .

"You pigs can't pin this crap on me," Ronnie said.

Ray backhanded him in the mouth. "Shut up!"

"Hey! That's police brutality!"

Ray slugged him in the gut. "You ain't seen police brutality yet, you no-good piece of . . ."

"Ray!" Billy Bob pulled him back. "Settle down!" He held Ray by both arms. "Relax. Count to ten." He watched him closely. "Now I'm gonna read Ronnie his rights, and get him into some clothes, and take him down to the station. I'll call for backup. You handle the ladies and the scene."

Ray nodded.

"You okay?"

Ray inhaled, exhaled. "Yeah. I'm fine. Thanks." He watched Billy Bob lead Ronnie away and wondered what had just happened. He had almost ruined his career, he realized, and come perilously close to giving a murderer a "get out of jail free" card by roughing him up. What had he been thinking? He wasn't sure and that scared him. He had been irritable lately. But this . . . it was more than irritability. It was reckless and unprofessional behavior.

He herded the ladies into the living room. "Have a seat," he told them. He read them both their rights and cuffed them, just in case they got any ideas about taking off on him, then went back down the hall. The kids were still sleeping peacefully, somehow blissfully ignorant of the chaos occurring around them.

Ray entered the master bedroom again and, upon seeing the bloody knife and the finger, felt the rage return. What sort of animal did such things? It was amoral. Sociopathic.

As Billy Bob assisted Ronnie with his pants, Ray bent and examined the finger. He shuddered as he imagined it being separated from Aana's hand with the huge knife. Closing his eyes, he said a short prayer—to the tuungak, to God, to whoever might be listening—wishing Aana peace and rest. When he opened his eyes, he looked at the finger for several seconds before his mind engaged and he noticed the absence of a ring. If it was indeed Aana's mikilgaq—the third finger of the left hand—it should have had a wedding ring on it. Unless Ronnie was not only a murdering SOB, but a thief: a man who robbed jewelry from corpses. What a monster!

"I didn't do anything!" Ronnie claimed as the cowboy helped him into a shirt.

"Shut up!" Ray told him.

He went over to the knife. It was three feet long with a wooden handle, the blade dark with a crust of blood. Why would you use something so large and cumbersome for the delicate job of removing a finger? Ray couldn't think of a good reason. But then, Ronnie had never been known for his smarts. Which is why, after committing the crime, he had returned to his house, within a stone's throw of the crime scene, and partied the night away with two women—two sleazy women, neither of whom were his wife—while his kids were asleep in the next room. And that was why he had left the murder weapon sitting there in plain view. The man was not only a psychopath, he was an idiot. A complete moron.

Ray returned to the living room and glared at the women. They were both rather pretty, but looked haggard.

"Who do you work for?"

"Ourselves," the redhead said.

"We're massage therapists," the blonde specified.

"Ah . . ." Ray nodded at the cover. Though there was such a thing as a licensed, accredited massage therapist, these bimbos were not it. "Just came by to give Ronnie a massage?"

They cut their eyes at each other. The redhead said, "We don't have to tell you nothin'."

"Fine. How about if I tell you something: You're going to be charged as accessories to murder."

"But we didn't do anything!" the blonde blurted out.

"Doesn't matter. If you were with the perpetrator before or after his crime and have any knowledge of . . ."

"We didn't know!" the blonde said.

"We didn't!" the redhead affirmed.

"All he said was he scared some old bag half to death."

"Some old bag?"

"Yeah. A neighbor lady that's a real pain in the ass."

"Scared her?"

"Yeah. He said it was funny."

Ray felt the anger surging again.

On cue, Billy Bob pulled Ronnie into the room by a cuffed arm. "I'll get Lewis in here to help ya," the cowboy told Ray.

Ray nodded, but didn't know what he was agreeing to. His attention was on Ronnie. It was all Ray could do to resist the urge to pummel him. When Billy Bob had him out the door, Ray said, "Oh, yeah. It was funny. It was downright hilarious. Your boyfriend there cut off the 'old bag's' finger, hid her body under a wheelbarrow, then put the finger in a glass on the nightstand, like a trophy."

"Geez . . . and we spent the night with him," the blond said, grimacing.

"What a sicko!" the redhead said.

"Yeah. But he'll get his. Life in prison. No possibility of parole. As accessories, you'll get . . . say . . . twenty years apiece."

"Twenty years? I'll be fifty-two!"

"Nah. If you behave yourself, you can get off in maybe seven to ten." He let that sink in before adding, "Or you can cooperate and do less. Who knows, maybe you'll get off with probation and a fine for solicitation."

"What do we have to do?"

"Tell us everything, agree to testify against Ronnie, comply with the wishes of the district attorney . . ."

They glanced at each other again. "Fine," the redhead said. "Whatever. We'll do it."

Ray nodded, satisfied. The women probably weren't involved. But having them testify about Ronnie's drinking and drug taking, and how he was fooling around with two "massage therapists" while his kids were in the house would serve to provide the jury with a character profile. It wouldn't be hard to convince them that such a man would murder a neighbor and find it "funny."

Lewis arrived a few minutes later and grinned when he saw the two women. "Lay-dees . . ."

"Of the *evening*," Ray specified.

"Aiyaa . . . dat not legal up here. You need to go to An-kor-ig, where dare's plenty-a johns and day more legacy on dat sort thing."

"Lenient," Ray translated.

"Dat what I say, legacy-ent."

Ray heard a noise and turned to see a small boy emerging from the hallway.

"Hey, there," he said, trying to look and sound friendly. It had to be a shock to wake up and find your home full of strangers.

"Where's Dad?"

"He's . . . uh . . . had to go downtown."

Another figure appeared behind the boy, then another, and another. None of the kids were older than eight and all had the grubby, life-weary faces.

"When was the last time you guys ate anything?"

They looked at each other and then back at Ray, as though he has posed a very difficult question.

"Do you go to school?"

The tallest child, a girl, answered, "Not anymore."

Ray started to ask them to get dressed, but realized they were—after a fashion. Two were wearing thread-bare sweatpants, the other pair had on jeans with holes in the knees. All of them had on dingy T-shirts bearing sports logos: Nike, Adidas, Reebok . . . with their grungy faces, they looked like waifs from a Dickens novel.

"Do you have shoes?"

They all nodded.

"Put them on, okay?"

"Where are we going?" asked the oldest girl, who was apparently the spokesperson.

"Downtown."

"To be with Daddy?" one of the little ones asked.

Ray was still fighting to come up with an answer for that one when a middle-aged woman came through the front door. It was Barbara Harris, the resident social worker. She nodded at Ray before going over to the children.

"Well, hello there. Who do we have here? What's your name?" she asked the oldest girl.

"Sarah."

"Sarah . . . that's a pretty name."

"Thank you," she peeped.

As Ms. Harris continued to draw the kids out, Lewis led the massage therapists out to his patrol car. Ray was watching, amazed at the smiles Harris was getting, when Jimmy Fowler came into the house. He was the newest member of the force, a fresh-faced kid just out of the academy in Anchorage.

"What do you got?" he asked, chest out, looking and sounding like a TV cop.

Ray quickly filled him in on the finger, the weapon, the boots . . .

"Sounds like a deadbang," Jimmy said.

"A what?"

"You know, open and shut. Deadbang."

"Uh . . . yeah." Ray had heard the term in a movie but never thought he would hear a real police officer use it. Or at least, he had hoped he wouldn't.

"I understand that Bill took the perp in."

Ray almost asked who Bill was, then realized Fowler meant Billy Bob. "I guess the first thing we need to do is . . ."

Fowler held up a hand. "The first thing *you're* supposed to do is go home."

"Excuse me?"

"Captain's orders."

"Home?"

Fowler nodded. "Until Monday. You got the weekend off."

"Why?"

Fowler shrugged. "I guess because . . . you broke the case." He shrugged again. "It's sort of like a reward."

Ray squinted at him, wondering if he were joking. "A reward?" It didn't feel like a reward. It felt like a punishment. His behavior with Ronnie flashed to mind. "Did Billy Bob say anything to the captain about the arrest itself?"

Fowler held up both hands. "Talk to the captain. All I know is that I'm supposed to relieve you and secure the scene."

"You're serious?"

"Captain's orders," he repeated.

Ray glanced around helplessly.

"Go on," Fowler prodded. "Go home. Enjoy the whale party."

"Festival."

"Right."

"The bedroom is where the knife and the . . ."

"Don't worry. I'm gonna sit tight until Bill gets back. Then we'll take pictures, bag everything, print the place . . . relax, Ray. We'll do you proud."

Ray wanted to ask why Billy Bob was still on the case. Why hadn't the cowboy been "rewarded" with leave time? But he knew Fowler's answer would be: Talk to the captain.

"Okay . . . well . . ."

"See you Monday," Fowler said cheerily.

"Yeah. I guess so."

"Take it easy." His radio squawked and he turned away to answer it, as though Ray were civilian and not privy to the conversation.

Feeling useless and a little like a boy being sent home from school for misbehaving, Ray left. He walked to his car, got in, and began driving back to Barrow, intent upon speaking to the captain. His curiosity and frustration got the better of him before he had gone two blocks and he picked up the radio. Betty answered his call.

"Barrow dispatch."

"Say Betty. It's Ray. I need to talk to the captain."

"He's in a meeting."

"With who?"

"That's whom."

"Betty . . . !"

"With the mayor. He asked not to be disturbed."

"Well then . . . I'll stop by the station and . . ."

"No. He also said that if you called in, to tell you to go home."

"Why? What did I do?"

There was a stretch of static.

"Betty . . . come on. It's me."

"I don't know what's going on, Ray. I think the mayor . . ."

"The mayor what?"

"All I know is that Ronnie Pilchuck was brought in with a bloody lip. He also says he's got a broken rib."

"Bull!"

"Billy Bob said Ronnie tripped getting into the squad car."

"He tripped?"

"Ray, Billy Bob thinks you hung the moon. He'd do anything for you, including lie through his teeth."

"I know."

"Do you?"

Ray silently acknowledged that he didn't appreciate the cowboy as he should. "So I'm being . . . disciplined?"

"Your guess is as good as mine."

"Was it the mayor's idea?" When she didn't answer, he prodded, "Betty . . ."

"You're going to get me into trouble."

"Listen, I'm coming in . . ."

"Don't, Ray. It's not a good idea." Static. "Honey, we all know you've been a little tense lately. Think of this as a chance to relax. Go on home, take your family to festival . . . you'll be as good as new by Monday."

No matter how it was couched, being relieved of duty felt like a slap on the wrist. "If I could just talk to the captain . . ."

"Go home, Raymond." Before he could argue, she added, "Dispatch out."

⨾➤ TEN ◄⨾

MAYBE BETTY WAS RIGHT, Ray thought as he wound through the neighborhood. Maybe he did need a rest. He *had* been tense lately. And he'd been having those weird, recurring dreams. Now, this murder . . .

He hadn't been out of Barrow in over a year and even though he'd lived there since he was in high school, it was still tough to weather the months of darkness, the intense cold, the bleak, flat expanse that surrounded the town on every side. Was a change of scenery the answer?

What about therapy? As much as he hated to admit it, Margaret had a point about seeing someone. Going to a counselor would probably help. But that was a little drastic, wasn't it? He wasn't loony. Just a little stressed. Once you went to a mental health practitioner, didn't you get labeled as a nutcase? In Ray's mind, it was tantamount to announcing that he couldn't handle life as an adult and was falling to pieces. Was he?

He pulled into the driveway and scolded himself for losing his temper with Ronnie. Murder or no murder there was no excuse for such behavior. If the captain wanted to, he could suspend him or worse.

Ray switched off the Blazer and sat for a moment trying to figure out why he was unraveling. He was thirty-five. Did that have something to do with it? Approaching middle age. Was this the start of a midlife crisis? He wasn't dissatisfied with his life. Or was he? Margaret had spent the past ten years bettering herself, going from a job as a social worker to getting her law degree and working for a Native firm. What had he done during that time? Nothing. He was still a beat officer with the Barrow Police. Nothing had changed. And nothing would change in the foreseeable future. He hadn't studied for the lieutenant's exam and hadn't seriously entertained the notion of doing so, despite the captain's persistent encouragement. Was that the problem? Lack of ambition? Of course, even if he made lieutenant, what then? He'd still be stuck in the department, riding a desk instead of patrolling the North Slope Borough. It was a dead-end job in a dead-end town, and at the moment, he felt like one big dead-end failure.

Where were these thoughts coming from? He shook his head vigorously, hoping to clear his mind. He had to stop this downward spiral. Think positive thoughts, he told himself.

He looked through the windshield at his home and imagined his wife, daughter, son and grandfather inside awaiting his arrival. He loved them and knew they loved him. That was enough, wasn't it? And today was festival. They could go and enjoy the blanket toss, the dancing, the special foods, the other ceremonies.

Today could be a blessing, he decided. If he allowed it to be.

"Carpe diem," he muttered, recalling *Dead Poets Society*. It was one of Margaret's favorite movies and though Ray wasn't big on poetry, he liked that Latin message: seize the day. That was what he had to do right now.

He got out and went inside. Keera and Freddie greeted him in the living room with squeals of delight, rushing to hug his legs. He picked them both up and carried them to the kitchen where Margaret was flipping pancakes. Grandfather was seated at the table, eating.

"Look who's home, Mommy!" Keera shouted.

Margaret turned and stared at him, asking with her eyes, What are you doing here?

"We, uh . . . arrested someone," Ray told her as he set the kids into their chairs.

"A bad guy?" Keera asked.

"Ba ga!" Freddie chirped.

"Yeah. A bad guy."

"Already?" Margaret asked.

Ray nodded.

"Who?"

"Um . . ." Ray glanced at the kids. "Onnie Ray, Ilchuck Pay."

"Who?" Keera said.

"Really? How did you get him so fast?"

"I'll tell you later."

"So it's . . . it's over?"

"What's over?" Keera wanted to know.

"Ba ga!" Freddie yelled, banging a fork on the table.

"I'm talking to your mother."

"Da-ddy!" Keera complained.

"Da-da!" Freddie mimicked happily.

"Well . . . that's good to hear," Margaret said. "Even though . . ."

"Yeah. I know," Ray said.

Margaret loaded four pancakes onto a plate and handed it to Ray. "Hungry?"

"Starving." He took the plate, sat down and began loading the pancakes with butter and syrup.

He took a bite, moaned his approval and was about to take another when Grandfather muttered, "You let anaun get way." The old man kept eating, never looking up. "Anaun fly way," he said between bites. When he finished what was on his plate, he tapped Ray's shoulder. "Why you not chase him?"

Ray looked at Grandfather, wondering how long it would be before the old guy was too much for them and had to be placed in a retirement or nursing home. He forgot things, got lost easily, was often confused. Now he was blathering gibberish.

"I not kinnaQ."

"I didn't say you were crazy," Ray replied.

"I talk 'bout anaun with savIk."

"How do you know there was a knife?"

"When Manaqtaaq-tinmiaq begin circle . . . no good."

"Raven is always doing bad things," Keera agreed.

Ray groaned. His daughter seemed to have inherited Grandfather's preoccupation with the spirit world. A few years earlier, she had "seen" Raven do something evil to a man and been dead set on convincing Ray of this. That it had turned out to be a bona fide crime didn't settle matters. Ray had been hoping she would grow out of it. But as yet, she hadn't.

"She right," Grandfather said.

Nothing like being ganged up on by a senile old man and a quirky seven-year-old. "Of course she is," he said, trying not to sound too patronizing. "Raven is the worst. When he shows up, the party is a bust."

"You make fun, Ray-mond," Grandfather said.

"Daddy's always being sarcastic," Keera told him.

"I am not," Ray objected. "Besides, you don't even know what that word means."

"I do too. It means . . . how you act, Daddy."

Margaret laughed.

"She got that from you," Ray accused.

"Maybe so, but it's true," she said, smiling. "You're the Dave Barry of Barrow. Except you're not as funny."

"Thanks," Ray groaned.

"Who Dave Bar-ry?" Grandfather wanted to know.

The phone rang and Ray rose to answer it, leaving Margaret to explain.

"Hello?"

"Attla?"

Ray's heart sunk. Here it came. He was about to be reprimanded. "What's up, captain?"

"Just wanted to touch base with you and say good job."

"Good job?"

"I know you're a heck of a cop, but . . . even I was amazed when Billy Bob brought in Ronnie."

Ray was speechless.

"Great work." The captain cleared his throat. "I also wanted to make sure you knew that your time off was not intended to be a slap on the wrist. I understand you

got a little physical with Ronnie. Which is understand-
able, given the circumstances. He's a loser and with the
physical evidence right there in his bedroom . . . if I'd
been there and it was my relative who had been murdered, I'd probably have beat him senseless. It takes a
big man to restrain himself like that."

"Uh . . . thank you, captain."

"You take it easy, enjoy the downtime, and have fun
at festival."

"Okay."

"Now, hang on a second, there's somebody else
who'd like to talk to you."

Margaret looked at Ray from the table. "Is everything okay?"

He shrugged, still a little stunned.

"Officer Attla?"

"Yes?"

"This is Mayor Hodish. I'd like to congratulate you
on a job well done."

"Well, thank you, sir, but . . . uh . . . it was a team
effort."

"Nonsense. According to Officer . . . uh . . .
what'shisname . . . the cowboy . . . ?"

"Billy Bob."

"Right. According to him, you single-handedly put
the pieces of the puzzle together and figured out that
Ronald Pilchuck was responsible."

"Not exactly, I—"

"A marvelous piece of police work, Officer Attla . . ."

"Really, I didn't—"

". . . Which deserves to be recognized. While the need
to keep this matter under wraps is now something of a
non-issue, I would like to publicly decorate you . . ."

Publicly? Ray thought. What did that mean?

". . . For your valor in the field."

"That's not necessary, sir."

"Oh, but I believe that it is, Officer Attla. You're a hero. Besides the men and women in law enforcement are too often overlooked. This affords us an opportunity to change that."

And for you to get up and make a speech at festival, Ray thought.

"So I have taken the liberty of scheduling an award presentation for this evening during the closing festival ceremonies." The mayor blathered on about the details: a band, photographers, media in droves.

When the mayor finally ran out of gas, Ray asked to speak to the captain again.

"Sure. See you this evening, Officer Attla."

"Uh-huh."

There was a pause. Then the captain grunted, "Yeah?"

"What's going on, sir?"

"You're being recognized for valor in the field," the captain answered.

"This is a crock. Why are you letting this happen?"

"Because I don't have any choice."

"It's ridiculous."

"Agreed."

"Is there some way I can . . . ?"

"Get out of it?"

"Yeah."

"Nope."

"But captain—"

"Just humor the guy, okay, Attla? Let him pin a medal on you and forget about it."

"Billy Bob should get one too then. And Lewis. And Fowler, for that matter. I didn't make the collar alone."

"I know. But the mayor seems to like the idea of handing out a commendation during festival, with the TV cameras and all. Especially to a local."

"You mean an Inupiat."

"Right."

"And since Billy Bob is a naluaqmiu, he's not considered a hero?"

"You're the image Hodish wants: young, brave, Eskimo."

"Not so young and not so brave." Ray thought for a moment. "What about Lewis?"

"You gotta be kidding. The mayor wouldn't share a stage with Lewis. He's afraid the nut would do or say something embarrassing and it would turn into a fiasco. Frankly, I don't blame him. Fowler's *too* young."

"And too white."

"Exactly. So . . . bottom line: you're the man for the job, Attla."

"I feel so honored," Ray said sarcastically.

"Good. Act that way when you shake hands with the mayor."

"Do I have to?"

"Of course not. But if you don't show up, you might as well not bother showing up for work Monday either. See you at the ceremony."

Ray hung up and blew air at the phone.

"What's the matter?" Margaret asked.

"You'll never believe it."

"What?"

"The mayor is going to give me a commendation this evening at festival."

"What's a commen-da-tion?" Keera asked.

"An award."

"For what?" Margaret asked.

"For arresting Ronnie."

"Who's Ronnie?" Keera wanted to know.

"On-nee!" Freddie shouted.

Margaret got up, her face full of excitement. "Ray! That's wonderful!"

"Is it?"

She embraced him. "You're a hero!"

"I didn't do anything . . . except my job."

"Not do job," Grandfather muttered.

"What was that?"

"I say, you not do job."

"Thanks. That makes me feel good."

"You get turn round, look wrong way."

Ray blinked at the old man.

"You get trip on you."

"Trip? You mean, trick?"

"Dat what I say. But no shame. Raven a trip-ster."

Geez . . . not Raven again, Ray thought.

"Even good tigurl get trip some-time. You good tig-url, Ray-mond."

"Yeah." He looked at Margaret. "I'm such a *great* policeman that I'm suspended until Monday."

"You're not suspended," Margaret argued.

Ray shook his head. "I gotta take a shower. Then I'll be ready to go down to festival."

Grandfather pointed at him. "You catch anaun—rull keeler."

"Yeah. I'll catch the real killer, right after my shower." Ray started to walk away.

"Ray-mond!"

Ray turned back around and saw that Grandfather was seething. "You no turn you tunu on me."

"Sorry."

"You so . . . crocky."

"*Cocky*. And no, I'm not cocky. I just . . . the case I worked this morning was difficult. Simple, but hard to handle, okay. And now, it's over. Thank goodness."

"Not over."

Ray was losing his patience. "It's tough for me to show you respect when you talk crazy."

"Ray!" Margaret warned.

"I kinnaQ to you, because you no ukpigun—you no be-leev. If you be-leev, den you see."

"Uh-huh."

"You see," Grandfather said, pointing a bony finger at him. "You see I right. Raven circling, circling. He not done. And you not done."

"I am for now. Is it all right with you if I take a shower?"

"You go," Grandfather said. He waved his hand in the air. "I send tuungak with you. Make you see."

"You do that." Ray went up the stairs to the bedroom and began pulling off his clothing. Grandfather had once been such an influence on him. Now he was merely an irritant, an annoyance. His old ways and beliefs were just nonsensical superstition and senility.

If only it were that easy, he thought as he took his hair out of his ponytail and went to the shower. If only the old man's magic spells and spirits and legends were true. If only Ray could flip a switch and see the answers behind the questions.

He twisted the water on and tried to decide, given a sudden and inexplicable dispensation of such supernatural ability, which question he would address first.

⇥ ELEVEN ⇤

RAY STOOD IN the shower, letting the hot water pour over his head, soaking his nearly waist-length hair. The commendation ceremony was a publicity stunt, he knew. Still, it bothered him to think that he would be singled out and cast as a hero when he had merely been doing his job—and not especially well or courageously. The case was a no-brainer, or, as Fowler liked to say, "Deadbang." Ronnie was known to be a violent drunk and the murder weapon had been sitting by his bed. And with the complaints against him, only a complete idiot would have missed him as a suspect.

Ray closed his eyes and ordered himself to stop thinking about it. He took up the soap and washed himself, then lathered his hair with shampoo. It was festival and for the time being, he was off-duty. He would de-stress, attend the events with his family, enjoy himself . . .

In his mind's eye, in a flash of motion and light, he saw himself out on the ice floes, clinging to the side of an umiak that was hurtling behind a snowmachine. In the daydream, he lost his grip, was slung toward the sea, couldn't stop himself, fell in . . . Underwater, as he struggled to find the surface, he saw Ronnie's face glimmer into view. Wearing an expression of shock, Ronnie pleaded, "I just tried to scare her!"

Ronnie's face wavered and disappeared, replaced by a void of black water. The void became a square and then a wooden frame. But there was no picture. There was a ruffling sound and a white shadow crossed the emptiness at the center of the frame.

Ray opened his eyes and swore. It wasn't enough that he was having a hard day in his sleep. Now he was seeing things when he was awake. Weird.

He turned off the shower and toweled off.

As he put his clothes on, he forced himself to think about something else. He thought of the festival—the blanket toss, the dancers, the feast held by the whaling crews . . .

This worked for a matter of perhaps thirty seconds. Then his thoughts drifted back to the case against Ronnie. It was so tight. So easy. Too easy? The pictures of the empty frame returned with a new meaning. A frame-up?

Ray recalled how the two bimbos had recoiled at seeing the finger in the glass. Why hadn't they seen it earlier? If Ronnie had committed the crime, then partied with the two women, they would have noticed something like a human finger on the nightstand. Wouldn't they? It could have been dark. And they were, no doubt, drunk. Maybe high. Still . . .

The more Ray considered it, the more it bothered him. The whole fit felt wrong. But why hadn't it felt wrong when they busted Ronnie? Because Ray was too busy playing the role of the bad cop? Too distracted by anger and grief? Maybe. Or maybe this was part of a growing delusion, something he needed to tell a psychiatrist: I'm second-guessing myself to death.

He pulled his hair into a ponytail and fastened it together with an ivory whale clasp Margaret had given him. "Nalukataq," he told the mirror over the dresser and himself and his overactive imagination.

"Who are you talking to?" It was Margaret. Standing at the door, she was giving him a look of concern.

"Nobody."

"You okay?"

"I'm fine."

"You sure? You look a little . . ."

"What?"

"I don't know. Like you're . . . I don't know."

He went over and embraced her. "Like I'm ready to go to festival and have fun with my family as a layman who isn't on duty and doesn't have to worry about police work until after the weekend?"

"That must be it."

"Is everybody ready?"

"Just about. We need to get some shoes on the kids and gather up some jackets."

"I'll go help with the shoes and try to get Grandfather moving."

"He's not going."

"What?"

"He says he's tired."

"Too tired for the whale festival? He hasn't missed one since he was born. He must be sick."

"He says he'll watch it on TV."

"Grandfather? *My* Grandfather? The man who dragged me to every festival and ceremony ever held, rain or shine, in sickness or in health? You gotta be kidding me. When I was ten, I got the flu and was puking up my guts. He still made me go to a Messenger Feast."

"So you told me."

"I barfed three times before we got home."

"And barely survived the ordeal." Margaret grinned.

"I'm serious."

"That's what's so funny."

"It's not funny. He's a lunatic when it comes to tradition."

"Maybe so. But the way *he* tells the story, you had an upset stomach and refused to stay home."

"Not true."

"And all that happened was that you turned a little green during dinner and spit out your muktuq."

"His memory is obviously failing."

"Uh-huh . . ."

"I'll go talk to him."

Ray went down the hall, pausing to help Keera find her shoes and to put socks on Freddie. He continued down the stairs and found Grandfather in the kitchen, reading the newspaper.

"What's up?"

Grandfather tipped his head back and examined the ceiling with wide eyes. "Up?"

"Stop it," Ray said.

"Stop what?" the old man asked.

"You go around acting like you don't understand. But I know better."

Grandfather grunted at him and directed his attention at the newspaper.

"Now what's going on?"

"Prez-dent say he cut tax. And wedder-man say it rain uvlaaku."

"You know what I mean. What's this about not going to Nalukataq?"

He shrugged. "Don't wanna go."

"Since when?"

"Seenz now."

"Why?"

The old man sniffed and turned the page.

Ray reached over and pulled down the paper. "Talk to me."

"What you wanna talk 'bout?"

"You."

"What 'bout me?"

"What's the matter?"

"Piunilaq."

"It's not nothing. Tell me what it is." Ray felt like he was coercing one of his children. "I want to know why you aren't going to festival."

Grandfather's eyes darted around the room and he sighed melodramatically. "Utuqqanaaq."

"You're old?"

"Yep."

"What does that mean?"

"It mean," Grandfather said, turning toward Ray, "I not 'member way I used to. It mean, I not find way home. It mean, legs hurt when I stand too long. It mean, I get fire in chest when I eat mikigaq. It mean, I bur-gen have 'round."

"You are *not* a burden."

"I bur-gen, like kisaq 'round neck. 'Round you neck, make you sink."

"Grandfather . . ." Ray felt horrible. He'd been testy

and acting out of sorts for a number of reasons, the least of which was having the old man in their home. Grandfather made things more complicated and was sometimes something of a pest, but he was not an anchor around Ray's neck. "If I made you feel that way, I'm sorry."

Grandfather looked at him.

"We enjoy having you here with us. You're part of the family. An important part of the anayuqaagiich."

The old man grunted, seemingly pleased with this.

"But you have to go to festival."

"Why?"

"Because. Because . . . you're one of the Elders, you're one of the last true keepers of the old ways. You have so much to offer . . . you're an example to the young people. You have to go." He looked at the old man. "Besides that, it'll be fun. There's nothing wrong with fun, is there?"

Grandfather shrugged. "Don't wanna be bur-gen."

"You're not a *bur-gen* and I want you to quit saying that. You hear me?"

He snorted and then grinned. "What? You my aaka, now?"

"I'm not your mother, but I am your grandson and I'm telling you that you're a valuable part of this family and of this community."

Grandfather let his head droop. "I gonna miss Aana."

"Me too."

"I like last dying nigrun. Like caribou go ex-pink."

"Extinct. And trust me, I know how you feel. Sometimes there's just no place for a man in this world."

They were quiet for a moment.

"Get your shoes on," Ray prodded.

The old man got up and shuffled to the living room for his shoes. Ray followed him.

"You fi-gur out 'bout Ronnie yet?" Grandfather asked.

"What about him?"

"He not keel-la."

"He sure looks like the killer. I found evidence to prove it right in his home."

Grandfather shook his head. "Not always way it look."

Ray watched him slowly and stiffly pull his boots on and had to resist the urge to offer assistance. That always angered Grandfather. Whether he could do something himself or not, he ardently and proudly refused help.

"Ronnie a bad anaun. He bad to his wife, treat her like qimmIq. Worse than dog. Lotta men good to qumm-mIq. He also bad for chid-ren. Bad for Utqiagvik."

Ray nodded. Utqiagvik was the original name for Barrow.

"But he not keela. 'Cept sef-keela. Drink sef to deaf, beat wife till she want to die and teach chid-ren drink and hit. Very bad. But not code-blooded keela."

"How do you know all this about Ronnie?"

"I hear 'bout com-plain to con-cil. From Aana and udders."

"Why didn't the council just call the police?"

Grandfather shrugged. "In old times, con-cil *was* po-lees and judge. What they say was . . ." He waved a trembling hand. ". . . Was end. No question. No talk. End. Whatever day say. End."

It's not that way anymore, Ray wanted to say. But he

didn't want to make the old man feel any more out-dated than he already did.

"What did the council do about it?"

"Day look at problem, dee-cide. Get rid Ronnie."

"What do you mean, get rid of him?"

"Day say he gil-tee of bad huz-bund and bad faud-da, break law, so must leave."

"And how did he react?"

"Uh?"

"What did he do when they told him that?"

"Didn't tell him yet. First, tell wife he in big trouble, cheat on her. Somebody see him wif Dor-thy Rud-dy."

"Dorothy Ruddy?" Dorothy had been a hooker out at the oil camps until she got too old for the work and was now living off welfare.

"His wife say she leave him, take chid-ren. They tell her: good. But when she try leave, Ronnie say he keel her and keep chid-ren."

"And you're trying to tell me he isn't capable of murder?"

"Ca-pa-bull?"

"You said he threatened to kill his wife."

"Sure. Yah. But dat his wife. Huz-bund tell wife all time, never do it. Wife make huz-bund life bad and . . ." He shrugged. "You get mad wit Margaret?"

"Mad, yes. In a murderous rage, no."

"Dat where it at when you arrest him. Wife gone to Kot-ze-bue. 'Fraid a-Ronnie, 'fraid take chid-ren."

"I think the council should coordinate these discipli-nary efforts with the police."

"Why?"

"Because we are entrusted with serving and protect-ing the community."

"But da council is leader to People. It da Inupiat voice."

Ray wasn't in the mood to argue or point out that few people paid much attention to the council nowadays. The council was on show during ceremonies and festivals, but was wielding less and less real power.

"You listen me," Grandfather told him. "I utuqqanaaq, mem-ree bad. But I still hear tuungak. I see ukpIk. Come take Aana Netsilik. I see Raven move, circle. Ronnie deserve be 'rested. Good he in jail. But he no keel Aana. He a . . ." He struggled for the word. "He a . . . 'look udder way' trip."

Look udder way trip? Ray thought. "You mean, trick? Oh, a distraction."

"I mean trip get you look udder way, while he do evil."

Ray nodded.

"We're ready," Margaret said from the entryway. She had the kids in their shoes and jackets.

"Okay." Ray reached for Grandfather's hand.

"I no need help," the old man said gruffly. With some effort, he rose and ambled to the entryway and out the door.

"So he's coming?" Margaret said.

"I guess so."

"Good. What did you say to him?"

"I told him that if he stayed here, he'd have to have your leftover meatloaf for lunch." Ray laughed and dodged a punch. "Come on, guys," he said, ushering the kids out. "Let's go to Nalukataq."

➤➤ TWELVE ➤➤

"I WANNA DO the blanket toss first!"

"Bank ta!"

Ray glanced back at Keera and Freddie, both of whom were strapped into their car seats. They were giggling and smiling, the exact opposite of Grandfather, who was in the back bench seat of the van, looking out the window absently, his face void of emotion. He looked old. Old and tired.

"Can we, Daddy? Can we do the blanket toss first?"

"Bank ta!"

"We'll see," Ray answered diplomatically.

As the kids cheered this, Keera for assuming "we'll see" meant "yes," and Freddie, just because, Margaret said from the passenger seat, "I'm glad you didn't have to work."

"Me too."

"It not right work Nalukataq," the old man said from the back. Though he claimed to be hard of hearing and slow of mind, he was still very quick when he wanted to be.

"Somebody has to watch the store," Ray said. He

found it interesting that the same man who was prodding him to put in more time on the Clearwater case didn't want him working today. His mysticism and his sense of tradition seemed to be at cross purposes today.

"What store you talk 'bout?" Grandfather asked.

In the old days, the town shut down for festivals. Stores closed, city hall closed, everything closed. But that was before the introduction of alcohol and television and consumerism. The People hadn't been perfect or sinless before the intrusion of white culture. They had, however, been less selfish and self-serving. Being enveloped by America meant being taught how to want things and accumulate them, emotions and activities for which they had previously never seen the need. It had taught them greed. It was unthinkable for the police to stand down on a holiday now. Who knew what might happen. Looting? Vandalism? Arson? Burglary?

As they approached the festival grounds, the sides of the road became crowded with parked cars and pedestrians.

"Geez . . ." Margaret gasped. "I've never seen them park out this far."

"According to the captain, there's quite a few tourists in town this year," Ray said.

They reached a standstill of traffic. Kids and adults on ATVs rolled past on the shoulder at regular intervals, the drivers laughing at the jam-up.

"You should arrest them, Daddy," Keera said.

"Oh, yeah? What for?"

"For driving on the side and passing on the right."

Ray looked back at her, impressed at her knowledge of road rules.

"That's against the law."

"Yes, it is, but . . . I'm off-duty and . . . it's festival, so . . ." When it came to ATVs, the policy was pretty much hands off. Unless they were being truly reckless and endangering the lives of others, Ray and his co-workers left them alone. There were too many in town to keep up with enforcement—almost like bicycles in some parts of Asia—and though a few people had been killed in ATV accidents, none of those had occurred within the city limits. They usually happened on hunting trips or out at the whaling camps and often involved alcohol as a contributing factor.

As they crept through the shops and storefronts of downtown, Grandfather grumbled from the back, "Should no work."

Almost all the shops were open, Ray noticed, many offering T-shirts and trinkets from sidewalk stands that were being overrun by souvenir seekers. A television crew was set up on the corner, the camera shooting a man with his back to the festival grounds, which were directly across the street.

"This is gross," Margaret said. "It looks like a circus."

"Circus?" Keera shouted.

"Sur-is!" Freddie yelled.

"Yeah," Ray agreed. "Ever since Hodish and his publicity campaigns, things have gotten out of hand."

"There's just too many people," Margaret said. "It gives me the creeps."

"Should no work," Grandfather muttered disapprovingly.

"We should have walked," Margaret complained.

"It's too far for the kids," Ray said. Actually, he was thinking, it was too far for Grandfather.

They reached a bottleneck at a wide vacant lot that was part of the festival grounds. It was three-quarters full of cars. Ray rolled the window down as a man in an orange vest approached them. "Can we park in here?"

"Sure. Five dollars."

"Five dollars? Since when is it five dollars?"

The man shrugged. He was a naluaqmiu that Ray didn't recognize. "You wanna park here or not?"

Ray dug his wallet out of his pocket. "You live here?"

"Heck no. I'm from Sacramento. I got hired on by Roth and they flew me up."

"Roth?"

"The Roth Science Foundation."

Ray handed the man a ten and watched him make change.

"Go on in," the man said, offering five ones. "The other guys will direct you to a spot."

Ray rolled the window back up and drove on. There was another man in an orange vest waving them forward, a third pointing at a place on the end of the row of cars, a good hundred yards away from the festivities.

Ray rolled the window down again. "Can I drive up and drop my family off?"

The man shook his head. "No traffic allowed up there."

"I've got two children, a woman, and an eighty-nine-year-old man . . ."

"Eight-eight!" Grandfather corrected.

"An *eighty-eight*-year-old man. Can't I just . . ."

"You can park it here or you can turn it around and find another lot."

Ray rolled up the window and turned into the slot. "Jerk . . ."

Keera and Freddie giggled.

"Ray . . ." Margaret warned.

"Well, he is."

"You should arrest him, Daddy," Keera suggested.

"I should at least have flashed him my badge. Telling me where I can and can't drive . . . in my own town . . ."

"Ray . . ."

He shifted into park, switched off the car and took a deep breath. "Okay . . ."

They began the rather involved process of disembarking: assisting Grandfather out of the back, unhooking Freddie, making sure everyone still had on shoes, coats . . .

When everyone was out and their attire approved by one or both parents, they began the trek to the festival grounds. A dozen yards later, Freddie demanded, "Care-wee! Care-wee!" Ray picked up him. Keera gave out at about the halfway point, feigning complete exhaustion. Ray handed Freddie to Margaret and put Keera up on his shoulders.

"I tired too," Grandfather said.

"I'm not carrying you," Ray said.

They followed the stream of foot traffic to the festival grounds overlooking the beach. The wind was blowing and the sky, which had been clear earlier, was now gray and overcast. Ray was glad they'd brought coats.

"Daddy! I see the blanket toss!" Keera shouted excitedly.

"Bank-ta!" Freddie chimed.

"There's a lady going way high." Keera gasped and pointed. "She's doing flips!"

"Oh, yeah?"

"She's really good!"

"And you think that looks like fun, huh?"

"Uh-huh!"

They made their way through the opening in the fence and waded into the sea of people. There were Inupiat, Ray knew, from all over the North Slope, as well as a far larger than usual collection of tanik.

"There's Hadie," Margaret said. She waved. "And Jed."

Even though the temperature was in the forties, many of the people had on their best caribou parkas for the occasion. The colorful flags of the various whaling crews whipped in the breeze high above the grounds. Makeshift plywood tables had been set up to hold the plastic-lined cardboard boxes of food brought in and served by the crews. After the Elders performed the blessing, the food would be served: muktuq, fish, miki-gaq, niglik soup, duck soup, crackers, bread, tea, coffee, Eskimo donuts . . .

Ray's stomach rumbled at the thought of all these delicacies and he realized that while he'd just had breakfast, he was still hungry.

"What are those?" Margaret wondered aloud. She was squinting at a long row of booths that had been set up along the beach. Several were selling food, others souvenirs. One had a sign that read: Eskimo Yo-Yos. Another said: Eskimo Dolls.

"Hodish's idea, no doubt," Ray grumbled. It reminded him of a crass flea market he had once seen in Anchorage. "Who else would think of debasing festival to this level?"

"Come on!" Keera began pulling them toward the blanket toss area where much of the crowd was congregated. Dozens of hands gripped the ogrook skin that had once covered a whaling umiak and was now a high-powered trampoline.

Ray and his family stood watching for a moment as the woman who had been flipping and doing di-dos in the air finished and a young man took her place. He was clutching a plastic bag in his hand.

"Candy!" Keera said.

It was traditional to toss candy from the peak of flight and let the children scramble for it.

"Atauchikun!" the crowd chanted in unison. "Altogether! One! Two! Three! Go!" And the young man was sent skyward, plastic grocery sack in hand.

"Hurry! We have to get some!" Keera yelled. She and Freddie began scrambling closer to the blanket.

As Margaret followed after them, Ray spotted Ernest Nilchick, a longtime friend and one of the whaling captains. Ernest waved him over.

"I'll be back in a minute," he told Margaret.

"Hurry, Daddy!" Keera called. "Or you'll miss the candy!"

"Cannee!" Freddie shrieked.

Ray walked over and greeted, "Happy Nalukataq."

"Same to you, Raymond," Ernest said. He was a large man with a round, happy face that was creased with a spectacular network of wrinkles. Wearing a dusty down coat and a ratty wool sailor's cap, he could easily have been mistaken for an indigent rather than an umialik.

"How was your season?"

"Good. Not as many whales as last year. Too cold, I think. But we got plenty. More than enough. The Bowhead is good to us."

"Always," Ray grunted. It was forbidden to complain about a whaling season, even if it was a terrible one.

"Say, I heard about Ronnie," Ernest said.

"You did?"

"Yah." He shook his head. "I knew he was no good."

Ray nodded, recalling that once upon a time, Ronnie had been on Ernest's crew. That was before he supposedly hurt his leg or arm or whatever it was and went on the dole and began drinking heavily.

"He's a drunk."

Ray nodded again, thankful that Ernest didn't add, just like your father. Ernest had been a friend of Ray's father. They had worked together before the former had succumbed to the lure of alcohol. After his father's death, Ray had come to look upon Ernest as something of an adopted uncle.

"It's good that he's in jail."

"I agree."

"He never was much for work. Mostly just a lazybones." He muttered something that Ray didn't catch before saying, "Shoulda seen him last night."

"Oh, yeah?"

"He was drunk as a skunk. No surprise he did something stupid. Something evil. He's an evil lazybones. And when he gets drunk, he gets mean. Last night, he was hollering at my crew while they were dancing out in Browerville."

"Is that right?"

"Sloshed. Drunk as a skunk."

"When was that?"

"Around . . . seven or eight. He could hardly walk. And then later, he had a couple-a girls with him. You know, the kind that make for bad times."

Ray blinked at him, his mind taking this bit of information and running with it. If Ronnie was "drunk as a skunk" at seven or eight, how would he have killed Aana later in the night? For that matter, how would he have cut off her finger, the ring finger only, if he was sloshed?

"It's good you arrested him. Very good for everybody. Get da trash outta the neighborhood." He sniffed. "Well . . . you and da family have a great festival. I'll be around to see your Grandfadder later. And be sure to come to get some of my muktuq, okay?"

"You bet, Ernest."

"It's da best. And my wife made mikigaq that's also da best."

"I believe it."

"Happy Nalukataq." He patted Ray on the back and set off toward the food area.

Ray pulled his cell phone out and dialed. He could see Margaret and Grandfather and the kids from where he was standing. The two adults were sitting on a picnic table bench while Keera and Freddie scampered in the gravel with dozens of other kids for loose candy. The line rang and a woman answered.

"Melissa?"

"Ray? What's up?"

"How are you coming on that autopsy?"

"I'm doing it as we speak. You're on headset."

"Any idea when you'll be done."

"I'm not supposed to comment on that."

"What?"

There was a pause. "I could get in trouble, Ray."

"With who?"

There was another pause. "I shouldn't be talking to you."

"Why not?"

"Because you're off the case."

"News travels fast around here."

"It's now 'need to know' only."

"Says who?"

Silence.

"Come on, Melissa. It's me, Ray. What's going on?"

"I could ask you the same thing."

"Huh?"

"All I know is that when I got back to the hospital, there was a message waiting for me that said I was to postpone the Clearwater autopsy until tomorrow."

"Tomorrow? Why?"

"Beats me. It also said the case was 'need to know' and that I wasn't to discuss it with anyone. Especially you."

"I was just interested in time and cause of death."

She didn't reply.

"Can't you tell me that?" When she didn't respond, he said, "At the scene you guessed that the time was around ten. Is that still good?"

He could hear her breathing on the line.

"Melissa . . ."

"Ray, I can't."

"Sure you can. You're not waiting on the autopsy."

"That's because waiting would be foolish. We'd lose information."

"Okay. Same story here. I need this information."

She groaned. "What for?"

He hesitated. "Because I . . . there's a chance that . . . I'm starting to wonder about Ronnie as the perp."

"Word is it was deadbang."

"It was. Maybe a little too *deadbang*."

"How much more do you have with the autopsy?"

"I'm finishing up right now. It was pretty straightforward."

"Can you meet me at Blackie's . . . in . . ." He checked his watch. "Half an hour?"

"I guess. But . . . Ray . . ."

When she didn't continue, he asked, "What?"

"We could both be disciplined for this."

"For doing our jobs?"

"You know what I mean."

"I'm willing to take a chance. How about you?"

She sighed at him. "Okay."

"See you at Blackie's."

➤➤ THIRTEEN ◄◄

"WHO WERE YOU talking to?"

Startled, Ray turned and saw Margaret standing next to him. She had snuck up on him. Or at least, approached without being noticed.

He slapped the phone shut and stood there feeling guilty—for failing to let go of the case after he had promised to, and for talking to Melissa. Why the latter bothered him, he wasn't sure.

"Ray?" She wasn't being overbearing, just curious.

"Uh . . . it was . . . work."

Her eyes narrowed. "I thought you were off for the weekend."

"I am. Sort of."

"Ray . . ." she complained.

"It's just a meeting."

"Ray . . . !"

"It shouldn't take long."

"Mmm-hmm."

He took her hand and kissed her.

"What was that for?" she asked suspiciously.

"For being so understanding." He grinned at her.

"You're incorrigible."

"I might take offense if I knew what that meant."

She slugged him. "You better make it quick, buddy, or you're dead meat."

"I will."

"Which? Make it quick? Or be dead meat?"

He kissed her again. "Yes."

"Are you taking the car?" Margaret asked him. "How are we supposed to . . . ?"

"Here." He handed her the keys. "I'll walk."

"To the station? It's a long ways."

Oops, Ray thought. He almost said I'm not going to the station, which would bring more questions and more chances for him to snare himself in a half-truth. "That's okay," he said. "I need the exercise." He walked over to the kids. "Hey, guys. Daddy has to work for few minutes."

"Daddy! Look what I got!" Keera displayed two fists full of hard candy.

"Da-dee!" Freddie yelled. He held out a single butterscotch candy.

"You have to share with him, you know that, right?"

Keera nodded. "I already did. I gave him the butterscotch."

"That's a start." He rubbed their heads affectionately and saw Grandfather glaring at him. "What?"

"Not right work festival."

"Yeah, well, sometimes you gotta do what you gotta do."

Grandfather waved him over and Ray groaned inwardly, expecting to be admonished for violating the old ways.

"Grandfather, things have changed and there are some occupations that require . . ." he started.

But the old man cut him off. "Come," he said motioning for Ray to lean down.

"What?" Ray groaned.

"Be careful bad anaun."

Oh, geez, Ray thought.

"He know you see him, follow him. Be much careful, Ray-mond."

"I will."

"Listen to tuungak. They keep you safe."

"Right."

He handed Ray something. It was a jade charm: the likeness of a whale. "You listen. Spirit of ingutuq guide. Young bow-head see, he guide."

"Thanks." He started across the gravel to the street and as he put the charm into his jacket pocket, his fingers discovered a plastic sack. The frowning woman. He had forgotten to turn it over to Lewis and Billy Bob. He checked the other pocket and found the note from the watering can. Maybe he could use these as an excuse to visit the station later.

He walked the three blocks to Blackie's and found the street and the café itself deserted. Apparently everyone had migrated to the festival grounds in anticipation of the feast. He slid into a booth by the window, then changed his mind. Though he was doing nothing wrong, there was no reason to advertise his meeting with Melissa. He chose a stool at the counter.

A middle-aged man with long black hair appeared in the open door to the kitchen. "What are you doing here?" he asked, rubbing his hands on his apron.

"Hey, Blackie."

"Why aren't you at festival like everybody else?"

Ray shrugged. "You are open, aren't you?"

"Barely. I gave Julie and Mike the rest of the day off. You should have seen this place a half hour ago. It was packed to the gills."

Ray glanced around at the empty chairs and tables.

"You bet. Naluaqmiut with manIk to burn." He laughed. "The best kind." He poured Ray a cup of coffee. "So what'll it be? With Mike gone, I can't do ya anything fancy. How about ham and eggs? A BLT? Soup? We got onion today."

"No, thanks. Coffee's fine."

Blackie nodded. "So what's up?"

"Not much."

He frowned at Ray. "You get in a fight with the nuliaq?"

"No."

"Where's your uniform?" Blackie peered around. "This a stakeout or something?"

Ray shook his head. "I'm off duty."

"Then what gives?"

After sipping his coffee, Ray answered, "I'm meeting someone."

Blackie's eyebrows fell. "Oh, yeah?"

"Yeah."

"Meeting someone . . . ? We talking about an anaun someone or a . . . niviaqsiaq someone?"

"We're talking about it not being any of your business."

"Ah . . . niviaqsiaq."

"It's not like that."

"Uh-huh." Blackie was clearly not convinced. "Don't worry." He pretended to lock his lips. "Mum's the word."

"It's not like that."

"Sure, sure . . . I understand."

"It's Melissa . . . I mean Dr. Bradshaw."

This caused Blackie's eyebrows to wiggle up and down. "Aarigaa! . . ."

"*Dr.* Bradshaw," Ray emphasized.

"She's a pretty thing."

"Blackie . . . it's police business."

"Sure, sure . . . I get it. You're meeting a young lady off duty, away from festival . . . on business. Yah. You don't have to beat me over the head." He turned away and began working on some of the dirty dishes that were piled behind the counter. "She's a pretty thing."

Ray gave up on him. If he wanted to think their meeting was something other than professional, let him. As long as Margaret didn't find out. Or the captain. Either way, he would be in big trouble.

Twisting on the stool, he looked out the window. There was no traffic on the street and parked cars lined both sides. In a minute he saw Melissa crossing toward the café. She came through the door and, after casting a glance over her shoulder rather suspiciously, took a stool next to Ray.

"We could catch it for this," she said.

"Good to see you too."

She twisted her head and scanned the street. "So what's so important?"

"I need the T-O-D."

"You told me that on the phone. And I told you, ten P.M."

"Couldn't have been earlier. Say . . . eight?"

She shook her head. "It would be a stretch to make it nine."

Ray nodded. "How about cause of death?"

"Blow to the head."

"Where?"

She tapped her temple. "She also had a contusion on the crown of her head. But that was older."

"What do you mean older?"

"I mean whoever did it, hit her there first. Probably knocked her down and maybe out. But then didn't kill her for a while."

"Could the shot to the crown have been around eight?"

"Maybe." She stopped as Blackie appeared and poured her some coffee. "Thanks."

"Let me know if you need anything," he said. He eyed them both before returning to the kitchen.

When he was gone, she told Ray, "The finger was close to the death blow."

"How close?"

"I'd say minutes. He took the finger and then killed her."

"At the scene, you said the finger was severed after death."

Melissa shook her head. "I said there wasn't enough blood. Which means the body was moved."

Ray sighed. "Okay . . . so, she was attacked around eight, the finger was removed, she was killed, then moved." He considered this for a moment. "Anything else out of the ordinary?"

"No. Except that I'm supposed to delay my report until tomorrow."

"Who ordered that?"

"No idea. It was handed down through the hospital administration."

"Does anyone know you did the autopsy?"

"I don't think so. I dictated my notes, but I'll wait until tomorrow to file the report."

They sat sipping their coffee and gazing out the window.

"Why are you starting to question Ronnie as the perp?" she asked.

"Well, for one thing, I was talking to one of the whaling captains. He saw Ronnie last night, around eight, falling down drunk."

"So?"

"So that's all."

She looked at him, obviously expecting more.

"How could he have murdered Aana at ten when he was out of it at eight?"

"You said he was drunk. Not passed out."

"Right."

She shrugged. "He could have dried out a little and . . ."

"Not Ronnie. He doesn't dry out. When he goes on a binge . . ."

"If he's a drunk," she countered, "then he has a high tolerance for alcohol."

"Yeah, but if he was that sloshed . . . how would he cut off her finger without damaging the rest of the hand?"

Melissa sighed at this. "Maybe he was just lucky."

"Or maybe Ronnie was pissed at Aana for filing a complaint against him with the council and for making anonymous calls to the department . . . maybe he even blamed Aana for his wife leaving, who knows? Anyway, he decides to get back." Ray thought for a second.

"What?" Melissa prodded.

"He told me when I arrested him that he was only trying to scare her."

"What's he supposed to say? 'Uh, yeah, sure . . . I did it.' "

"No. But . . . what if he was telling the truth? What if he was only trying to spook her? He shows up drunk, feeling mean, gets violent, hits her on the head. She falls, he freaks out, thinking he killed her, and runs."

"And comes back later when he's a little more sober, cuts off her finger, and puts her in the shed?"

"No. Somebody else comes back later and does all that."

"And just who might that be?" she asked skeptically.

Ray sagged. "No idea."

"This is exactly why you're off the case, Ray."

"Why?"

"Because you won't let go. Once you get a hold of something . . ."

"I know. I get tunnel vision. My wife complains about that."

"It's a good trait in a cop," she shot back. "It means you aren't satisfied with easy collars and easy answers."

He shook his head. "I'd be happier right now if I knew Ronnie did it."

"I think he did, Ray." Melissa's beeper went off. She checked it, then groaned, "Uh-oh . . ."

"What is it?"

"EMTs are bringing in someone from the festival grounds: seven-year-old with a fracture to her arm."

"Seven-year-old?! Girl or boy?"

"Doesn't say."

Ray tossed some money at the counter and they hurried outside. As they were trotting across the street, a car horn sounded. Ray flinched and looked behind them. It was a police cruiser with Billy Bob at the wheel. He rolled down the window.

"Say, partner. Where you running off to?"

Ray took Melissa by the hand and pulled her toward the cruiser. After loading her into the backseat, he hopped into the front.

Billy Bob looked at Melissa with wide eyes. "Where's Margaret?"

"Take us to the hospital," Ray ordered. "It's an emergency."

Billy Bob shifted into gear and accelerated down the street. After they had screeched around the corner, he asked in a whisper, "What's going on, Ray?"

"I don't know."

➤➤ FOURTEEN ◀◀

BILLY BOB FLIPPED on the siren and the lights and raced along the empty streets to the hospital. Pulling up to the ER entrance, he asked, "Is somebody hurt?"

An ambulance was sitting outside, the back doors still hanging open. Ray scanned the parking area for Margaret's van.

"There are other seven-year-olds in Barrow, Ray," Melissa told him as they got out and started for the door.

"I know," he said. But he had a bad feeling.

"You want me to sit tight and wait on y'all?" Billy Bob called out the car window.

Ray hurried through the double doors without answering. A pair of EMTs were standing at the admittance desk. Ray had known both men since high school.

"Was it Keera?" he asked.

They nodded.

"I knew it!"

"But she's fine, Ray. Just a broken arm. It wasn't a compound or anything."

"I knew it," Ray repeated. "She fell off that stupid blanket toss." He turned to Melissa. "I told Margaret she was too little for it."

They went to the waiting room and found Grandfather sitting with Freddie in his lap. Grandfather shook his head at Ray and frowned. "I tell you dere e-vil happ-ning."

"Come on," Melissa said. She led Ray through a door marked "Hospital Personnel Only."

They passed several empty exam rooms before reaching a nurses' station.

"Morning, Dr. Bradshaw," the nurse said.

"Good morning. Can you tell me which room the Attla girl is in?" Melissa asked.

"Four."

In room 4, Margaret was standing next to Keera, who was lying on an exam table, smiling. When she saw Ray, the smile grew.

"Daddy!"

"Hi, honey," he said in a sympathetic tone. He looked at her arm, which was in a splint device to keep it immobilized, then looked at Margaret. "I told you she was too small for the blanket toss."

"I didn't do it on the blanket toss," Keera said, sounding far too happy for someone with a broken arm.

"How'd it happen?" Ray looked to Margaret for the answer.

"She and one of her friends . . ."

"Jessica," Keera said.

". . . Followed some other kids out onto the floes."

"The floes?!"

"Just right there by the beach. They were jumping

back and forth across those really shallow leads
and . . ."

"And I slipped and hit a big chunk of ice, Daddy."

"Ouch!"

"It didn't hurt that much," Keera claimed. "But it
made my arm into a V."

Ray made a face.

"Must have broken both bones," Melissa surmised.
She introduced herself to Margaret and Ray thought he
noted a glimmer of recognition in Margaret's eyes. He
had told her about working with a Dr. Bradshaw
before, but had not described her in detail.

"Ray didn't mention that you were a woman," Margaret said, smiling without amusement. Under her
breath, in Ray's direction, she added, "And a beautiful
one at that."

Another doctor entered the room carrying an X-ray.
He greeted Melissa with a quiet, "I thought you were
off."

"So did I."

"Well," he said to Ray, "you must be the father. I'm
Dr. Hamilton."

Ray shook the doctor's hand.

Dr. Hamilton stuck the X-ray onto a lightbox affixed
to the wall and flipped it on. A skeletal picture of an
arm appeared. The two main bones were neatly
snapped in half midway between the elbow and the
wrist.

"That's your arm, Keera," he told her.

"It is?"

"Yes. And see right here and here? That's where it's
broken."

"Will she require surgery?" Margaret asked.

He shook his head. "It's a nice clean break and since no joints are involved, we'll just set it and cast it."

"I get a cast?" Keera gasped.

"You certainly do."

"Mommy, remember when Samantha had a cast? And everybody got to sign it?"

Margaret nodded.

"This will be great!" She turned to Ray. "Daddy, I get a cast!"

"Wow." Ray was amazed at how well Keera was taking this.

"It'll take a little while," the doctor told them.

"I don't mind," Keera said. "As long as I get a cast. Samantha's was purple. Can I have a purple one?"

"You can pick whatever color you'd like."

"I want purple."

The doctor left and, after a little smile of sympathy, Melissa left too.

Ray said to Margaret, "You want to stay with her, or . . ."

Margaret nodded.

"How about if I take Grandfather and Freddie home."

"Good idea. I was a little nervous about leaving Freddie with him."

"I saw them in the waiting room. They're doing fine."

"Good." She sighed and drooped a little, then shook her head at Ray.

"I know," he said, feeling the same relief that Keera was okay, but the nagging fear that hung around after your child hurts themselves seriously in such an innocuous situation. Keera had been through other, much more dangerous things, with apparently little lasting impact. In fact, Ray thought, her experiences had apparently toughened her, resulting in the very positive attitude evidenced today.

"I'll come back with Freddie after I get Grandfather home. We can trade off watching him if we need to."

"Okay," Margaret said.

Ray bent and kissed Keera on the cheek. "I'll be back in a little while, honey. You hang in there."

"Oh, I will Daddy. Especially if I get a purple cast."

"You're a trooper," he told her. He left and found Melissa waiting for him in the hall.

"She'll be fine," Melissa assured.

"Really?"

"Oh, yeah. Kids heal fast. And that break . . . if you have to break a bone, that's how to do it. Nice and clean. She'll be good as new after six weeks in that purple cast."

"Yeah, *purple.*" He shook his head, wondering why anyone would want to call attention to a broken limb by wearing a colorful cast.

"Hey, she's a girl. She probably has lots of clothes to match. That's important. A plain old white cast would clash."

"We wouldn't want that," Ray agreed sarcastically as they went back down the hall.

When they got to the waiting room, he scanned the chairs and said, "Thanks for your help—with Keera and with . . ." His voice trailed off when he realized that Freddie was sitting all alone in a chair. No Grandfather.

Ray rushed over to him. "Hey there, champ." He picked Freddie up. "Where's Grandfather?"

Freddie smiled brightly and pointed at the exit.

Ray looked around the room again. "Did he go to the bathroom or something?"

Freddie continued to point.

"Did he go to get you a snack?"

"Ampa," Freddie said, jabbing a finger at the door.

"He couldn't have . . ." Ray muttered.

"What's the matter?" Melissa asked.

"My Grandfather. He . . . uh . . ."

Freddie pointed enthusiastically. "Ampa!"

"He might have wandered off."

"Does he have Alzheimer's?" she asked.

"He's just getting senile. Forgetting things . . ." Ray looked at Freddie. "Important things."

"Has he been to see anyone?"

"No. He hates doctors. Except for anjatkut."

Melissa made a face. "What?"

"Shamans. Grandfather's one of the elders. He believes in the old ways, the tuungak . . . you know . . . the whole nine yards."

Melissa nodded.

"Could you watch Freddie for just a second?"

"Sure." She sat down and picked a toy up from the end table. "Hey, Freddie. How are you?" Freddie went right to her.

Ray went through the lobby and checked the lavatory, then the cafeteria. No Grandfather. When he got back to Melissa he shook his head. "I don't know where he is."

"Ampa!" Freddie said, pointing at the door.

"I'll have security search the hospital."

"I'd appreciate that."

Melissa went to the admission desk and picked up the phone.

"What's become of Grandfather, Freddie?" Ray asked, still scanning the area, expecting the old man to come shuffling up at any moment.

"Go!" Freddie chirped, pointing at the door.

"Did Grandfather go outside?" Ray asked him.

Freddie nodded at him. When Melissa returned, Ray said, "He might have left the building."

"I've got security checking each floor. You want me to help you look outside?"

"If you wouldn't mind."

"What's he look like?"

Ray told her, nearly certain that no one else fitting his description would be wandering the streets. All the old people who weren't bedridden were at festival.

"Ampa!" Freddie said.

"Don't worry, Freddie," Melissa said in a comforting tone. "We'll find your Grampa."

They went through the glass doors to the sidewalk. The ambulance was gone, but Billy Bob's cruiser was still parked under the awning. Ray walked over and tapped on the driver's window. Billy Bob glanced up from a newspaper and rolled the window down.

"Is ever-tang all right?"

"Did you see Grandfather out here?"

Billy Bob glanced around. "Naw. I shore didn't. But . . . to tell you the truth, I was busy catching up on the baseball scores and wasn't payin' much attention."

Ray looked up the street one way, then the other. All was quiet: no cars, no pedestrians. Every few seconds, pieces of music came to them on the breeze. Festival music, he realized. The dancing had begun.

"You want me to call in a missing person?" Billy Bob asked.

"No. Just sit tight. I may need you to give him a ride home, if we can find him."

"Didn't you lose him a couple weeks back, down at the grocery store?"

"I didn't lose him," Ray shot back defensively. "He just walked off."

"I'll take this direction," Melissa told Ray, nodding to the left. "You take that way. We'll do the block and meet on the other side of the hospital."

"Okay." Ray held out his hand for Freddie, but the boy took hold of Melissa's hand and smiled at him.

"I don't mind," Melissa told him.

Ray started up the block, his anger rising. As if a murder investigation *and* festival *and* his daughter's broken arm weren't enough . . . now *this*. Add to that the fact that he was tired, already out of sorts—stressed or a little depressed or going through a midlife crisis, whatever the heck it was—and you had the makings of an explosion. He walked briskly along, taking deep breaths, telling himself that he needed to relax, but knowing that he might well blow up when he located Grandfather. He loved the old man dearly and was grateful for his upbringing and for the important things he had taught Ray about The People and their ways. But he could be incredibly infuriating. Especially in these last few years as Grandfather's faculties had begun to deteriorate.

Growing old was hard, Ray thought, eyes raking the street, the alleyways, the side doors of the hospital. Maybe that was part of his problem. Seeing Grandfather go downhill, feeling his own body begin to slow down a little, taking a long, hard look at the road laid out before him . . . not liking what he saw. How did people endure it? How was Grandfather keeping despair at bay? He had little to live for. What kept him going?

Ray realized that in his self-absorbed state, he had failed to take the old man's emotional state into consideration, much less ask about it. He decided to try and be more understanding, to be more empathetic, to open up some sort of dialogue with the person who had played such an important role in his life. If he failed to do this, he would regret it always. And there wasn't that much time left to work on their relationship, was there? This thought made Ray sad and served to dissipate his anger.

It returned, however, as a sense of utter frustration and irritation when he reached the other side of the block and saw Melissa and Freddie standing there, waiting on him.

"Nothing?"

Melissa shook her head.

"Where could he be?"

"Maybe he went back to the festival."

"And left his great-grandson alone in the hospital?"

Melissa shrugged.

Ray blew air at the deserted street.

"He could be over at the museum."

"He could be anywhere."

"It's right across the street. If he went out the main ER door, it's a straight shot."

"I guess it's worth a look." They walked back around to the ER entrance and crossed the street. Inside the patrol car, Billy Bob was hidden behind the paper. Ray whistled, got no response, whistled again. The cowboy finally lowered the paper and squinted out at them. He rolled down the window. "Find him?"

"Not yet. Keep an eye out."

They went into the museum, Melissa holding one of Freddie's hands, Ray holding the other. The interior, like the streets outside, was empty. A big banner declared that a new exhibit was on show: Dance of the Whale, sponsored by the Roth Science Foundation.

They walked to the information desk and Ray greeted Mrs. Hucheck, the curator. She was in her sixties, very talkative and terribly farsighted.

"How is the Attla family on this fine festival day?" She smiled at Freddie, then the smile disappeared as she noticed that the woman with them wasn't Margaret.

She recovered quickly and said hello to Melissa.

"Actually, we're looking for my grandfather."

"You've come to the right place."

"He's here?"

"He's in the Whale Hall, enjoying our new exhibit."

"Thank goodness."

"And I must say, it really is a fine one. Probably the most elaborate, and, though it may be a little crude to say, the most expensive display we've ever hosted. The Roth Foundation went all out and the result is quite spectacular. I just wish more people had stopped by to see it."

"Maybe they will after festival," Ray said, trying to disengage from the conversation.

"Unfortunately, by then it will be too late," she went on. "It will be moving on tomorrow to start an impressive tour schedule."

"That's great," Ray said, not interested in the slight-

est. He made a move for the Whale Hall and was
stopped by her upheld hand.

"I should explain that we're not talking about small
towns. Oh, no. It will stop in Seattle, Los Angeles, the
Smithsonian in Washington, DC . . ."

"That's great. If you'll excuse me . . ."

"Then on to New York. After that, it heads overseas
to London, Paris and finally Vienna."

"Fascinating," Ray said.

"They're touting it as the biggest thing since King
Tut."

"Oh, yeah?"

"You remember: the artifacts of the Egyptian
pharaoh Tutankhamen that were recovered in Egypt
and displayed in the eighties."

"Right."

"In fact, there was a movie crew in here just yesterday. From the Discovery Channel." She paused to
emphasize the importance of this. "They're producing
a special on the exhibit."

"Hmm . . . that's something."

"And several Barrow residents will be in the program, including yours truly." She smiled proudly.

"Congratulations. Listen I need to . . ."

"It really is a spectacular exhibit. Which is why
you'll want to take some time and really appreciate the
artifacts and informative materials." She handed them
a brochure. "You'll find a self-guided tour in there. Or
if you'd like, you can rent these personal tape
recorders . . ." She held one up.

"This will do fine," Ray said, tapping the brochure.
He wasn't planning to spend any longer with the
exhibit than it took to get Grandfather out the door.

"That will be twenty-five dollars."

"What?" Ray thought she had to be joking.

"I'd wave the entrance fee," she said in a hushed tone, "if it were up to me. But it's not. The Roth Foundation requires that we charge for all visitors."

"We're just going in to get Grandfather."

"I understand."

"Good."

"Thirty-five dollars." She stood there, waiting. "Or if you'd like to go in alone, it will only be fifteen dollars."

"Only . . ." Ray got his wallet out and paid her. "You guys stay here."

Melissa nodded.

The phone rang and Mrs. Hucheck answered.

"If you have any questions, please let me know," she whispered to Ray.

"I'll be right back," he told Melissa. Ray went through the turnstile and beneath the Dance of the Whale banner. He had heard about the arrival of the display. It had been heralded in the paper and described as a very detailed history of The People and their dependence on the bowhead whale. School kids had been brought in and Mayor Hodish had performed the ribbon cutting ceremony. However, Barrow wasn't much for highbrow things like museum exhibits, especially those that cost $15 a pop, and Ray knew of no one who had actually seen it.

He entered a large room with a high ceiling that was decorated with colorful cloth banners and an enormous replica of a bowhead. The exhibit was very attractive, incorporating a number of interactive displays, a movie running on a television inset in the whale's belly. Along the walls were brightly lit cases full of pots, jewelry, and photographs. Music was playing in the background, along with the haunting song of the bowhead.

And there in the midst of it all, seated on a bench beneath the wide mouth of the beast, was Grandfather.

➤ FIFTEEN ◄

"GRANDFATHER." HE WALKED up and touched him on the shoulder.

The old man flinched and looked up at him.

"What are you doing here?"

For a long moment, it seemed that Grandfather didn't know who he was.

"Are you all right?"

He squinted at Ray, then turned his attention back to the closest display. "I found it."

"Found what?"

"Da qitiqliagun."

Ray sighed and rubbed his face with a hand. They'd been through this before. In moving Grandfather's belongings from Nuiqsut to Barrow, an old ring of his had somehow been misplaced. They had searched the boxes for two days and Ray had gone back to Nuiqsut to check Grandfather's ivrulik, all to no avail.

"We've been over this, Grandfather," he said. "Your ring . . . it's gone. I'm sorry but . . ."

"Not mine."

"What are you talking about."

He lifted a bony finger and aimed it at the display. "Hers."

"Her who?"

"Hill-ree Clearwater."

Ray twisted his head at the display. There were a number of ivory and jade pieces, several rings, some necklaces, even an ulu knife, all somehow incorporating the shape of a bowhead whale. A card in the corner explained that some of the artifacts were on loan from the Fairbanks museum, others donated by various private individuals, all now in the care of the Roth Foundation.

"Did Aana give some pieces to the foundation?" Ray asked wearily.

The old man shook his head.

"Then it obviously isn't . . ."

"On da end." He pointed.

Ray stepped over and examined a small but attractive ivory ring. It had been meticulously carved to form a single whale curling in upon itself to touch head to tail.

"What about it?"

"Da hers."

"It may look like her ring, but . . ."

"Not look like. *Is*."

"Okay, whatever." He looked Grandfather in the eye. "Do you realize what you did?" He waited, but Grandfather was focused on the display. "You left Freddie alone in the hospital." He paused again, but Grandfather refused to acknowledge this. "Did you hear me?"

Grandfather pointed at the display again. "Day took Hill-ree ring."

Ray decided that Melissa was right. They needed to

get Grandfather in for an exam. Getting him in would be a trick since he hated doctors and medicine and all things modern. But Ray would figure out a way.

"UkpIk say, it here."

It was sad, Ray thought, when a proud, noble man was reduced to this. Hearing voices. Being visited by snowy owls.

"An-suh apiqqun."

"What question?" Ray groaned.

"Why Hill-ree have die."

"Tuungak speak and ukpIk come. Help find keel-a."

"The tuungak are always a big help," Ray muttered.

"You no mitaagun 'bout tuungak."

"Oh, I wouldn't think of joking about the spirit," Ray shot back. "Come on. Let's get you home."

"UkpIk try show you what—what. But . . ." The old man shook his head at Ray. "You too much citee-fy."

"I'm what?"

"Drive car, watch Tee-Vee, listen ray-deeo."

"So?"

"Forget who you are."

Ray opened his mouth to reply, to launch into a rebuttal speech and argue that it was a new century, a new millennium and the world had changed. But he knew that no matter what he said, Grandfather would not budge from his position. The old ways were the best ways to him. To most elderly folks, no matter their cultural heritage, Ray thought. Maybe he too would be like that one day. Maybe he and Freddie or Freddie's kids would debate the same basic issues. He hoped not. He hoped that he would be more open to change than that.

"I know who I am," Ray finally said.

"Then why you no quviasuun?"

This struck a nerve. "Who says I'm not happy?"

"No one say. I see."

He tried to mask the fact that this was a very accurate assessment. Either Grandfather was a good guesser, or his powers of observation were as keen as they had always been.

"You try fill uumman," he said, tapping his chest, "with A-mare-eeka. But that only make miser-bull."

"Is that right?"

"You try fill with savaak. But savaak no-good."

"Don't start about my job. I'm proud of what I do."

"Try fill with anayuqaagiich. But make miser-bull too."

"I love my family!" Ray said, growing defensive.

"Nakuaqqun, but day not fill. Still killaQ—hole. Only Great Qaummaq fill dark place." He tapped his chest again. "Only Great Qaummaq make you see . . . feel. Take away miser-bull. Make quviasuun—joy inside-out."

Ray sighed, tiring of this bit of superstitious mumbo-jumbo and, simultaneously, trying to fight off a nagging sense that the old man was on to something. Though he didn't believe the spiritual baloney about a Great Light anymore, Ray did acknowledge the fact that man was more than just body and mind. There was something else, call it a soul, something intangible but very real that longed to be satisfied. And while his family and his job were able to provide him with a certain degree of happiness, there was still something lacking. A future. A purpose. A destiny. But he wasn't about to admit this to Grandfather.

"You listen ukpIk. He know."

"Okay," he said, trying to humor the old man.

"You listen, Raymond. No joking."

"Right."

"And let qaummaq fill dark place."

"Sure."

"Pro-mise."

"I promise," he said, not sure what he was promising.

"You see."

"Great." He took Grandfather by the arm. "Let's go home."

"What 'bout qitiqliagun?"

"What about it?"

"It belong Hill-ree."

Ray sighed. "It's not hers. Not unless she donated it."

"Day steal it."

"They who?"

"The keel-a and da udder one. You gotta catch."

Ray shook his head. "Even if someone stole her ring . . ."

"Day steal it," Grandfather repeated determinedly. "Stealed her entire mikigaq. Stealed qitiqliagun right off her."

Ray blinked at the old man. How did he know that Aana's ring finger had been "stolen"?

With some effort, Grandfather rose and approached the display case. Tapping the glass, he said, "Dat her qitiqliagun."

"Why would someone take her ring and put it in a museum exhibit?" Ray thought aloud.

"That what you gotta find out."

Ray looked at the ring through the glass. "It must just look like hers."

"Dat hers."

They stood staring at the ring for a moment before Ray took Grandfather by the arm and led him back to the lobby.

"What did you think?" Mrs. Hucheck asked with a bright smile. "Isn't it wonderful?"

"It's great," Ray said. "But I have a question."

Mrs. Hucheck seemed delighted by this.

"When was the exhibit set up?"

"Set up?"

"Yes. When did it arrive? When was it assembled, and when did it open to the public?"

"Let's see . . . it arrived last Thursday and we opened it on . . . Saturday."

"See?" Ray said to Grandfather. "It couldn't be Aana's ring."

"It her ring," Grandfather insisted.

Mrs. Hucheck looked at them curiously. "Is there a problem?"

"No. Just a disagreement."

"He killuq," Grandfather told Mrs. Hucheck.

"I'm not wrong."

"Wrong about what?" Mrs. Hucheck asked.

"It's a long story."

"Hill-ree Clearwater qitiqliagun in dere," Grandfather said, pointing.

"It can't be," Ray said, biting off his words. The old man was really getting on his nerves.

"It in dere."

"The exhibit was set up a week ago. It couldn't be in there even if someone did . . ."

"Explain to him that the exhibit has been here since last Saturday," Ray instructed. "Tell him that nothing has been added since then. Please."

"Well," Mrs. Hucheck began, "actually . . . some members of the Roth Foundation did make a few slight changes."

"When?"

"Last night. I got a phone call at about . . . oh . . . I'd say it was eleven. Yes, it was eleven, because I was watching the news and they were doing a special report about how illegal drugs are showing up in elementary schools in Anchorage. Elementary schools! Can you imagine? Little children, getting hooked on cocaine and marijuana and all sorts of terrible things."

"About the phone call?" Ray prodded.

"Oh, yes. Anyway, they called and said they needed to make some adjustments to the exhibit."

"At eleven o'clock at night?"

"That's exactly what I said. I asked them why it couldn't wait until morning. But they were insistent. So . . ." She shrugged. "I told them to come by for the key and they did."

"Who's *they?*"

"Mr. Roth and two of his people. They said they wouldn't be long, and they weren't. Just a few minutes later, they came to return the key."

"What was it they changed?"

"At first, I couldn't tell much of anything. Then I finally noticed that the ring exhibit was different."

"How so?"

"Well, one of the spots for a ring had been empty. I remember them saying that the piece had been lost in transit from Fairbanks. But apparently they found it and added it back in."

"It hers," Grandfather mumbled.

"Thank you, Mrs. Hucheck," Ray said.

"Come back anytime," she chimed.

Ray signaled Melissa and Freddie, who were sitting on a couch near the door, and started toward the exit with Grandfather.

Out on the sidewalk, Melissa said, "What took so long?"

"It hers," Grandfather repeated.

Melissa looked to Ray, obviously expecting an explanation.

Ray frowned. "They made adjustments to the exhibit last night. Around eleven. They added a ring."

"A ring?" Melissa shrugged. "So?"

"It belong Hill-ree Clearwater," Grandfather said.

"You're not saying that . . . that they . . ." Melissa said.

"No," Ray answered. *"I'm* not saying that at all. *He* is." He nodded at Grandfather.

"It is possible, I guess," Melissa said.

"But not probable in the least."

"How does he know about your aunt?" Melissa asked in a whisper.

"Ukplk tell me," Grandfather said, proving once again that his hearing was quite sharp.

"The snowy owl told him," Ray translated with heavy cynicism.

"Dat right," Grandfather said. "And he tell you, Raymond. If you listen. He tell you."

➤➤ SIXTEEN ◀◀

RAY LED GRANDFATHER, Melissa and Freddie across the street to Billy Bob's patrol car. After he loaded his son and the old man, Ray told Melissa, "Thanks. For helping with the case, and for helping with . . ." He waved at the backseat.

"No problem."

"I appreciate it."

When Ray started to get into the car, Melissa stopped him. "What are you going to do?"

"Take them home."

"I mean about that ring."

Ray shrugged.

"What if it is Mrs. Clearwater's?"

"I don't think it could be."

"But what if it is?"

"What if it is?" he countered.

"If it is, it means that whoever killed Mrs. Clearwater did it to get that ring."

Ray frowned at this. "Which doesn't make any sense. The ring is valuable, as an artifact and an antique. But . . . not worth someone's *life*."

158

"You already said you didn't think Ronnie committed the crime."

"I didn't say that."

"You intimated it."

"So?"

"So now there's this ring business."

"No. There's this crazy *Owl* business. There's a big difference. My Grandfather . . . he's always been different. And now . . ."

"I think you should at least check into it."

"You do, huh?"

"Yeah. There's something strange about the whole thing."

"I agree. And he's in the back seat." Ray nodded at the old man.

"You know what I mean."

Ray did, but still didn't know what to do about it. "I'm not on the case."

"That didn't stop you from meeting me to talk about the autopsy."

Touché, Ray thought.

"I just think you should look into it."

"You're tenacious, aren't you?"

She smiled as though this was a compliment. "You bet."

"I'll see what I can find out," he said without enthusiasm.

"I'd like to help."

He frowned at her. Melissa was very intelligent and obviously talented in piecing things together. She would probably be a great benefit to him. But she was also pretty and charming and likable. A little too likable.

"All I'm going to do is make a few phone calls and maybe go down to the station. I can handle it."

"How about if I babysit? I can watch Freddie for you. And Grandfather."

Ray considered this, then decided it wasn't a good idea. What if Margaret came home with Keera and found Melissa "intruding" on her territory. Besides, the next door neighbor, Mrs. Chu, their usual babysitter, would do just fine. She was a Filipino widow who never attended the Native festivals. She was good with Freddie, and Grandfather liked her, which was a big plus.

"No, we've got someone for that."

"Then how about . . . I could introduce you to Paul."

"Paul who?"

"Paul Roth, Chairman of the Roth Foundation."

"You know him?"

She nodded. "He came in yesterday with Montezuma's revenge."

Ray wasn't familiar with this term. "With what?"

"Diarrhea. I treated him. The foundation has a booth set up over at the festival grounds. He said I should stop by and say hello, that he had some sort of thank you gift for me." She shrugged. "Might be useful to talk to him."

"It might," Ray admitted. He finally caved. "Okay, I'll run these guys home and get them situated. Could you check on Keera for me?"

"Sure."

"Let's meet by the blanket toss in . . ." he checked his watch. "At noon."

"Okay." She smiled again, clearly excited about being part of the investigation.

"Remember," he cautioned, "this is unofficial."

"Mum's the word," she said, putting a finger to her lips. "See you there." She went into the hospital.

Ray climbed into the patrol car. "Can you take us home?"

"On one condition," the cowboy replied. He started the car and pulled out of the ER driveway with a jerk. "Tell me what in blazes is goin' on."

Ray shook his head. "I'm not sure." It was the truth. He wasn't certain what was going on in terms of the Clearwater case and he was even less certain of the course of action he was taking. Not only was he going against orders, putting himself at risk of disciplinary actions on the hunch of a senile old man, but he had just agreed to do so in the company of a woman that he found quite attractive. He knew this had something to do with his blues of late and that it was an illusion. Allowing anything beyond friendship would be a tragic mistake.

"Watch," Grandfather told him from the back seat. "Be care-ful."

"Huh?"

"Be care-ful, Ray-mond." The old man looked him in the eye. "You walk sikuliaq. It break, you go in tag-iuq. Not get out."

Ray's reoccurring nightmare flashed to mind: clinging to the umiak, losing his grip, sliding helplessly toward the water, falling through the ice into cold darkness, being engulfed by a sense of sheer terror.

"Go slow, care-ful. Listen to ukpIk."

Billy Bob looked at Ray. "Listen to *what?*"

Ray waved him off. "Don't ask."

When they got home, Ray got out and assisted

Grandfather and Freddie up to the door. After unlocking it for them, he went back to the police cruiser. "Thanks for the ride."

"Anytime."

"I'll catch you later."

"Hang on a sec," Billy Bob said. "I wasn't kiddin' about wantin' to know what's up with you. Now what you do on your own time is your own business. But as your partner, I think I gotta right to know if somethin's up."

"Who said something was up?"

"Come on now, Ray. This is Billy Bob you're talkin' to."

"I realize that. That accent and the hat gave you away."

"I ain't jokin' around."

"I know."

"So what gives? Are you working undercover, or what?"

"Undercover?"

"I heard that doctor lady ask you about a case. Now I know you've been taken off of homicide. So it has to be somethin' else." When Ray didn't say anything, he prodded, "I won't tell nobody. And I might even be able to help."

"Thanks. If I need help, I'll let you know."

"You better," he said in a threatening tone.

"I will."

"Okie-dokie. But you heed your Grampa, now. Be careful, you hear?"

"You bet."

As he watched Billy Bob drive away, Ray decided that he was a lucky man. He had a wife who loved him, two great kids, an eccentric but caring Grandfather, and a number of good friends, not the least of which was Billy Bob. The cowboy was clumsy and downright slow on occasion, but he was loyal to the bone and would do anything for Ray. Anything. Add to the list of good things a job that Ray was good at and usually enjoyed, and you had the makings of happiness. Right? Then why was he so down lately?

When no answer came, he turned and went into the house. After making a quick call to Mrs. Chu, he set Grandfather and Freddie up with a Barney video. For some inexplicable reason, they both loved the purple dinosaur. It was one of the few things that could make the old man laugh. The entertainment value was lost on Ray. He could hardly stand to listen to the stilted dialogue and silly songs.

Mrs. Chu arrived minutes later bearing a plate of what she described as Filipino wontons. She insisted they were going to waste at her house and needed to be eaten posthaste.

Ray thanked her and explained that either he or Margaret should be back in a couple of hours.

"Take your time," she said cheerily. In a lower voice, she added, "I keep an eye on your grandpapa."

Ray laughed. Mrs. Chu had been making eyes at Grandfather, occasionally openly flirting with him, for months and the old man had yet to notice.

"He's a good man," she said.

"Yes, he is," Ray agreed. He went and told Freddie goodbye and received an energetic hug in return. He told Grandfather goodbye and got "Move! Can't see Bah-nee!" in return.

Ray left Mrs. Chu in charge and went out to his

Blazer. It suddenly occurred to him that the van was still at the festival grounds and Margaret had no way of getting home. Using his cell phone, he called the station and got Betty.

"Say, is Lewis around?"

"No. He's on patrol."

"Could you patch me through?"

"Only if it's a personal call."

"Betty . . ." he complained.

"You better not be working."

"I'm heading for the festival."

There was a long pause. "Swear?"

"Swear."

"Because you sound like you're onto something."

"I do?"

"Yes. Your voice gets kind of . . . I don't know . . . *serious* when you're working."

"Betty, I just need to ask Lewis if he can arrange to have someone drive my van to the hospital."

"The hospital?"

"It's a long story. Just patch me through . . . please?"

"Okay," she groaned, "hold on."

Ray waited, thinking that by the time he got Lewis and made the arrangements, he could be there and drive the van to the hospital himself.

"Yah?"

"Lewis, Ray."

"Hey. What-up?"

"*What-up*? You sound like you're from east L.A."

"Every-body sayin' it."

"Not everybody," Ray insisted. "Listen, I need a favor." He told Lewis about the van and Keera.

"Sure. No prob."

"Prob?"

"Dat slang."

"No kidding." And *dat* stupid, Ray thought. "Thanks."

"Hey, you wanna go out on floes wit me dis weekend?"

"What for?"

"Hunt nanuq."

"Polar bear? Are you nuts? At this time of year?"

"But I gotta new rifle and Johnny Salik tell me I can use his camp. Gotta boat too. We go out there wit my brudder-in-law. He got a good snow machine to pull us."

Again Ray's nightmare came flooding back.

"We set up on ice and use boat to track dem. Sleep on da ice and stay couple days."

"Sounds like a great time."

"Aarigaa! You bet. Da best!"

"But I'll pass."

"Ray . . ." he whined. "Gonna be fun."

"You can tell me all about it when you get back." *If* you get back, Ray thought. Lewis was something of a menace when it came to the outdoors. Ray had learned his lesson on an expedition into the Brooks Range a few years earlier and wasn't about to trust Lewis again. As a cop, he was dependable and quick-witted. As a hunter . . . run for cover!

"Aiyaa . . ." Lewis sighed.

"Talk to you later."

He hung up and drove through the empty streets. When he got to the festival grounds, he saw a handwritten sign: Lot Full. "Perfect," he muttered. He made a block and looked for a space on the street. But there wasn't one. Circling, he wound up parking back near the hospital.

It was still twenty to twelve and he needed to check on Keera anyway, so he went in through the outpatient entrance. Snaking through the corridors, he found the ER wing and was headed for the admit desk when he saw Margaret and Keera in the waiting area. When Keera saw him, she lifted her injured arm high.

"Look Daddy! Purple!"

He nodded at the cast and rapped it with his knuckles.

"Isn't it cool?"

"Very cool. If you have to wear a cast, that's the kind to get."

"I get to wear it for six whole weeks."

"Wow."

"I can't wait to show Jessica and Aime and Kaitlan. And Samantha!"

Ray looked to Margaret. "How you holding up?"

"I'm tired."

"You want to go back to the festival, or . . ."

"Definitely *or*."

"You'll miss the muktuq."

"I'll live."

"I called Lewis and he's bringing the van over."

"Okay." Margaret sagged. Then she shot him a puzzled look. "What are you going to do?"

"Billy Bob drove us home and I drove back in the Blazer. Mrs. Chu is watching Freddie and Grandfather."

"You didn't answer my question, Ray," she said suspiciously. "What are you going to do?"

"Um . . . I have an errand . . ."

Before he could concoct a vague explanation, Melissa came striding up. "Oh, good. You're here. I was about to walk over to the festival grounds. You ready?"

Ray felt his cheeks flushing.

"An errand, huh?" Margaret asked, eyebrows raised.

"Okay . . . it's work," he admitted. He knew that attending to police business while supposedly off-duty would irk her, but not as much as the idea of going to festival with Melissa. He explained briefly, trying to fashion the bizarre happenings into something resembling a whole: Ronnie's condition at the time of Aana's death, the Dance of the Whale exhibit, the ring, the outside chance that it could have been Aana's . . .

When he finished, Margaret nodded as though she understood. She stood up, hugged Ray, and whispered, "I trust you."

"I know."

"I think you're the best cop in town."

"Just in town? What about in the Borough?" he joked.

She pulled back and looked up at him. "If you think somebody else did it, then . . . I believe you."

"It's just a hunch."

"Call it whatever you like. The bottom line is still the same. Somebody killed Aana. And you have to catch them, Ray."

"I'm trying."

ANAQASAAGIAQ

(AFTERNOON)

*In the gentle passage
of morning to noon
a beating of wings
urges the sun
to fly away home.*

GRANDFATHER ATTLA

➤➤ SEVENTEEN ◄◄

IT WAS TWO minutes after twelve when Ray and Melissa arrived at the crowded Nalukataq grounds. The festival was in full swing and great throngs of people were gathered at the various activity sites. A woman was performing impressive acrobatic tricks at the blanket toss area. Closer to the beach, a whaling crew was dancing to the steady beat of the seal-gut drums. Another crew was serving those seated at the picnic tables, doling out Native delicacies from cardboard boxes. The booths were doing a land office business hocking trinkets and several new attractions had been set up: a sign offering kayak rides in the Beaufort Sea, a lemonade stand, a display of whale hats and T-shirts, even a row of Coke machines.

According to the paper, the chamber of commerce was expecting attendance to reach the five thousand mark this year. Scanning the crowd, Ray decided that for once, their estimate was close to the truth. There were at least that many, possibly more, counting children, all milling about taking in the festivities. The tourists were easy to spot by their dress and the photography and video gear slung about their necks and cradled on their shoulders. The locals were recognizable not only by their attire and distinctive physical traits, but also by their unabashed jocularity. Nearly everyone was smiling, laughing, truly celebrating the bounty of the whale. Which was as it should be, Ray thought.

Before the commercialization of Nalukataq, it had been a simpler affair not only in terms of size or scope, but in the sincerity and overriding sense of joy. Winter was over. With the help of the bowhead, they had survived another brutal season in the north. Now it was time to honor the spirit of that great and marvelous beast.

This, Ray thought, glaring at the lines at the souvenir stands and the kids putting change into the vending machines, was over the top. It would have truly grieved Grandfather. Actually, it bothered Ray a little, too. There was something sad about seeing a pure and good-natured event adulterated by a desire to make a profit. How long would it be before the hospitality of the whaling crews was replaced by naluaqmiut from Outside selling burgers and buffalo wings?

"What a mob," Melissa said.

"I remember when it was just the local families—no more than a few hundred people. But this . . ." Ray looked out over the sea of heads. "How are we ever going to find Mr. Roth?"

Melissa pointed at a banner next to the picnic tables.

" 'Dance of the Whale,' " Ray read. It was a slightly smaller version of the banner at the museum. As they began making their way over to it, pushing through the knots of people, Ray realized that the banner was part of a display. A board under the banner listed options for supporting the exhibit. Contributors of $25 to $99 were rewarded with a stuffed whale. Those who coughed up $100 to $499 received a 24-carat gold whale pin. Those willing to hand over $500 to $999 got a signed whale lithograph in return. The heavy hitters—$1,000 and up—could choose between an original ivory whale sculpture and a two-night vacation package to see Dance of the Whale in Seattle—airfare not included.

Ray wondered if Mr. Roth realized that most of the Inupiat were below the median income, quite a few languishing around the poverty level. Some of them still lived off the land. He doubted that more than a handful of residents could come up with $50 bucks for the cause, much less $1,000. Maybe in New York—but not in Barrow, Alaska. He decided that they had to be going for the tourist trade, trying to play on their obvious interest in all things Eskimo.

"That's him, right there," Melissa said. "The one in the suit."

Ray leaned and looked through the bodies at a rather handsome Hispanic man of about his own age. This surprised him. He had been expecting the stereotypical CEO: white, overweight, fifty-five or so. This guy looked a little like Ricky Martin, except more mature and sophisticated.

Melissa pushed through the people until they were standing directly in front of the whale banner, across a long, narrow table from Roth and two people wearing polar fleece whale masks.

One of the masked attendants greeted, "Happy Nalukataq!"

The other handed them a brochure and launched into a spiel about the exhibit that hit the basic points that Mrs. Hucheck had already covered, but with a much smoother, snappier presentation.

Roth interrupted with, "Dr. Bradshaw!" His eyes lit up and he reached to shake her hand. "It's great to see you."

"How are you feeling?" she asked.

He patted his belly. "Much better. Thanks to you. This woman is a life saver," he told Ray.

"This is a friend of mine," she said, turning to Ray. "Raymond Attla, Paul Roth."

"Nice to meet you," Roth said, still smiling.

"We saw the exhibit this morning," she told him.

"And what did you think?"

"Very nice."

Roth looked to Ray for a review and Ray nodded. "Nice."

"It was ten years in the making," he said. "Ten *long* years to collect the artifacts, organize them, and present them with the flair and the authenticity we were looking for."

"We?" Ray asked.

"The members of the foundation."

"The Roth Science Foundation," Ray acknowledged. "Which is . . . what?"

"A nonprofit company formed with the specific purpose of making significant archaeological finds accessible to the public. You may have read about or seen the Louis Leakey tour, or the People of Darkness exhibit, uh . . . the China Then and Now exposition . . . ?"

Ray nodded, though he wasn't familiar with any of

these. He had heard of Leakey, but the rest were foreign.

"Dance of the Whale is the pinnacle of our efforts to date," Roth explained. "It mixes the rich and rather mysterious heritage of the Inupiat with the wonderful mythology of the bowhead to form what I believe is a winning combination that will capture the public's interest."

Ray nodded again, amazed at how smooth and compelling this guy was. He could have been trying to get rid of a used car, or offering shares of stock and either way, the listener would be hard pressed to resist. His words were almost unnecessary. Just the expression on his face, the contortions of his mouth, the way he looked at you, implying that he was not only passionate about the subject, but cared about you as a person. Ray glanced over and saw Melissa smiling in a dazed sort of way, as though Roth were a movie star or a famous celebrity.

"You say you collected the artifacts?" Ray inserted when the man paused for breath. "From where?"

"All over the Arctic: Greenland, Canada, Alaska, Siberia . . ." Roth answered proudly. "It was an arduous chore, but ultimately a very rewarding one."

"Not all Natives hunt bowhead," Ray pointed out.

"True. But we concentrated on the coastal peoples."

"Were the artifacts donated, or . . . ?"

"A few were donated; some were purchased. Others were excavated by members of the foundation. We actually funded six archaeological dig sites."

"And when the exhibit has run its course," Ray wondered, "where do the pieces go?"

"Many will be donated to various museums after the tour, including the museum here in Barrow."

"That's very generous of you," Melissa said, seemingly bowled over by the man's presentation.

"Not so much generosity as a respect for the indigenous peoples of the far north, as well as a profound desire to keep history alive."

It sounded good, Ray thought to himself. A little too good. Either this guy was a selfless, altruistic friend of The People, or he was a very polished snake-oil salesman. It was tough to tell which.

"Which is why we solicit funds from the public. Though we have grants from the federal government and also the support of various companies such as Ford, Sears, and Coca-Cola, we depend on the gifts of private individuals to continue our work."

He paused and the smile grew. "But don't feel pressured to make a donation. I'm not after your wallet," he told Ray. "In fact, after what Dr. Bradshaw did for me, I'm the one who's indebted."

"It was nothing," Melissa said.

"Oh, it was something, all right. I wouldn't have been able to be here today or make the trip to Seattle if it hadn't been for you." He took her hand and shook it appreciatively.

Ray noticed that Melissa was blushing.

Roth then turned and took one of the gold whale pins from the display. "Here. I'd like you to have this."

"No. Really . . . I couldn't."

"It's just a small token of my appreciation, Dr. Bradshaw."

"Well . . ." She accepted it reluctantly. "Thank you."

"No. Thank *you*." He smiled at her and then plucked up a stuffed whale. "Do you have children, Mr. Attla?"

"Yes. A daughter and a son."

Roth snatched another whale. "Here you go."

"Oh . . . uh . . . no, that's . . ."

"Go on. They're stuffed. They won't bite."

Ray took them. "Thank you."

"My pleasure." He reached into his jacket. "And here." He extended a pair of laminated cards. "I intended to give you one yesterday, but didn't have them with me at the hospital."

Ray and Melissa each took a card.

"They're passes for the exhibit, in case you want to go back, or if you get a chance to catch it in the Lower Forty-Eight. They're good for as many times as you want to use them."

"Thank you."

A cell phone rang and Ray reached into his jacket. But it wasn't his phone. It was Roth's.

"If you'll excuse me." He shot them a winning smile as he answered the phone.

"Have a good day," the two attendants chimed from under their fleece masks.

Ray and Melissa waded through the throng of people to a spot of relative calm adjacent to the lemonade booth.

"Now that guy is good looking," she said.

"You think so?" Ray asked, feeling a little jealous.

"Oh, yeah. Could have been an actor."

Maybe he is, Ray thought. He examined the stuffed whales. "Quite a charmer."

"He certainly is."

"You think he's on the level?"

"Not for a second."

Ray grinned, once again impressed with Melissa's investigative abilities. "I got the impression that you liked him."

"What's not to like. He's a hunk and he's charismatic as all get out. But . . ."

"But what?"

"But I wouldn't trust him as far as I could throw him."

➤ EIGHTEEN ◀

"YOU KNOW ANYTHING about him?"

"Not much," Melissa answered. "Just that he's head of the foundation. And he's friends with the mayor."

"The mayor?"

"Yeah. Hodish came by the hospital to check on him yesterday. But I'd already seen him and written him a script."

Ray glanced back at Roth. "How does he know the mayor?"

Melissa shrugged. "The mayor knows everybody. And he's so PR oriented . . . I wouldn't be surprised if he had a hand in getting the exhibit up here for festival. He might have finagled the whole thing for all I know."

Ray produced a phone, flipped it open, and dialed. When a female voice answered, he said, "Hey, Betty."

"Raymond Attla," she scolded.

"What?"

"You're off duty."

"Yes, ma'am."

"Then why do you keep calling the station?"

"I miss you, Betty."

"Uh-huh . . . either that, or you think we can't run the place without you."

"Can you?"

"What do you want?"

"I need a favor."

Betty groaned.

"I need you to run a background on a guy named Paul Roth."

"R-O-T-H?"

"Yeah. Also . . ." He waited as she sighed at him. "I need some information on the non-profit he chairs, the Roth Foundation: how long they've been around, what they do, etc."

"Anything else?" she said rather testily.

"I'd do it myself except, well, I'm off duty, so . . ."

"Uh-huh . . ."

"I really appreciate it, Betty."

"Uh-huh . . ."

"You're the best."

"Uh-huh . . ."

Ray laughed at her. "Talk to you in a little while."

"Yeah . . ."

He hung up. When Melissa looked at him expectantly, he explained, "She's gonna run it through the computer for me." Ray glanced back at the Dance of the Whale booth again and saw the mayor talking with Roth. Both were smiling.

"I can't stand that guy."

"Who?"

"Hodish," Melissa said, nodding in the mayor's direction.

"Join the club."

"How did he get elected?"

"No idea."

Ray's eyes wandered from the booth to where the dancers were performing. Though they were obscured by the crowd, he could see an occasional head bobbing along to the beat of the drums. Several professional video cameras were aimed at the dancers. One was marked ABC, another bore the letters of the Anchorage PBS station. A third had a Science Channel logo. On the other side, a film camera with a thick lens was mounted on a ten-foot-high tripod. A man up on a ladder had his eye to the viewfinder and was panning the area.

"That must be the documentary crew," Melissa said.

Ray watched as the man on the ladder moved the camera to follow the movements. "They're making a documentary," he mumbled.

"That's what I just said."

He thought for a moment. "Didn't Mrs. Hucheck say that they shot the whale exhibit yesterday?"

"Yeah. So?"

"So if Grandfather is right, and that's Aana's ring in there . . ."

"We might be able to tell from their footage?"

Ray cut his eyes at her, wondering about the use of the word "we."

"Problem is, that's a thirty-five-millimeter camera," she said.

"What's wrong with that?"

"It shoots film stock. Not video."

"I don't understand what you're saying."

"I'm saying that you have to have the film developed. They might not have the reel from yesterday developed yet."

"Come on." He started off.

"Where are we going?"

He noticed the "we" again but let it slide. "To find out."

They pushed their way through the crowd, toward the spot where the tripod was set up. There was a woman standing at the bottom of one of the legs wearing headphones and holding a microphone on a long boom. She was intently studying gauges on an audio unit.

"Excuse me," Ray said. When she didn't look up, he tapped her. This drew an upraised hand and a curt, "Shhh!" Ray noticed that a thin mike extended from the headphones. He looked up and saw that the cameraman was wearing headphones too.

"Come out slowly, then give me wide for five," she whispered. A few moments later she whispered, ". . . And . . . *cut*." She relaxed a little and turned toward them as the man on the ladder began to descend.

"Are you from the Discovery Channel?"

She held a finger up at him, then addressed the cameraman. "How much do we have left on that cartridge?"

"Maybe . . . a third."

"Okay. Break and set up over at the picnic area. In fact . . . let's go hand-held over there. You can do a walk-through. Then we'll set up and do a couple of short interviews."

The man nodded and went back up the ladder. The woman took off her headphones, quickly collapsed the boom and began coiling cable.

"Discovery Channel?" Ray asked again.

The woman nodded without looking at them.

"Did you shoot the Dance of the Whale exhibit yesterday at the museum?"

Another nod. She finished with the cable and lifted the unit and the boom and began walking quickly away.

"I was wondering if we might be able to take a look at your uh . . . your film," Ray asked, trying to keep step.

The woman glared skeptically at him over her shoulder.

Ray pulled out his ID. "Ray Attla, Barrow PD."

The woman slowed a little and sighed. "I showed the guy all our permits yesterday."

"I don't care about your permits. I need to look at the film you have of the museum."

"What for?"

"It's a police matter."

"In case you haven't noticed, we're a little busy at the moment. It's just Jeff and me, and we're busting our buns to try and get all of this."

"I understand. But it's important."

Reaching the picnic area, she set the unit down and began pulling out plugs and inserting them in new outlets like a switchboard operator.

"We're conducting a homicide investigation," Ray finally said.

This caught her interest. "Really?"

Ray nodded.

"You tell the network crews yet?"

Ray shook his head.

The woman smiled. "If I show you our footage, can we do a piece on the murder?"

"For the Discovery Channel?"

"No. For the networks." She put down the boom and offered her hand. "Jean Carter. I'm producing the doc on the festival, but I'm freelance. When I'm not working for PBS or Discovery, I do stuff for CBS and NBC News. I even had a short on *60 Minutes* once."

"Congratulations," Ray said. "Now, about the museum footage . . ."

"Right. No problem. As long as you let us put together an exclusive on the crime."

"I don't think that would be in good taste."

"Suit yourself. No story, no museum footage."

"I could get a court order."

"Have at it." She turned her attention to the audio unit. "By the time you put that together, we'll be long gone, halfway back to New York."

Ray balked. "Okay. You can do your report. But only *after* the case is closed."

"Cool. I might be able to put something together for *Dateline* or *20/20*."

"But I need to see the museum film."

"One-thirty," she said, adjusting her equipment.

"One-thirty what?"

"That's when the dailies come back. Meet me at the Brown around one-thirty. Room 317."

The cameraman came up lugging the camera.

"Set up wide and we'll get some file stuff."

"But you said hand-held . . ."

"I know what I said. I changed my mind."

The cameraman sighed and went back for the tripod.

Ray and Melissa watched the producer for a moment before turning away. Ray checked his watch. It was almost 12:30.

"What are we gonna do for an hour?" Melissa asked.

"You hungry?" he asked, watching women dole out food in the picnic area.

"Starving. I skipped breakfast to do the autopsy."

"Ever try muktuq?"

Melissa shook her head. "Is it good?" She asked this as though whale meat couldn't possibly be worth eating.

"Come on." Ray led her into the maze of tables and they found two spots in a section marked Kickbush. "Joe Kickbush is one of the old-timers, Grandfather's generation. And he's still an umialik."

"A what?"

"A whale boat captain."

Two middle-aged women appeared, one carrying a plastic bucket, the other a stack of paper plates and plastic utensils.

"How you doing, Raymond?" the latter asked as she handed them each a plate and a fork.

"Fine. And you, Miss Ruth?"

"I always good, but very, very good on festival."

As the other woman dolled out chunks of muktuq and mikigaq, she asked, "How you grandfather, Raymond?"

"He's well, Mrs. Crenshaw," Ray said, not wanting to go into the details of his memory lapses.

"Where he at?" Miss Ruth asked.

"He was here earlier, but went home to rest."

"Aiyaa . . ." Mrs. Crenshaw lamented, "we all need rest after Nalukataq. So much quviasuun."

Melissa looked to Ray for a translation.

"Joy," he said.

"You wait for Cap-n Joe to bless food 'fore eat it."

"Yes, ma'am."

When the women had moved on, Melissa made a face at her plate.

"It's good, but it takes some getting used to," Ray encouraged.

"Let me guess. It tastes like chicken?"

Ray pointed to the muktuq, which was black and looked a little like the underside of a mushroom. "This is boiled whale meat." He pointed at the other. "This is fermented tongue and blood."

"You gotta be kidding."

Another woman, this one wearing a name tag that read Kickbush Crew, set Styrofoam cups in front of them.

"Quyanaqpak," Ray said.

Melissa smiled and nodded. "What is it?"

"Niglik soup."

"Dare I ask what niglik is?"

"Goose."

"Oh . . . smells good."

"It *is* good."

A man came along and put scoops of something resembling mincemeat onto their plates. "Enjoy!"

"Oh, we will," Ray said, amused by Melissa's reaction to the new substance. "Akutuq."

"Which means . . . ?"

"Eskimo ice cream. Haven't you tried that before?"

"No." She stabbed it with the fork and examined it suspiciously.

"It's whipped seal fat with pieces of caribou meat in it."

"Yummy," she said without enthusiasm.

Ray was still laughing at this when a bent old man

shuffled up. He was smiling broadly, his face a network of deep wrinkles.

"Paglagivsi!" he said in a whisper of a voice.

"Thank you, Captain Kickbush," Ray responded politely. "It's a privilege to share in your bounty."

"Whale good to us. Give many gifts." He grimaced. "Where Kee-ra, Al-fred?"

"They were here earlier," Ray explained.

"They try my niqi?"

"I'm not sure, sir."

"You tell 'em come back and try. It da best!" He jabbed a trembling finger at the muktuq. "Dat da flippa and fin."

Ray nodded. Meat from the flipper and fin was considered a delicacy.

Turning his attention to Melissa, Kickbush asked, "How you Mar-gar-et?"

"Oh, uh . . . I'm not . . . I'm . . ."

"She's fine," Ray said.

The man nodded happily. "Now I bless food, give thanks God and agviQ. We have good season but next year be better."

"Of course," Ray agreed.

Captain Kickbush launched into a paragraph of Inupiaq. His voice was too quiet for Ray to catch it all, but he did hear the word "thanksgiving" used several times, along with "joy" and "gifts of the bowhead." Kickbush finished with a hoarse "Amen!," then hissed at them, "Enjoy!"

As he shuffled up the line to the next table of guests, Ray picked up his fork and cut off a piece of muktuq. He sampled it and moaned his appreciation.

Melissa just sat there, eyeing her plate skeptically. "Did he really mean that about the flipper and fin."

Ray nodded, entertained by the fact that she was out of her element and suddenly didn't seem so sure of herself.

She waved her fork at the food. "Let's see . . . flipper and fin . . . tongue and blood . . . whipped seal fat . . ." She dropped the fork and lifted the Styrofoam cup. "I think I'll stick with the soup."

➤ NINETEEN ◆

"HEY, THIS IS GOOD!" Melissa said, after sipping her soup.

"Told you."

She hesitantly tried a few flakes of muktuq. "Interesting." She started to try the mikigaq, but shook her head. "Nope. I draw the line at tongue and blood."

Ray laughed at her.

"They do this every year?" Melissa asked.

"Don't tell me this is your first Nalukataq."

"Isn't it obvious?"

"I thought you'd been here for . . . a year or so."

"Just under. I came up last June." She tried a little more muktuq.

"What brought you? I mean, why take a job in Barrow?"

"I did an internship at the Native Hospital in Anchorage in med school and . . . I don't know . . . I guess I just fell in love with Alaska."

Ray glanced around, wondering what, aside from the people, there *was* to fall in love with in Barrow. It was flat and barren and had a rather forsaken look.

Even the sea was without romance: a gravel beach, a few floes, and an expanse of waveless water.

"And this place . . . what a surprise."

"Why's that?" Ray asked, finishing his mikigaq. It was juicy and delicious.

"Well, I expected to find a closed, primitive, aboriginal people."

"And that's not what you found?"

"No. The Inupiat are very intelligent and open and accepting, and they know more about survival in the north than most whites."

"You plan on staying?"

"For now." She drank more soup before asking, "So what exactly is Nalukataq all about?"

"It's a chance to express gratitude to the bowhead for providing sustenance."

"Seems like quite a party," she said, looking around.

"It's a little different this year. Usually it follows a strict order. First there's the blanket toss, then the food is served, then the crews dance through the night. I'm not sure why they decided to run things simultaneously this time," he said, waving at the blanket toss, that was still going, and the dancers, and the picnic area where hundreds of people were appreciatively chewing. "There aren't usually nearly this many tanik either."

"Tanik?"

"Tourists."

"Well, they've been running TV commercials for months," Melissa said. "I've got dish service and I saw them on the Anchorage station, the Seattle station . . ."

"I think the mayor was behind that. He seems to have this vision for transforming Barrow into some kind of Arctic Circle resort town or something."

"Well, I have to say that Nalukataq is a fascinating event."

"It was more fascinating before all these people showed up," Ray grumbled. He finished what was on his plate, tried the soup, and then pulled out his cell phone. After dialing, he heard the line ring twice before Margaret answered.

"Hey."

"Where are you?"

"The festival grounds."

"How's it going?"

"It's going," he answered. "How's Keera?"

"If it wasn't for the cast, you'd never know she had a broken arm. She's having Grandfather draw a picture on it right now."

"Oh, boy."

"Any developments?"

"Nothing solid yet."

"I take it you're calling to say you won't be home for lunch?"

"I'm shooting for dinner at this point."

"Ray . . . I hate that this happened at festival."

"Me too."

"Be careful, okay."

"I will. Talk to you later."

"I love you."

"I love you too," Ray said quietly.

When he hung up, Melissa asked, "How's Keera?"

"She's fine."

"Good. Kids heal quickly."

Ray was stuffing the phone back in his jacket pocket when it rang. He answered it with, "What is it, honey?"

"It's just me, *darling*," Betty shot back.

"Oh, hi, Betty. What do have for me?"

"Paul Roth," she said, "AKA Juan Rodriguez. Originally from Tijuana."

"Mexico?"

"Right. Arrested in the mid-nineties on drug running charges. Didn't stick. Changed his name a couple years back and started the Roth Foundation."

"A couple years?"

"Uh . . . two and a half, to be exact."

"I knew it," Ray muttered.

"Now the Roth Foundation," Betty continued, "is more complicated. As far as I can figure out, they make nothing, sell nothing of any great value, and yet somehow afford to be generous patrons of the arts."

"Investors?"

"Maybe."

"Could it be a front company or something?" Ray asked.

"Or something. Oh, and get this. About six weeks ago they made a donation to a certain re-election campaign fund."

"Let me guess: Mayor Hodish."

"Yep."

"How much?"

"One hundred thousand dollars."

"You're kidding!"

"Nope."

"Geez . . ."

"Ray, you need to let the captain in on this."

He didn't respond.

"It sounds like . . . well, you know what it sounds like."

"Yeah."

"Which means you could be in big trouble." She waited. "Ray? Are you listening to me?"

"Yes, ma'am."

"Want me to patch you through to him?"

"No."

"Raymond . . ."

"I have a couple of leads to run down. Then I'll drop by the station."

"Don't be the Lone Ranger on this."

"See you in a little bit."

He hung up.

"What did you find out?" Melissa asked.

He glanced around, then collected their plates. "Let's go for a walk."

They got up and made their way through the people to the beach.

"What?" Melissa asked.

He conveyed the information he had just gleaned from Betty.

"So the Roth Foundation is like a . . . a fake?"

"I don't know."

"What does that have to do with Aana?"

"I don't know," Ray repeated.

"*Does* it have anything to do with Aana?"

"I don't know."

"Why would the mayor get in bed with Roth, or Rodriguez, or whoever he is?"

Ray raised his hands in a gesture of ignorance. He checked his watch and was about to suggest that they head for the Brown to meet the documentary producer when he heard feet crunching the ground behind them. He turned to see Justin running up.

"Uncle Ray!" He had a blue ribbon around his neck

with a gold medal suspended from it. "I've been look-ing all over for you," he said.

"Well, you found me." Ray reached over and fin-gered the medal. "First place," he read. "Congratula-tions."

Justin looked down as though he had forgotten he was wearing it. "Oh . . . yeah." He frowned. "I wasn't going to do the race, but . . . then I started thinking of how much Aana liked to watch me run and how much she encouraged me, and all. So . . ." He shrugged. "I did it for her. And it helped. A little. I took first with a new PB."

"PB?"

"Personal Best."

"Wow. That's great."

"So what's going on? With the investigation, I mean."

"Not much. We arrested Ronnie. He's being charged with murder one."

"But he didn't do it," Justin said.

"And just how do you know that?"

"I got to thinking. Ronnie is a jerk and a drunk but . . . if he killed Aana, it would have been because he was ticked off at her, so it would have been, you know, spur of the moment." Justin shook his head. "That wasn't spur of the moment," he said, sounding much older and more mature than his fourteen years.

"It wasn't, huh?" Ray said, impressed by the boy's capacity for reasoning.

"No, Uncle Ray. It was planned out and then care-fully hidden." Justin shivered slightly. "It wasn't a spur of the moment thing."

Ray nodded at him. The kid was bright.

"And another thing. The good luck face. It was knocked off the wall and broken."

Ray reached into his pocket and fingered the charm.

"But when we went back, it was gone. And then you found it under her, fixed with glue. Which means that whoever broke it was an Inupiat who respects the tuungak."

Ray considered this. It wasn't bad logic, except that the glued charm didn't mean the murderer had been respectful of the spirits. It meant that whoever had cleaned up after the murder had been. The idea that the attacker and the one who covered up the attack were separate people had been rattling around in Ray's head for quite some time. Still, it didn't quite line up and it certainly wasn't enough to exonerate Ronnie. He could have assaulted the woman in a fit of rage and then someone else could have tried to hide it. Which still didn't make sense to him.

Another thought occurred to him. "Could you identify Aana's ring if you saw it?"

"Her whale ring?" Justin asked.

"Yeah."

"Maybe. It was ivory, with a bowhead on it. Uncle gave it to her when he became umialik."

Ray pulled one of the exhibit passes out and handed it to Justin. "Go over to the museum and take a look at the Dance of the Whale display. There's a case full of rings. Check them out."

Justin accepted the pass, looked at it, then looked up at Ray curiously.

"You want to help with the investigation, don't you?"

"Yes, sir."

"This will help." Ray examined his watch again. "We'll meet you at Blackie's in . . . say, an hour."

"But what am I . . . ?"

"Just take a good look at the rings, okay?"

"Okay." He trotted off down the beach.

"Let's get over to the Brown," Ray suggested. He and Melissa cut across the gravel to the street where parked cars lined the shoulder. They waited as a latecomer in an old Ford slowly rolled past, trolling for a space. Behind it was a patrol car. Ray recognized the driver as Lewis. The cruiser stopped right in front of them and the window came down. Lewis grinned cockily out at him.

"Hey, man, what you doing?"

"Hey, Lewis."

Lewis's smug expression faded slightly as he noticed Melissa. "What you doing?" he repeated more softly. His eyes shot back and forth between them.

Ray hesitated. He wasn't in the mood to deal with Lewis's mouth, or to explain why he was with Melissa, or to admit that he was working the case through a back door.

"Uh . . . Keera had an accident."

The curiosity drained from Lewis's face, replaced by an expression of concern. "She okay?"

"She's fine, now. She broke her arm playing on the floes."

"Aiyaa . . ." Lewis muttered, shaking his head. "Dat happen to me once when I hunting nanuq. I stumble and slip, break leg. 'Member cast?"

Ray nodded. It had happened back in high school and instead of making Lewis more cautious, it had strangely had the opposite effect, transforming him into a daredevil and a thrill-seeker.

"Where you headed?" Ray asked.

"Blanket toss," he said with a mischievous grin. "Gonna be highest, like last year. And year before."

"You're the man," Ray said.

"You bet. I da man."

"Be careful," Melissa cautioned.

Lewis's eyes narrowed. "Can't be careful if you want to win." He smiled again. "I gonna win."

"You might want to keep an eye on the festival crowd, while you're there," Ray said, knowing that was why the captain had allowed him to go on patrol.

"Sure, sure. I do that too."

"Happy Nalukataq."

"Aarigaa! Most happy Nalukataq!"

As he drove off, Melissa said, "So there's a contest to see who can go the highest on the blanket toss?"

"No," Ray answered. "He just can't stand for anybody to outdo him."

"Maybe I should call over and have them prepare an ER room for him."

"Not a bad idea."

They walked the four blocks to the Brown Hotel, their steps accompanied by the thumping of the festival drums. When the wind changed, they could hear the whaling crews moaning, "Ah ya ya na ha ya ya . . ." In Ray's mind, he could see the men in their dirty down coats and ballcaps and jeans, bobbing and swaying, knees bent, arms outstretched like giant birds.

The Brown looked as if it had closed for the day. There were no bellmen outside the hotel and the lobby was quiet. A lone employee, a woman of about forty, was working at a computer behind the counter. She never looked up as they made their way to the elevator.

"Room 317, right?" Ray said, hitting the button.

"Right."

The elevator chimed and they got on. Ray punched 3. When the doors finally lurched shut and they started up, he said, "I hope this isn't a wild-goose chase."

"Never can tell," Melissa said. "It's the same with medicine. Sometimes you spin your wheels a lot, ruling out things. People get impatient with that but . . . it has to be done, otherwise you might miss something important. Something life-threatening."

Ray nodded at the comparison. It was a good one, except that, in his thinking, medicine was much more exciting than police work. Outside of the occasional bust, his days were spent cruising Barrow, giving out parking citations and ensuring that kids went to school. It wasn't exactly glamorous or invigorating.

He realized that this was something new: dissatisfaction with his job. He had never before voiced this, even to himself. Didn't he love being a cop? The answer had always been yes. Until . . . what? What was going on with him?

The elevator opened and they got off, following the numbered doors to 317. Ray knocked. When no one answered, he knocked again.

"Maybe she's not back yet."

"Maybe," he grumbled. His mood was going sour. He was beginning to think this was a big waste of time and energy. What if he was just bored, ready for a change, and that was why he was traipsing around town trying to prove that a man known for being a vio-

lent drunk and wife beater was innocent of a crime that
fit him like a glove. And perhaps that was why he was
doing so in the company of a woman whom he liked,
found attractive, enjoyed being with.

What was happening here? Was he manufacturing
this case to fill some inner need—a pathetic attempt to
placate an identity crisis?

He reached and tried the knob. It turned and he
opened the door a crack. "Hello?"

No answer.

He knocked and pushed it wider.

"Ms. Carter?"

They stood in the threshold, peering into the room.

"Ms. Carter?"

The bed was made and an open suitcase was sitting
on the floor of the closet, the clothes neatly arranged.
There was a 35-mm camera on the nightstand.

"We better wait," Melissa said.

"Stay here." Ray stepped in, not sure why he was
violating this woman's privacy and unable to put into
words the strange but very heavy sense that something
was wrong.

He glanced in the closet, then out the window that
offered a view of the Chukchi Sea.

"What are you looking for?" Melissa called from the
door.

He didn't answer because he wasn't sure. There was
a film viewing machine set up on the table with film
threaded through the spools. On the nightstand was a
35mm camera. Next to it was a consumer grade Sony
video camera. Kneeling, Ray checked under the bed
and found an empty aluminum film canister. A label on
the canister said: Barrow #2 Rush.

Ray got up and set the canister on the bed.

"What is it?"

He was facing the bathroom and the door was shut. "Ms. Carter?" He walked over and rapped on it, somehow certain that there would be no answer. "Ms. Carter?"

"I think we should go down to the lobby and wait for her there," Melissa suggested with a nervous edge in her voice.

Ray tried the knob but it wouldn't turn. He bent and examined the lock. It was a simple device that required only a paperclip or a bobby pin to release. He pulled a miniature Swiss Army knife from his pants pocket and extracted the plastic toothpick. After fiddling with the lock for a moment, he heard it pop. He twisted the knob. "Ms. Carter?"

Pushing the door open, he saw a naked body reclining in the bathtub. "Oh, I'm sorry," he apologized. But before he could turn away, he saw that there was no water in the tub. The face was obscured by the shower curtain. There was a thin rivulet of blood running down the neck and shoulder. "Ms. Carter . . . ?"

He glanced back at Melissa and was about to wave her inside so that she could administer first aid, if the woman was still alive, when something impacted the back of his head. He heard a loud crack and saw Melissa's expression change from trepidation to horror.

Suddenly the carpet was rushing at him and he fell into darkness.

➤➤ TWENTY ◀◀

"HANG ON!"

The snow machine revved and the umiak jerked. Ray clung desperately to the side, a reluctant hooky-bobber. This was a bad idea, his mind kept repeating. He looked over and saw Lewis grinning maniacally.

"Why are we doing this?"

Lewis laughed and his dog, Vader, jumped up at Ray, licking him in the face.

"Down!" Ray scolded the dog. What had he been thinking when he agreed to accompany Lewis out on the floes? Lewis? And with a dog, no less. Having a dog in a whaling camp was taboo, an invitation for bad luck. Though Ray wasn't all that superstitious, he didn't like to tempt fate or the tuungak or God or whoever was in charge of such things. Why take chances?

The snow machine was putting up a rooster tail of ice crystals that showered Ray's eyes and cheeks. The driver was going fast. Too fast. He tried to figure out who it was, but couldn't. The man was wearing a white parka, a white ski mask, white gauntlet mittens and white bunny boots. No whale would spot him coming.

Suddenly the driver made a hard right turn and the trailing umiak nearly turned over. It was all Ray could do to hang on. The umiak swerved radically from side to side and Ray was in the process of adjusting his grip when the dog's head shot up over the edge of the boat, teeth bared. Ray reflexively let go and went skidding out across the ice. Sliding on his back, boots in front of him, he could see a lead widening, as if to swallow him. He tried to dig his heels in, drag his gloved hands, but he continued to accelerate toward the opening of water. With only a dozen meters of ice left, one of his boots caught on a chunk of ice and he spun around so that his head was pointing at the sea. Miraculously, he managed to slow himself until he stopped with head and shoulders hanging off the ice. He stared down at the deep blue water, panting, still panicked, watching as tiny waves leapt up the side of the floe, as though trying to reach him.

He lifted himself up with his arms and was about to stand when the ground beneath him shifted. There was a sound like wood splitting and the shelf of ice tilted toward the water. He didn't have time to jump away or find a handhold or even take a breath of air before he was underwater.

Strangely, he wasn't cold. Just heavy. His arms and legs were drawn up into a ball and he was sinking like a rock. Drifting down into the darkness, he realized that he was going to die and also that his body might never be found. He would probably be swept under the ice and far out into the Arctic Ocean.

"Ray . . ."

The voice was clear and crisp and somehow comforting. Ray blinked into the blackness and saw a light approaching. The light became two lights, then two eyes. It was a bowhead whale.

"Ray . . ."

He answered, "Yes," without ever speaking. And without thinking, he reached and grabbed one of the mighty flukes. As it pulled him through the water, he could feel the beast's power and knew that he was safe.

Other lights appeared. Other eyes. Other whales. There were ten, twenty, a hundred. Ray had never seen anything so beautiful or felt so at peace.

In the next instant, he was one of them. AgviQ gliding gracefully through the water, changing direction at will, spinning his massive girth with an agility and a freedom that was utterly amazing to him.

"Ray . . ."

The voice was a beacon, summoning him.

He aimed his broad head at the surface and began to pound the massive fluke. Up he went, shooting through a cold and comforting space without stars. He saw the surface and then suddenly broken through it and was airborne. Flying. Breaching. He exhaled in a tremendous explosion of air.

"Ray . . ."

He opened his eyes and a face slowly materialized. A woman's face. A beautiful woman with a look of distress.

"Margaret . . . ?"

"No, Ray. It's Melissa."

He tried to sit up.

"Lie still," she ordered.

He relaxed and pain surged down the back of his head, into his neck. The face above him went yellow and Ray almost fainted.

When the stars finally dissipated, he saw Melissa and beyond her, a popcorn ceiling. The hotel room, he recalled. He craned his head a little and before the stars returned, saw the bathroom and a smear of blood on the tile floor.

"Don't move," she cautioned.

"I won't." He cringed as his vision tunneled down and he grew nauseous. When the wave of pain had passed, he asked, "What happened?"

"The guy coldcocked you."

"What guy?"

"The guy hiding in the bathroom."

Ray closed his eyes and tried to remember but all he could see was a school of whales. Slowly something else materialized: the naked, lifeless body of a woman.

There was a rustling noise and Ray opened his eyes to see two men entering the room carrying equipment boxes. One of them had a handlebar mustache and both were wearing vests emblazoned with: Barrow EMT.

"Long time no see," the clean shaven one said as he bent over Ray.

He blinked up at the man and realized that he had been at Aana's that morning.

"What do we got, Dr. Bradshaw?" the other asked.

Melissa explained Ray's condition in medicalese, ending with, "He might need a few stitches. I can't tell with all the blood."

"Is it bad?" Ray asked as the man with the mustache carefully lifted his head and examined the wound.

"Nah," he answered. "My son fell off his ATV last week and got a bigger gash."

They had him sit up and he watched as the room wavered.

"You okay?" the other EMT asked.

"No," he answered. "My head feels like it was stomped by a caribou."

"I know a guy that had that happen once," the man said, laughing. "Couldn't see straight for a week."

"I'll bet."

They dabbed at the cut, washing away the blood and irrigating the wound.

"Ouch!" Ray complained. "That stings!"

Ignoring this, Melissa moved in to check the patient. "It's not as bad as it looked. You just bled like a stuck pig. You don't need stitches."

The EMTs nodded their heads and applied a thick bandage with tape.

"But you were unconscious so you may have a slight concussion."

"Want us to take him in for a CAT scan, Doc?"

Melissa made a face, then shook her head. "I'll keep him under observation."

Ray felt a strange thrill at those words. In a James Bond film they might be taken to mean . . .

"You're the doc." The EMTs began packing up their cases. They stood in unison and swore in unison as they stared into the bathroom.

"What the . . . ?" the man with the mustache wondered.

"There's a . . . uh . . . a body . . . in the . . . uh . . . bathtub . . ." the other one stuttered.

"I already called the police," Melissa informed.

The image flashed into Ray's mind again: the whales and the body. Now the body had a face and it was looking at him.

The EMTs approached the tub cautiously. "Who . . . ?" one of them asked.

"Film producer from Outside," Melissa said.

"What happened?"

"Don't touch anything," Ray warned.

"Are you sure she's dead?"

Melissa nodded grimly.

The man with the mustache cursed. "What is it with today? We don't have a death, even from natural causes for weeks. Haven't had a murder since . . . what? Last summer?"

"Yeah," Ray grunted. He had worked the case.

"And now, suddenly, we've got two in a matter of hours."

"Bizarre coincidence, huh?" his partner said.

"It's not a coincidence," Ray muttered.

"Can you stand?" Melissa asked him.

"I can try." She and the EMTs assisted him to his feet and he stood there, holding onto them as the room vanished into a swirl of golden sparkles.

"Sit down on the bed," Melissa advised.

"No," Ray said, resisting the pull of her hand. "This is a crime scene." His vision slowly cleared and when he was sure he wasn't going to throw up, he said to the EMTs, "We'll need you to transport her to the morgue, after we've swept the place."

The men nodded, and looked back at the bathroom, obviously horrified.

"We'll wait downstairs," the one with the mustache said.

As the EMTs were heading for the door, Lewis and Billy Bob hustled up, hands on their holstered weapons. They both had bewildered expressions on their faces.

"She's in there," Ray said, aiming a thumb at the bathroom. As he did, he turned to look in that direction and his colleagues gasped at the bandage.

"Aiyaa! What happen to head?"

"Ray, buddy, are you okay?"

"I'm fine."

They looked to Melissa for confirmation. "Concussion."

"Geez, Ray . . ." Billy Bob gasped.

Lewis pointed at the blood on the bathroom tile. "Aiyaa! Who dat?"

"I think that's mine," Ray confessed.

Carefully stepping around the small puddle, Lewis leaned to look into the tub. "Aiyaa!" he repeated. "Who dat?"

"Her name is Jean Carter," Ray explained. "She's a producer with the Discovery Channel."

Billy Bob quickly examined the bathroom, the body, the blood, then turned back looking a little pale. "What's going on, Ray?"

"It's . . . complicated."

"We're not in a hurry to go anyplace," the cowboy said.

"I'll tell you about it in a sec. First, print the place," Ray said. He was about to ask Melissa to see if she could come up with a cause of death before they had to move the body, when Billy Bob interrupted.

"No. First, you need to tell us what we got here. And how you stumbled onto it."

"What? Are you saying I'm . . . ?"

"I'm saying you're an off-duty cop who spilled some of his blood right next to a corpse."

"I was here," Melissa said. "She was dead when we came in."

Billy Bob gave Melissa the once over and Ray could almost read his thoughts: *not only are you off duty, but you're running around with a pretty girl who is not your wife and you wound up in a hotel room with her.*

"It's not what it looks like."

"I hope not," Billy Bob said.

Lewis went for the evidence kit, and when he came back, Billy Bob took Ray and Melissa downstairs to the lobby for a debriefing session that bordered on an interrogation. Ray wasn't offended. He would have done the same thing. The cowboy was just being thorough and going by the book, something a lot of cops neglected to do and later regretted.

After they finished with their accounts, Billy Bob sat looking at his notepad. "Let me get this straight. You think Ronnie is innocent?"

"It's possible," Ray stipulated.

"And you think the knife and the boots and the . . . the . . . *you* know . . ."

"Finger," Melissa said.

"Right. You think they were planted at Ronnie's."

Ray hadn't put his suspicions into words until now and it sounded rather farfetched. "Maybe."

"And whoever it was that killed Miz Clearwater, they did it for her jewelry?"

"For her wedding ring," Ray explained.

"Now this here lady," he said, jabbing his pencil at

the ceiling. "Miz Carter . . . she was killed because she was making a movie?"

"Uh . . . kind of," Ray said. The more he thought it over, the less sure he was.

"And you were here to look at her movie?"

"The museum footage."

"But when you got here, she was dead and this mystery man was there too and he hit you on the noggin' and got away clean?"

Ray looked to Melissa for confirmation. All he remembered was seeing the carpet come at him.

"Right."

"You didn't see his face because he had on a black ski mask."

"White."

"Huh?"

"It was a white ski mask and a white parka and white gloves."

Billy Bob noted this on his pad.

Ray suddenly recalled his dream again: the snow machine driver dressed all in white. Not only was it disturbing to have a recurring nightmare like that, but this one had been even more elaborate: the water, the whales showing up, him becoming a whale. It was a little like a story grandfather used to tell involving a man who turned into a salmon and was then caught by his own people. Or maybe it wasn't like that at all.

"He hit Ray and then pushed past you."

"He knocked me back against the wall," Melissa said.

"And you didn't chase after him?" Billy Bob asked.

"No."

"And why was that?"

"For one thing," she answered a little tersely, "he had an ice pick in his hand."

"Oh, that's right."

"And for another, Ray was lying there bleeding. Being a doctor, rather than a cop," she said slowly and deliberately, "I figured that giving first aid would be much wiser than running after an armed assailant."

"You did, huh?" he asked absently.

"Yeah, I did."

There was a long pause as Billy Bob reviewed his notes.

"You do believe us, don't you?" Ray asked.

The cowboy looked up at them. "It's a whopper of a story . . ."

"It's the truth!" Melissa said, losing patience.

"I didn't say it wasn't. I just said it was a whopper." He sniffed at his pad. "But . . . well . . . of course, I believe you. Why wouldn't I? Dr. Bradshaw here is a well respected medical professional. And you . . ." He looked at Ray. "You're my best buddy and the reason I'm in Barrow. The reason I'm alive, for that matter." He told Melissa, "Ray has saved my skin a number of times. I owe him big-time."

"So we're not under arrest?" she asked.

"Arrest? Heck, no. You're witnesses and you've supplied important information to an ongoing investigation."

"I'm on this case," Ray told him.

"That's for the captain to decide."

"I don't care about the captain. I'm on this case. Now you can help me or you can get in the way. It's up to you."

Billy Bob shook his head. "You're gonna get me in a heap of trouble."

"I'll take full responsibility."

"Oh, you will, will ya?"

"We're wasting time. Whoever killed this woman isn't going to hang around town waiting for us to catch him."

"Wouldn't be too smart if he did."

Ray got up. "Why don't you go home," he told Melissa.

"You gotta be kidding. I'm in this too."

"Melissa . . . it's getting dangerous."

"So? You should try working the ER sometime. Besides, I have to watch you for signs of head injury." Before Ray could object, she said, "You're stuck with me."

"Suit yourself," he muttered, thinking he could do worse than to have a beautiful woman looking after him. He had the distinct feeling that the danger of investigating with her was as much a matter of physical chemistry as it was the possibility of physical harm.

Ray led them to the elevator. "Let's see if Lewis turned up anything."

➤➤ TWENTY-ONE ➤➤

WHEN THEY REACHED room 317, they found Lewis repacking the evidence kit.

"Anything?" Ray asked, closing the door behind them.

"Lotta prints . . . day all look da same. Prolly da victim."

Ray glanced over the prints. Lewis was right. The whorl patterns were very similar.

"The attacker was wearing gloves," Melissa reminded them.

"I don't suppose he left any other calling cards."

"He do it real clean," Lewis said.

"How about the c-o-d?" Ray asked Melissa.

"I know cause of death," Lewis boasted.

"Oh, yeah?"

"Sure. Guy poke hole in temple. Not much blood but kill her real good."

Melissa nodded in agreement.

"We got us pro-fession hit here."

Ray scoffed at him. "And just how do you know that?"

"I see how it done. Too clean for re-gular kill."

"It is clean," Melissa agreed.

"Since when are you an expert on homicide?" Ray asked Lewis.

"I study up."

"Where?"

"I watch *Law 'n Orda.*"

"I watch *ER*," Ray countered, "but that doesn't make me an expert on emergency medicine."

"I tell you, dis guy good. He know what he doing."

Ray went into the bathroom and glared down at the body. The woman looked different than she had a few hours earlier. It wasn't just that she was naked. It was that her face had lost something. Life, Ray decided. He squinted at the hole in her head. The temple area had been punctured and blood ran in a trickle down her neck and shoulder, disappearing under her back.

There was a knock at the door. A voice called, "Jean?"

Ray walked over and pulled the door open.

"Sorry I took so long." It was the cameraman. He was looking down at a tray of cellophane-wrapped sandwiches. "The FedEx place was closed, so I . . ." He glanced up and stopped. Drawing back, he checked the number on the door. Satisfied that it was the right room, his eyes darted from Ray to Lewis and Billy Bob to Melissa. "What's going on?"

Lewis started toward him. "Dis a crime scene, you go away."

"Crime scene?"

"It's okay," Ray told Lewis. He motioned for the man to enter.

"Where's Jean?" He glanced around, then saw the

bathroom, the blood on the floor. "Oh, God . . ." Dropping the tray, he rushed for the bathroom door. Ray and Billy Bob converged to stop him.

"Jean!"

He muscled them back far enough to see the body in the tub. "Oh, God . . . ! No! No! Jean!" He struggled for several seconds, then suddenly gave up, his whole body deflating. He was breathing erratically, on the verge of tears. "She's . . . she's not . . ." He turned to Ray, pleading with his eyes. "She can't be!"

This was that part of being a cop that Ray hated. Telling the survivors that their friend or relative had been in an accident, had succumbed to a heart attack, had frozen to death . . .

"She was murdered," Ray said.

The man shook his head, as if this couldn't be possible, then burst into tears. Billy Bob helped him to the edge of the bed.

"Take it easy," the cowboy said. He sat down next to the man. "Take it easy."

"Who dis?" Lewis asked Ray in a whisper.

"The cameraman," Ray whispered back.

"Look more like da boyfriend," Lewis said.

Ray nodded his agreement. Not that you wouldn't be saddened and shocked by the sudden, violent death of a co-worker. But this guy was really broken up. He looked like he had just lost someone close to him.

"Wonder where he was when she was getting life stolen from her."

Lewis wasn't particularly good at investigation, Ray thought, but he did have one valuable trait along those lines: he suspected everyone. Sometimes it was easy to make assumptions and let people slip through the cracks. But this guy, no matter his emotional state at the moment, had to be placed at the top of the suspect list. At least for now. The victim was from out of town and wouldn't be at risk for a crime of this nature unless she had either seriously ticked off someone—like, say, her partner/boyfriend here—or had been robbed. No other motive seemed to present itself.

"Get some pictures," Ray told Lewis. He motioned for Melissa to assist him. "When he's done," he said to her, "see what you can learn from the body."

Lewis got the camera. "Don't let him run off," he said, glaring at the cameraman.

Ray pulled a chair over from the table and straddled it backwards, facing the man. As he waited for the man to collect himself, Ray's eyes drifted to the closet. There were two suitcases in there, he realized: one sitting open, the other closed and positioned against the wall, partially hidden by the closet door. He also noticed that the clothes hanging on the bar were comprised of a woman's jacket and a man's sport coat.

"I just . . . I can't believe this . . ." the man sniffed. "I can't believe she's . . ." He nearly broke down again.

"I know this has to be a shock," Ray said. "But we need to ask you a few questions."

He looked at Ray with dead, empty eyes.

"What's your name?"

"Jeff Adams."

"I'm Officer Attla." Ray twisted and extracted his wallet to show him his ID. He introduced Billy Bob and Lewis before asking, "What's your relationship to Ms. Carter?"

Jeff clamped his eyes shut. "She's my boss and . . ." He paused, breathing hard. "And we're . . . we *were* . . ." He began to cry again. "Why would anyone . . . ?"

Billy Bob patted him on the shoulder. "It's gotta be tough."

Ray noticed a gold ring on the man's left hand and struggled to recall if there had been one on the victim's left hand. "You two were . . . married?" he tried.

Jeff shook his head.

"Engaged?"

Another shake.

"*Involved?*"

He nodded. Exhaling heavily, he said, "But please don't let that get out."

"Why not?" Ray said, already knowing the answer.

"Because . . . I'm . . . I'm married."

Billy Bob removed his hand from Jeff's shoulder and shot him a disapproving look. "So you two, you and Ms. Carter, you were adulterers?"

This surprised Jeff. "Well . . . no . . . I mean, we . . ."

Ray waved the cowboy off. This wasn't the time for moral judgments. "How long have you been together?"

"About six months. We've collaborated on three projects. When you travel and work together like that, it . . . I don't know. It just happens."

"It just happens?" Billy Bob asked indignantly. "Bull. You don't just break your promises to your wife because you happen to be with someone else."

"Billy Bob . . ." Ray warned.

"Well, you don't. You make a conscious decision to betray your sweetie. It don't just happen."

Ray started to tell the cowboy to stuff a boot in it,

but Jeff said, "You're right. It was a conscious decision. Things aren't that good at home. We've been having trouble. And Jean . . . she's so spirited and free
and . . . geez . . . who would kill her?"

"Any ideas on that?" Ray asked, trying to sound as
nonchalant as possible.

"Not one."

"She didn't have any enemies?"

"Jean?" he asked, as though this were ludicrous.
"No."

"Anybody get bad press from one of your films?"

"Sure. We did a thing for *60 Minutes* that tore a new
one in the insurance industry."

"Is it possible that someone from that piece was out
for revenge?"

"I don't know. I suppose. Maybe. But this is a
strange place to come after us."

"Why's that?"

"Barrow, Alaska? We've been in New York, Seattle,
Washington, DC, doing all these assignments. It would
have been so much easier to do it down there."

"This is more remote, fewer cops, wide open country, easy to hide, to escape," Ray pointed out.

Jeff shrugged. "I don't know."

"You two were sharing this room?"

"Yes."

"Anything missing?"

He glanced around at the equipment boxes, then at
the suitcases in the closet. "Doesn't look like it."

"What about this?" Ray handed him the empty film
canister.

Jeff examined the label on the outside. "It's one of
the daily reels."

"Where's the film?"

"Probably on the viewer." He got up rather shakily and went to the table where a machine with two reels was set up. Flipping a switch, he waited as the fan hummed and a light came on. Ray watched as he hit a button and the film began to advance. An image appeared on the small screen at the center of the device: men setting up flags at the festival grounds.

"This is old. Day before yesterday."

"Where's this one?" Ray asked, tapping the empty canister.

"I don't know."

"What was it of?"

"This one . . . ?" He examined the label again. "It was from yesterday. The stuff I shot out at the floes."

"What about the museum footage?"

"It didn't come back yet."

"But it was supposed to, right?"

"Yeah. We only got one of the two rolls. Some kind of screw up at the lab in Anchorage. They're sending it on the five o'clock flight. Supposedly. If they didn't expose the whole thing or something."

"Why would they do that?"

"They're just not the most competent bunch I've ever seen. We're used to working with top-notch labs down in the U.S."

"This is the U.S.," Billy Bob pointed out rather defensively.

"You know what I mean."

"So the museum footage is due back at five?" Ray confirmed.

"Yeah."

Ray looked at the empty canister. Was it possible

that someone had killed Jean Carter for that footage? Had they taken the other reel by mistake, thinking it had the museum on it? Was there something incriminating on the reel due in at five? Incriminating enough to commit murder? Why not just steal it? Why kill a woman?

"Was there anything strange or out of the ordinary about the work you did at the museum yesterday?"

"I wasn't there."

"Yesterday? At the Dance of the Whale exhibit?"

"Jean shot that. I was out at the point. One of the crews was bringing their boats in from camp and they offered to let me ride along."

Ray nodded. Had Jean seen something that got her killed?

"It wasn't a tough shoot—just background, static stuff of the exhibit, a few shots of the locals, nothing fancy. Besides, she worked camera before she started producing. She could do this whole piece without me if she wanted to."

Could have done, Ray's mind corrected him. From the look on his face, Jeff was thinking the same thing, switching his words to the past tense.

"Where was you when she getting killed?" The question came from Lewis who was standing with his hands on his hips, as though challenging Jeff.

"We split up when we finished at the festival. I went to pick up the reels at the airport and she said she'd meet me at the hotel."

"Why didn't she go with you?" Lewis wanted to know.

"She had a headache. And she was supposed to meet Officer Attla and the lady." He pointed at the bathroom.

"What time was that?"

"I don't know . . . forty-five minutes ago."

"It took forty-five minutes to make the pickup?" Ray asked. The airport was only ten minutes away.

"After I got the reel, I had to ship a production outline to the Discovery Channel, then I picked up some lunch for us." He looked at the sandwiches and drinks which were still lying on the carpet.

Melissa appeared in the bathroom door. "Ray? Could I talk to you a minute?"

He nodded at her. "Clean up the mess," he told Lewis. "Then get him something else to eat."

"And some coffee," Billy Bob threw in.

"What I look like, slave?"

"Please," Ray said.

Lewis leaned in and whispered, "We gonna arrest him?"

"I don't know yet. But don't let him run off."

Lewis winked at him. "Ten-forty."

"That's ten-four."

"Uh?"

"Nevermind."

Ray went into the bathroom. "Got something?" He looked down at the body and cringed.

"Lewis was right about the c-o-d."

"Was he right about it being a pro hit?"

"Maybe."

Ray leaned down and examined the hole in the woman's temple. It was grotesque, an obscene violation to an otherwise peaceful face. The woman could have been asleep.

"Ice pick to the temple," Melissa said.

"Geez . . ." Ray studied it for another moment wondering what would possess someone, even a trained killer, to do something so barbaric as to pierce the side of another human being's head with an ice pick.

"Anybody could do that," Melissa pointed out. "But here's the clincher." She gestured toward the top of the toilet where a hair dryer was lying on a stack of fresh towels.

"What about it?"

"It's plugged in," she noted.

"So?"

"So the mirror is way over here." She took two steps to the left. "Who's going to stand at the commode and dry their hair?"

"What does that have to do with it being a hit?" It took a second for this to dawn on Ray. "It was going to be a fake suicide?"

"Looks like it. The killer knocks her out . . ." She pointed out a bruise on the neck. "Choke hold or something. Sticks her in the tub, planning to turn on the water and toss in the dryer. Zap!" She pointed out a piece of hotel stationery on the counter next to the sink. "This might have been for a note."

"Except we surprised him."

"Yeah. So he had to kill her quickly and efficiently. Which he did. And then he had to get out, which meant putting you down."

Ray tried to visualize this scenario. It made sense. Sort of. The attack, the setup, the unexpected intrusion, the panicked escape . . . "I still don't get why. What's the motive?"

"I can tell you a lot from the scene and from the condition of the body, Ray. But I can't tell you that."

TWENTY-TWO

RAY LEFT THE bathroom and went to the evidence kit. Lewis had repacked the camera and other equipment. Filed in a slot next to the film was the set of Polaroids. Ray fanned through them: the body from different angles, close-ups that were slightly out of focus, shots of the wound that were also rather indistinct . . . what they needed was a better camera. Actually, what they needed were fewer murders, Ray decided. Except for this strange and ominous day, they seldom broke out the kit, much less had to nail down a murder scene.

Near the bottom of the stack of photos he found one of the hair dryer. You could see the plug in the wall. In the very last shot, you could see the paper and pen reflected in the mirror, along with Lewis's shoulder.

"Whatcha lookin' fer?" Billy Bob asked.

"Just making sure Lewis did the whole scene. How's Jeff doing?"

"He's hurtin'. And I know I'm not always the best judge of character, you know me, Ray, too soft-hearted, but I think it's genuine."

"You do, huh?"

"Yessir, I do. Those ain't pretend tears he's cryin'. That man is in some serious pain."

Ray glanced at Jeff. The man's face was pale, his eyes red and teary. Ray tended to agree with the cowboy. It didn't look like an act. Besides, it didn't fit. Why would he kill his partner? Unless . . . maybe she threatened to tell his wife about the affair? That could potentially motivate a man to kill someone. But in this fashion? With such premeditation?

Ray walked over to him. "Back to the museum footage. You said you were shooting out at the point while Jean was filming the exhibit?"

"Right."

"Isn't the exhibit the focus of your documentary?"

"The exhibit and the festival."

"Then why weren't you running the camera at the museum?"

"I told you, it was just background stuff."

Ray made a face. "The centerpiece of your project is background?"

"No. We were going to shoot more over there today, when the insurance guy showed up."

"What insurance guy?"

"The exhibit is covered by Lloyd's of London. They've got a policy for like . . . twenty million bucks."

"You're kidding?"

"No. Apparently the artifacts are so rare and delicate that they warrant that kind of coverage."

"What's the insurance man going to do?"

"He's coming to verify the authenticity and value of the items."

Ray considered this. "And you were going to film him doing that?"

"Right. It would make great footage: taking out various items and checking them with a magnifying glass. That kind of thing."

"And if something turned out to be fake?"

"We planned for that contingency. If that happened, we would cut it up into two separate features: one about Nalukataq for Discovery and another on the scandal for *20/20* or one of the other news programs."

"Clever," Ray said. "When's the insurance man doing his thing?"

"Three."

"Maybe we should be there for it."

"What's the point? There won't be a piece now. Not without Jean."

"Even if she was killed as part of a cover-up?" Ray asked.

"What do you mean?"

"She was killed purposefully. For a reason."

"What reason?"

"I don't know that yet. But in order to figure that out, we need your help."

"We do?" Billy Bob asked.

"I want you to film the insurance verification."

"What's the point?" Jeff said glumly.

"The point is . . ." Ray wasn't sure what the point was. Somehow, Aana's murder and Jean's murder were tied together. Or at least, his gut told him so. He had no proof. Aana had worked at the museum. Jean had been filming a documentary of an exhibit at the museum. That was the only tie between the two women. Aana's ring had been stolen. Jean's reel was missing. What did that mean?

Lewis entered with a tray of sandwiches and coffee.

He offered the tray to Jeff and the man accepted a cup of coffee. As Lewis doled out the rest to Billy Bob and Melissa, Ray picked up the empty film canister and frowned at it.

"They think they got the footage of the museum," he thought aloud.

"Who?" Billy Bob asked.

"Whoever it is who's going around killing people."

"Dee udder," Lewis said, shaking his head. "We already catched him. He in jail."

"We already arrested a *suspect*," Ray said. "A suspect who claimed he didn't do it."

"He had da weapon and da . . ."

Ray waved him off.

"Was it an ice pick?" Jeff asked with a horrified expression.

"No," Ray said. He was about to move the discussion away from the other murder when Lewis blurted, "It was a whaling knife."

"You mean one of those huge machete things?" He looked like he was about to be sick.

"Day not just big. Day sharp too."

Jeff turned and threw up on the carpet.

Either he was a great actor, on a par with DeNiro, Ray thought, or the guy was what he appeared to be: a distraught soul who had just lost a friend/colleague/lover and had no stomach for homicide.

"Excuse me a sec," Billy Bob said, starting for the door. His face was pale and he kept swallowing. "I need to use the rest room."

"While you're down there," Ray instructed, "talk to the manager. Find out if he saw anyone come up here."

"A man in a white parka, white boots, white gloves, and a white ski mask," Melissa specified.

"Sure thang," Billy Bob said, hurrying into the hall and away from the talk of bodies, blood, and weapons.

"Lewis," Ray directed, "secure the scene and call Jimmy. Have him take Jeff to the station for a deposition." He waited until Jeff had wiped his mouth and was breathing regularly again. "We'll need to know her next of kin."

"Gotta arrange to ship da body," Lewis added helpfully. "Or we gonna do autopsy?"

Adams almost lost it again. Covering his mouth with a hand, he muttered, "Oh, God . . . oh, God . . ."

"Nice," Ray grumbled at Lewis. "Notify the captain and see how he wants this one handled." He turned to Adams. "Mind if one of us films the insurance procedure?"

He shrugged, obviously not caring what happened from here on out.

"Where's your camera?"

"In the car," Adams sighed. "But . . . unless you've shot film before . . ."

"Hard to operate?"

"Not hard, but you have to know about light meters and f-stop settings. I mean . . . I guess I could do it, it's just . . ." He put his face in his hands and began to weep.

"What you gonna do now, Mr. In-Charge?" Lewis asked with a scowl.

"I guess we'll skip the insurance thing." Ray checked his watch. "I have to meet someone."

"Who?"

"Someone."

Lewis sniffed resentfully at this. "What I say if da captain asks 'bout you?"

"Tell him I've got something for him," Ray said, hoping that at some point he really would have something tangible for him. "And tell him I'll check in with him later."

"When later?"

"Just later."

Ray signaled Melissa and she followed him out of the room and down the hall. As they stood waiting for the elevator, she said, "I've got a theory."

"You do, huh?"

"Yeah. It goes like this: the Dance of the Whale exhibit is a crock." She paused, then said, "Something happened at the museum yesterday, something that could potentially expose that and someone had to do something to cover it up. Something like killing two women."

Ray chuckled.

"It's not that farfetched."

"It's not that. Actually I was thinking along the same lines. But . . ."

"But what?"

"But it's full of holes: somebody did something to someone when something happened somewhere. It's a string of blanks."

"We just have to fill them in."

"*Just?*" Ray said, resorting to the stairwell. "You make it sound easy, like working a crossword."

"It's kind of like that. I keep getting the feeling that we know more than we think we do."

Ray smiled. She was so like him, same intuition, same problem-solving strategy, it was almost spooky. "Me too," he admitted.

"What if Ronnie didn't kill Aana? And what if whoever did, also . . ."

"Yeah," he agreed. "But we're missing motive. Not to mention who might have that motive."

"I'm telling you, it has to do with the exhibit."

"Maybe."

As they approached the door to the main floor, Billy Bob came through it. His face had color again.

"Anything?" Ray asked.

"Nope. The manager was in his office and didn't see nuthin'."

"It was worth a shot."

"What now?"

"Stick around and help Lewis wrap things up."

"Shorely. Where you off to?"

"I'm chasing down a lead."

"Oh, yeah?" He looked at Ray, apparently expecting an explanation.

"I'll check in with you later."

"Okey-doke dokie," he sighed. "Ain't this just the worst sort of thang to be happenin' on festival—or anytime, for that matter."

"It certainly is."

The cowboy continued up the stairs and Ray and Melissa exited into the lobby. They reached the street and began making their way to Blackie's café. En route, they passed a dance group, then a whaling crew. The former was dressed in traditional Native garb, caribou jackets and mukluks. The latter were wearing their work clothes, white parkas with white gloves and white boots.

"You think it was a . . . ?" Melissa wondered.

"Could be but . . . I doubt it," Ray said. He could tell they were on the same wavelength. "What better disguise on festival day? If you want to blend in, why not dress like a whaler?"

"Why do they wear white anyway?" Melissa asked, watching the whalers trail away toward the festival grounds.

"To blend into the ice floes and keep the whales from seeing them."

"Camouflage."

Ray nodded. Camouflage was precisely the word. And it seemed to encapsulate what the perpetrator of the two murders was doing: blending into the environment to keep from being seen. Pieces of his dream skittered through his mind—the man on the snow machine, dressed in white. A whaler. Or someone who wanted to be taken for one. But that was just a dream.

They arrived at the café and found Justin in a window booth, nursing a mug of hot chocolate. There was only one other patron there and he was sitting with his back to them at the counter. As Ray and Melissa were sliding into the seat across from Justin, Blackie came out of the kitchen bearing a large slice of pie. He set the plate in front of the boy with a frown and a click of his lips.

"I didn't order . . ." Justin started to protest.

"On the house. Same with the cocoa." Blackie sighed and looked at him sadly. "In memory of your aana."

"Thanks." Justin looked up at Ray and his eyes widened. "Are you okay?"

"I'm fine," Ray answered, reaching to finger the bandage on the back of his head.

"What happened?" Blackie asked.

"Somebody coldcocked me."

Blackie shook his head in disgust. "What is this world coming to?"

Ray shrugged, not sure how to answer the question.

"A fine woman like Hillary Clearwater not safe in her own house? Here! In Barrow? And people go around assaulting the police! I tell you, this country of ours is going to hell in a handbasket." He huffed again.

"How'd you find out about Aana?"

"I told him," Justin admitted sheepishly. "I didn't mean to, but . . ."

"It's okay," Ray told him.

"You ask me," Blackie went on, "we ought to commemorate her passing by postponing festival. Hillary Clearwater was one of the last of the old ones, the folks who carry on traditions of The People. The least we can do is make sure everybody knows that and pauses to show respect. It's the least we can do."

"Her death is part of an open investigation," Ray explained.

"A moment of silence, prayers by Elders . . . It's the least we could do. You ask me . . ."

Ray cut him off. "Blackie, I feel the same way you do. But there are other issues here that . . ."

"Issues?" he said, making it sound like a dirty word. "What sort of issues are more important than dignity of Hillary Clearwater?"

"Her death will be made public in due time."

"Due time?" he grumbled. "That's a load of whale dung."

"Yeah," Ray said, "I agree. But my orders are to keep it quiet for now. So I'd appreciate it if you could do the same."

"Keep it quiet . . ." he muttered, leaving the table. "A woman goes to qilak, and we gotta *keep it quiet.* What has the world come to?"

When Blackie had disappeared into the kitchen, Ray asked Justin, "Well . . . ?"

"It was her ring, Uncle Ray."

"You're sure?"

"Yes, sir."

"You're absolutely positive?" Ray asked. "It couldn't be a ring *like* Aana's?"

"Could be a duplicate," Melissa suggested.

Justin shook his head. "It had the same scratches, the same worn places . . . that's her ring."

Ray blew air at the window.

"If it is her ring . . . why is it in the museum?" Melissa asked.

"I don't know," Ray said, his frustration growing. "I don't know."

➤ TWENTY-THREE ◄

"WHY STEAL A ring and put it in an exhibit?" Justin asked. "And why kill Aana? Why not just take the ring and leave her alone?"

They sat there, all three of them looking out the window as though the solution might present itself out on the street.

Blackie returned with coffee. "You wanna order?" he asked rather brusquely, obviously still ticked about keeping Aana's death a secret.

"No, we're fine," Ray told him.

"How 'bout you, Justin? More pie?"

Justin looked down at the plate and the slice of pie he had barely touched. "No, thank you."

"You need anything, you give a holler."

"Thanks."

Blackie went over to fill the cup of the man at the counter.

"Here's what I'm thinking," Ray said. "I'm thinking that there's something on the film reel that explains things." Actually, he thought, it wasn't so much that he believed this to be the case as he *hoped* it to be.

"Do you think Ronnie took Aana's ring?" Justin asked.

Ray shook his head.

"Then who did?"

He shook his head again. It was a vicious circle, *who* leading to *why* leading to *who* again.

"Why don't you arrest the people who do the exhibit?"

"For what?"

"For . . . having a stolen ring."

"How do we prove it's stolen?" Ray asked.

"It belonged to Aana."

"But unfortunately she isn't here to identify and claim it."

"Couldn't Justin and your grandfather do that?" Melissa asked.

Ray considered this. Would the testimony of a kid and a senile old man be enough to convince a prosecutor to press charges against the Roth Foundation? "They'd probably just feign ignorance and say they didn't know who the ring belonged to or where it came from. It isn't enough to tie them to the murders."

"There was more than one?" Justin asked.

Ray nodded and pulled out his cell phone. He dialed and got Margaret.

"How's she doing?" he asked.

"You'd never know she broke a bone, that's for sure. Hang on."

Ray waited and a second later, Keera said, "Hi, Daddy!"

"You sound good."

"I am good."

"How's the arm?"

"I've already got four autographs!"

"Four? Wow."

"And Grandfather's picture is cool. When are you coming home?"

"Miss me?"

"I want your autograph."

Ray laughed. "I'll be home later."

"Hurry up, while there's still good spaces left on my cast."

"Okay." There was a clunk and Margaret was on the line.

"How's it going?"

"Not good."

"What's the matter?"

"I'll tell you later."

She paused. "Be careful, Ray."

"I'm being careful," he assured her. He decided that this was not the time to tell her about the lump on his head. He told her goodbye, hung up, and dialed again.

"Barrow Police. Brinkley speaking."

"Hey, Mitch. It's Ray."

"What's up, Ray?"

"I need a favor."

"Now there's a surprise." Mitch Brinkley was an old college buddy of Ray's. "What is it this time?"

"I need to see Ronnie."

"Is that right?" Brinkley actually laughed at this.

"What's so funny?"

"Well, it's just that I have this memo in front of me that says under no circumstances am I to let Officer Raymond Attla see the prisoner."

"You're kidding."

"The captain's no dummy, Ray. He knows that you

won't let this thing slide. You do your best police work
when you're on vacation."

"Are you saying he expected me to stay on it?"

"Huh?"

Ray suddenly felt like an idiot. How had he missed
it? His abrupt removal from the case had been the captain's way of asking Ray to look into the matter, without constant oversight. Which meant . . . what? That
the captain trusted Ray's instincts, that he expected
Ray to catch the subtle wink in abrupt dismissal and
arrest the killer?

"Ray? You still there?"

Ray shook his head, trying to clear it. Or was he full
of himself? What if the captain had meant what he said
and wanted Ray to leave it alone?

"Ray?"

"Yeah, I'm here."

"Listen, I'm sorry, but orders are orders."

"Mitch, it's me. Ray. I'm telling you I need to see
Ronnie."

"Ray . . ." he whined.

"I'll owe you one."

"You'll owe me mortgage payments and grocery
bills if I lose my job for this."

"You won't."

"Easy for you to say."

"I'll take full responsibility."

"Whoopee. That always sounds good, but . . ."

"It won't take long. I just need to ask Ronnie and his
two lady friends a few questions."

"You missed your bet with the ladies."

"What do you mean?"

"They made bail and walked."

"Great . . . well, I guess Ronnie will have to do. Be at the back door in ten minutes."

There was a huff on the other end.

"You'll be there, right?"

"I'll be there," Brinkley sighed.

Ray hung up and stuffed the phone into his jacket. He was about to explain to Melissa and Justin that he had work to do, work that didn't involve them, when Melissa's beeper went off. She checked the number and slumped a little.

"Your captain knows about 317."

"What's 317?" Justin asked.

"Was that for an autopsy?"

Melissa nodded.

"An autopsy?" Justin said. "Of who?"

Ignoring him, Melissa got up. "So you're going to talk to Ronnie?"

"Yeah."

"Maybe we could meet up after . . ." She waved her hand in the general direction of the hospital and then at the police station.

"Maybe," Ray said, thinking that her involvement wasn't necessary. He enjoyed her company and she had a good mind for figuring things out, but now that a second body had been found . . . He caught himself. *Second body*. What if the two murders were unrelated? What if one had been a simple robbery? Perhaps the robber couldn't get Aana's ring off, so he cut it off. And the other an aborted sexual assault?

"Where? What time?"

Ray ran a hand over his face. "Uh . . . I don't know." He looked at his watch, still hoping not to include her. With bodies popping up everywhere and Ray running a rogue investigation, there was a growing risk to both life and career. The best thing for her to do was go home and forget about it.

"I'll be a couple of hours. What with the paperwork and all. How about if we meet right here at say, four forty-five? That way we can head to the airport for the five o'clock pickup."

Justin was squinting at them, struggling to keep up. "What pickup?"

"That's fine," Ray said without energy. He fully intended to stand her up.

"You better be here," she warned.

"You don't have to do this," Ray said.

"I know." She smiled at him and left.

Justin watched her go, then looked at Ray. "You like her, don't you Uncle Ray?"

Ray felt his face flush. "She's a nice lady." As an afterthought, he added, "And a good doctor."

"Pretty, too," Justin said.

"I guess."

"But not as pretty as Aana Margaret."

Ray grinned at him. "Not even close."

Justin pushed his pie plate away. "I'm ready."

"For what?"

"To go over to the station."

"You're not going."

"Sure I am. You said I could help."

"You already did, by going to the museum."

"I want to keep helping until you catch the guy."

"Going with me to the station wouldn't be helping."

"Then what am I supposed to do?"

"Why not go back to the festival? Hey, you're supposed to dance, aren't you?"

"I told them I wouldn't be there. I just . . . I don't feel like dancing."

"I understand," Ray said. He didn't feel like dancing either. He was tired and frustrated and rather confused. While the coffee hadn't alleviated his fatigue, it had aggravated the ache that had been throbbing through his head since his close encounter with the murderer. What a day, he thought, gently massaging the bandaged area. Two deaths, Keera breaks her arm, Grandfather runs off and leaves Freddie alone . . . and it was only mid-afternoon.

"Come on, Uncle Ray. Take me with you."

"No. This is official stuff."

Justin shook his head. "How can it be official if you aren't officially on the case?"

Smart kid, Ray thought.

"Give me something to do. We gotta catch this guy."

"What if we already did? What if Ronnie killed Aana?"

"I don't think so."

"Why not?"

"I just . . . I've got a feeling."

Ray rubbed his eyes. Everyone had a feeling. Grandfather felt like the tuungak were displeased, that the spirit of the whale was grieved, that Owl was on the move. Melissa was convinced that the real killer was still on the loose. Ray had a hunch that Ronnie wasn't guilty and that the two deaths were somehow related. Now Justin was jumping on the bandwagon. Lots of feelings, but no hard evidence.

He suddenly remembered the insurance verification that was scheduled to take place at three.

"You know how to run a video camera?"

"No."

"Wanna learn?"

Ray took Justin back to the Brown and made him wait in the lobby while he retrieved the video camera from Jean Carter's room. He took the tape out and put it in his pocket, then led Justin across the street to purchase a new 8-mm cartridge.

"What am I supposed to do?" the boy asked as Ray showed him the buttons and demonstrated how to hold it.

"Just shoot what you see."

Justin tried the camera on his shoulder. "They do documentaries on these little things?"

"Actually, they use a film camera, but we're kind of doing this on the fly." He finished with the how-to briefing. "Got all that?"

"I think so."

"You still have the museum pass?"

"Yes, sir."

"Good. Now the important thing is that you stay put and watch what goes on. Even if you can't get the camera to work or you run out of tape, hang out until the insurance business is over."

"Okay." Justin nodded importantly.

"That would a great help to me."

"What should I do when I'm done?"

"Let's see . . . how about if you wait for me at the ice cream place next to the museum. Okay?"

"Yes, sir."

Ray walked Justin to the corner and as they prepared to part ways, he instructed, "Be careful and keep your eyes open."

"I will, Uncle Ray. You can count on me."

"I know I can." He watched Justin stride off, thinking to himself what a bright future the kid had. He was smart, determined, and very dependable. He would succeed at whatever he chose to pursue.

Ray walked to the alley and, after checking the street, jogged the final block to the rear door of the station. He rapped on the metal twice before the door clicked open.

"Hurry up," Brinkley said nervously.

"Where's the captain?"

"He went out on that homicide." He led Ray quickly along the back hall. "What's going on?" he whispered.

"I don't know."

"We haven't had a murder in . . . what? Eight months?"

"Ten."

"And now we've got two within hours of each other?"

"Bizarre, huh?"

"Our stats are gonna bite. That's like a two hundred percent increase in violent crime in a single day. The mayor will have a cow and if it keeps up the captain will get canned. We all might."

"It won't keep up."

"How do you know?"

"I'm working on it."

They reached the lock up area and as Brinkley was hitting the switches to unlock the series of security doors, Ray asked, "How'd the ladies get out?"

"I told you, they made bail. It was like a couple hours after they came in."

"They had a hearing that fast? On festival day?"

Brinkley shrugged.

"Who paid?"

"Their bail?" He shrugged again. "No idea. I wasn't in yet. I got the story in pieces from Fowler and Betty. Apparently some guy just walked in and handed over the money."

"How much?"

"Twenty thousand a piece."

"Cash? That's a little odd."

They continued through security doors until they reached a hallway with three cells. Ray could see someone lying on the bed in the first one. As Brinkley was shutting the door behind them, the man rose up and glared at them.

"Hey, Ronnie," Ray said, trying to keep his tone even. He had already decided that the best strategy for getting him to talk was to imply severe punishment.

Ronnie slung his legs to the floor, but didn't say anything.

Brinkley opened the cell door and after Ray stepped inside, clanked it shut again. "I'll be back in ten."

Ray waited until he heard Brinkley exit the hall.

"What do you want?" Ronnie said. There was no belligerence in his voice, only resignation.

"I want to talk."

➤ TWENTY-FOUR ◀

"I ALREADY TOLD you everything." Ronnie was sober now and sullen. Sitting on the edge of the cot, he had his head in his hands.

"Tell it to me again."

"What's the point?"

"Did you kill Hillary Clearwater?"

"No," he moaned.

"Then that's the point."

Ronnie raised his head. "You mean . . . you mean, you believe me?"

"Not yet. Convince me."

"Right . . ." He dropped his head again.

"Take me through last night."

Ronnie huffed at the floor. "I went to her house. Spooked her, as a prank. Left. Hooked up with the ladies and . . . that's it."

"No. Start back a little further. And go slow. I want to hear everything."

Ronnie leaned back against the wall, frowning.

"You still unemployed?" Ray asked.

"No."

"Where you working?"

"Over at the hotel."

"Doing what?"

"Janitorial services."

"Which is what, exactly?"

"Keeping the halls clean, taking out the garbage, stocking the maids' closets . . ."

"Did you work yesterday?"

"Part of the day."

Ray waited. Getting Ronnie to talk was not easy. "Why only part of the day?"

"I hurt my shoulder again." He patted his right shoulder.

"Again?"

"That's why I can't whale anymore."

Ray nodded, though he was pretty sure Ronnie's whaling days had been curtailed by two things: sloth-fulness and alcohol.

"What's wrong with your shoulder?"

"Torn rotator cuff."

Ray lifted his eyebrows, surprised Ronnie could regurgitate this bit of medical jargon. The guy had never even finished high school.

"That's what the doc called it."

"Pretty painful?"

"Oh, man . . . hurts like heck and gets stone stiff by evening."

"But somehow, you were limber enough to be with those ladies."

"Barely," he said, his face somber, as though they were discussing a serious task.

"So you flared it up at work?"

"Yeah. Stocking the upper shelves of the kitchen

with cans." He rubbed his shoulder again. "I had to call it a day."

"Then what?"

"Then I went home for a while."

"What time was that?"

"I don't know . . . around . . . three?"

"And you went straight home?"

"Well, first I went over to the Clark for something to eat."

The Clark was the nicest restaurant in town, and Ray doubted that Ronnie could afford it, even with a job *and* the assistance of the state.

"I got a cousin works there. He comps me if I come in between lunch and dinner."

"Good deal." He was tempted to ask what Ronnie's kids were doing while he was eating comp meals at the Clark, but didn't want to throw a wrench into the account.

"Yeah. So I get free eats. And these are good eats, not fast food." Ronnie was starting to open up. "You gotta wear a tie in that place."

"Do you own a tie?"

"Used to. But now I just borrow one from Jack, my cousin. They got extras over there in case you forget."

"Did you eat with Jack?"

"Naw. He was busy. So I sat there all by my lone-some and had a T-bone." His eyes lit up at the memory. "Just as rare and tender as you could please."

"Was anybody else there?" Ray asked, offhandedly. He was stringing this out, waiting until Ronnie was comfortable before delving into the more important account of his visit to Aana's.

"Not when I come in. But later on, a tanik showed up." He paused. "That made it a really good deal."

"What do you mean?"

"Well, this guy paid me cash money to answer some questions." His eyes lit up again. "Twenty dollars!"

"What kind of questions?" Ray asked, growing more interested.

"About Barrow, where to go to see the festival and all. Like I was a travel agent or something."

"Oh . . ."

"And he wanted to know if I could tell him where to get good jewelry."

"What kind of jewelry?"

"Authentic Inupiat. You know, antiques, old stuff."

"What did you tell him?"

"I said the Gilded Cage was a good place to go. They got lots of ivory and jade and all."

Ray was about to move him along to his time at home and how he came to be sloppy drunk when Ronnie added, "And I told him about a couple of the old ones who have stuff like that, said they might be interested in selling—for the right price."

"Old ones?"

"Harry over at the grocery store is always talking about making money off his mother's pots, and Carson, the old man down at the YMCA . . . I heard him say how he wished he'd gone into business pedaling necklaces and bracelets and all to the naluaqmiut."

"What about Hillary Clearwater? Did you mention her name?"

"Uh . . . I might have."

"But she hasn't ever talked about hocking her heirlooms, has she?"

He shook his head sheepishly.

"Then why drop her name?"

"Because . . ." He hesitated. "Because I wanted to get back at her for butting into my business. I thought having a souvenir-happy tourist show up at her door would be funny." He looked at Ray. "I didn't kill her. I didn't do it."

"What did you say about her?"

"Same thing I said about all of 'em: that she had some nice stuff she might like to unload. I mean, all them people are old as dirt, and poor as dirt too . . . why wouldn't they want to make a few quick bucks, right?"

Ray resisted the urge to emphasize need to respect these "old as dirt" people for their role in keeping the heritage and ways of The People alive. "Did you tell him where she lived?"

"Who?"

"Hillary Clearwater."

"Uh . . . maybe. I think."

"You think?!" Ray willed himself not to lose control. "Okay, so you told this stranger about Aana . . . I mean, Hillary. You said she had some jewelry." He took a deep breath. "What did he look like?"

Ronnie shrugged. "Like a tanik."

"By that do you mean white, African American, Asian, Hispanic . . ."

"Naw. None of those. He was more like . . . uh . . . Spanish or something."

"That's Hispanic." Paul Roth's face came to mind.

"It is?"

"I don't suppose he introduced himself?"

"Naw."

"Was he tall, short, bald, have a mustache . . . ?"

"Uh . . ." Ronnie got a nervous look on his face.

"Well?"

"I don't really remember that well."

"Why not?"

"Uh . . ."

"Ronnie . . ." Ray urged. "Do I have to emphasize that you are dangerously close to going down on a murder charge?"

Ronnie began to breathe harder and beads of perspiration appeared on his forehead. "I could get in a lot of trouble . . ."

"You *are* in a lot of trouble."

He seemed to vacillate for a moment. Finally he said, "Okay. I was drunk. I remember talking to the man . . . sort of . . . and I remember him paying me, but . . . the rest is . . . sometimes I forget things when I'm drinking. It's like parts of my memory just fall out."

"It's called a blackout," Ray explained. "It's one of the signs of alcoholism."

"I ain't no alcoholic!" Ronnie shot back.

"Right. Your cousin. Is he the one who got you the booze?"

Ronnie shrugged.

"I'm serious about the murder charge. It fits you like a glove."

He sighed heavily. "Jack can get just about anything: Jim Beam, tequila, rum . . ."

Ray made a mental note to shut down the Clark after the investigation and throw Jack and the manager and anyone else he could possibly pin something to into the can.

"Anyway, after that I went on home."

"You think," Ray scoffed.

"Well, I remember getting there and seeing another notice from the council waiting on the door."

"What kind of notice?"

"About me disturbing the peace . . ." He raised his hands, dismissing it.

"Just disturbing the peace?" When Ronnie didn't answer, Ray said, "I can get a copy of it."

"And possession of a banned substance . . ."

"Alcohol," Ray specified.

"And . . . beating my wife . . . and soliciting." He cursed. "That aunt of yours is the reason my Doris left me."

Ray laughed bitterly. "I've seen your sheet, Ronnie. *You're* the reason she left. Beating the hell out of a woman and cheating on her tends to have that effect."

Ronnie fumed for a moment. "Old Mrs. Clearwater just had to stick her big nose in where it didn't belong."

"Okay, you got the notice," Ray said, trying to keep him on track, "and it made you angry. So you dug the knife out of your whaling gear, went over and killed her."

"No. Not the last part. The rest is right, but . . . I only wanted to scare her."

"Details, Ronnie."

"I got the knife," he said more slowly, "and the mask one of my kids made and I went over there and knocked on her door. I was only trying to scare her."

"But . . . ?"

"But she slammed the door in my face. And that really made me mad. So I went in there after her. And . . . and . . ."

"And what?" Ray asked, his temper growing hot. He could envision Aana cowering before this raging drunk.

"And I just meant to scare her, but . . ."

"But you accidentally killed her?"

"No!" he shouted. "I just . . . I hit her. Not very hard. Sort of a slap. But she fell and . . ."

Ray clenched his jaw, fighting the desire to rise in posthumous defense of Aana and pummel Ronnie with his fists.

"I didn't kill her. I just knocked her down. She was still alive when I left."

"You're sure?"

"Positive," he answered, desperately.

"You said you were drunk. And that you were having blackouts. How do you know she was alive?"

"Because that scared me sober. I didn't mean to hurt her. I just meant to scare her."

"If you're telling the truth and you didn't kill her . . ."

"I didn't!"

"You could still be prosecuted. You're guilty of harassment, assault, breaking and entering . . ."

"Better than murder."

Ray took several breaths, calming himself. "Why didn't you call 911?"

"I was scared."

What a coward, Ray thought. Only a coward would hit an old woman in the first place. And then to run away and not call for help . . .

There was clunk in the hall and Ray heard the door swing open. "You done yet?" Brinkley's voice called.

"Almost."

"Ray . . ." he pleaded.

"Give me a couple more minutes."

The door clanked shut.

"Okay, so she's lying there unconscious and you just . . . leave her there."

Ronnie nodded, obviously ashamed.

"Then what?"

"Like I said, it scared me. I needed a drink. So I went back down to the Clark. And that's where I met the ladies. They were dressed real fine and they kept looking over at me and . . . man, they were hotties. The next thing I knew, we were going back to my place together."

"How?"

"How what?"

"How'd you get home? Did you walk? Did you drive?"

"Uh . . . I think they had a car."

"Did you tell them about what happened?"

"You mean with your aunt? Uh . . . I don't remember."

"Convenient how your memory goes in and out, isn't it?"

"I know I talked a lot, but . . . I don't know what I said. I was pretty out of it. In fact, I don't even remember being in bed with them."

"You don't?"

"No. After I got into their car, it all just . . . it got real blurry."

"Maybe you told them about how your wife ran out and how you got another notice from the Council and then you got mad again and went over and finished off my aunt."

"No!"

"But you can't be sure because you blacked out, right?"

"I'm sure I didn't kill her."

Ray looked at him with disgust, uncertain whether he could trust anything that came out of the man's mouth.

The hall door opened again. "Ray! Hurry up! The captain's back!"

"I'm done," he said.

As Brinkley unlocked the cell door, Ronnie said, "You believe me, don't you?"

Ray glared at him.

"Ray . . . I mean, Officer Attla. I swear! I'm telling the truth."

"Are you?"

"Yes! I didn't do it. I only wanted to scare her."

"But you hit her, knocked her down and threatened her with a whaling knife while you were so drunk that you can't remember what went on."

"I remember that I didn't kill her!"

"Uh-huh . . ." Ray walked out of the cell.

"You've got to believe me!"

Ray followed Brinkley out of the lockup.

"I didn't do it!" Ronnie called just before the door slammed shut.

"Didn't do it, my eye," Brinkley scoffed. "What a scumbag. He's guilty as sin."

Ray glanced at him but didn't say anything. He still hadn't made up his mind about Ronnie. Yes, the man was a wife-beater, a drunk, an adulterer, a loser. But was he a murderer?

➤➤ TWENTY-FIVE ◄◄

"TOO BAD YOU'RE off today, Ray," Brinkley said as he walked him hastily to the rear exit.

Off wasn't exactly accurate, Ray thought. "Why's that?"

"We could use you. We got the festival, crowd control, people getting hurt at the blanket toss, on the ice . . ."

"Including my daughter," Ray inserted.

"Oh, yeah? Sorry to hear that. Is she okay?"

"She's fine. Just a broken arm."

"Good."

"You guys can handle festival without me," Ray said, slipping out the door.

"Festival, yeah. But now we got these burglary reports popping up."

Ray froze. "Burglaries?"

"Four in the last hour. Probably kids or maybe tourists. I don't know. Funny thing is, all they took was jewelry. And, so far, only from old people."

"Like who?"

"Let's see . . . Sue Una, Martha Ahvakans, Harry

Nageak, and Carson . . . uh . . . what's his last name? Lives over at the Y."

"Malguk."

"Right."

Ray's mind went over the names. Not only did they incorporate the two people Ronnie had mentioned to the white tourist, but he was pretty sure that they were all either homebound or very close to it. The perfect victims. "Are they all right?"

"Oh, they're fine. Just mad as hornets that somebody got their stuff."

Ray was about to ask what items had turned up missing when he heard the captain's voice call, "Brinkley!"

"Take it easy, Ray," Brinkley said as he closed the door on him.

As Ray walked back to his Blazer, he told himself that he would eventually have to face the captain. Hopefully he could put it off long enough to scrape up something significant—a clue, a piece of evidence, a break of some kind—to justify his going against orders.

He continued to have the feeling that he already knew enough to figure out what was going on and who was behind it. But for some reason, he couldn't quite put it together. This frustrated him and scared him a little. Maybe he had lost his edge.

He shook this off, telling himself not to be silly or self-indulgent. He was simply in a bit of a slump, personally, professionally, even physically. The small, but noticeable layer of padding around his waist was testimony to this. Maybe it was a test, he thought. Maybe the tuungak or God or the gods of destiny or all of the above were challenging him to see if he could get over this hurdle and successfully navigate through the middle and second half of his life. Or maybe he was just tired and needed another cup of coffee.

He picked one up at a little stand a block from his truck. Ray didn't recognize the man inside. According to a sign behind the coffee pot, the owner/operator was from Point Hope.

"Happy Nalukataq!"

"Same to you," Ray said without enthusiasm. "I'll take a bagel too."

"Great festival this year, uh?" the man said as he selected a bagel from the display case.

"Yeah."

"I come all the way from Point Hope for it."

Ray nodded. If the festival was so great and he had come so far, why was he cooped up in this little stand a half mile from the celebration? Obviously his interest in Nalukataq was financial.

"How come you're not at festival?" the man asked, handing the bagel and the coffee across to Ray.

"I'm working."

"That makes two of us. I think every other person from here to Siberia is off today." He shook his head sadly. "What do you do?"

Ray considered this. What *did* he do? He was a cop. But what did he actually *do*? What made him get up and go to work in the morning? "I . . . I help people. Or at least, I try to."

"You a fireman?"

"No." Ray took the bagel and paid the man.

"Doctor?"

"Huh-uh." Ray thanked him and started up the street.

"Uh . . . paramedic?" the man guessed.

"Nope."

"Lawyer?" he called.

"No." Ray laughed at this and at the fact that the man hadn't thought to try "policeman." That was probably because it wasn't always considered a helpful occupation. Enforcement was a large part of a law officer's job nowadays. They made arrests, gave tickets, investigated crimes . . . but Ray liked to think that by doing these things he was nevertheless helping people, helping to protect the community and make it a safe place to live. He had thought that way ever since he started with the department. But now . . . what did he think now?

He got to the Blazer and sat inside chewing the bagel. He hadn't realized how hungry he was and suddenly wished he'd purchased two of them. He washed it down with the coffee, which was very hot but very thin. The man from Point Hope was making a profit charging a buck for a small Styrofoam cup of brown water. Though it was almost void of taste, hopefully it was not void of caffeine. Ray needed to be jolted out of this malaise. He needed to be alert and to think clearly if he expected to fulfill the mayor's edict: solve the murder, now two murders, before the end of festival.

He started the car and drove past the festival grounds. The crowd seemed to have grown in size. The lot had disappeared, obscured beneath a sea of humanity. The blanket toss was going again and a man was sailing high into the air, performing ski jump maneuvers at the peak of each toss. The food area was the most heavily congested, the tables full with hundreds sitting on the ground. The dancers were dancing and a throng of tourists were capturing their every movement with a fleet of video and still cameras.

Reaching the Point road, he felt a slight pang of loneliness. Even when it wasn't festival, he felt that out here. It wasn't a bad thing, just a sense of isolation. To the left, the Beaufort was a tranquil lake for a few hundred yards, then the violent floes reached up in sharp blue fingers. It really did look like the top of the world. That was one reason he had never aspired to live in Browerville. From his home, he couldn't see the edge of the earth like they could up here. There was something wrong with that, as though you were gazing into a forbidden place. If not forbidden, at least, forbidding. Ray didn't like to be reminded at every turn that he lived in a spot on the globe where the land gave up and relinquished itself to the sovereign rule of water and ice.

In the rearview mirror, he saw a sedan. Probably an elder resident who had grown weary of the celebration and knew they wouldn't last for the remainder of the afternoon.

Maybe that was what he needed, he thought as he reached the turnoff to Browerville. A break. A nice, long rest . . . and a change of scenery. Or maybe something more severe and final. Was it time to move on? He tried to imagine himself in Fairbanks or Anchorage. No. That wouldn't work. As severe as the climate and seasons were up here, as ugly and flat and uninhabitable as it sometimes seemed, it was his home and always would be. A vacation then? Time away? Where?

He reached Ronnie's ramshackle house without coming to any decision and as he got out of the car and approached the door, he attempted to conjure up a level of focus and concentration that he had been unable to

attain thus far on this case. He carefully surveyed Ronnie's array of ATVs and snow machines, wondering if
any of them actually ran. Didn't look like it. Parts were
scattered across the yard and pieces were missing from
all the engines. One ATV was tireless, another upside
down and minus the rear axle. Two of the three snow
machines didn't have throttles, the other was without a
steering mechanism.

He went to the porch and ducked under the yellow
police tape. The door was unlocked. He stepped inside
and glanced around. The living area was exactly as he
had left it. Walking down the hall, he found the bedrooms undisturbed. The bed was unmade in Ronnie's
room. The only change was the absence of the weapon,
the boots, and the glass with the finger in it. Ray shivered at the memory.

The children's bedroom was a mess. Clothing was
scattered on the floor along with dingy toys and food
wrappers. Ray doubted that Ronnie would get the kids
back even if he beat the murder rap. He was guilty of
neglect, if not abuse.

He was going back down the hall toward the living
room when he saw a car pass by outside. The sedan. It
was a white Honda Accord. Out of habit, he tried to
read the tag, but the car made the corner before he
could.

In the kitchen, he stood with his hands on his hips
and asked aloud, "What am I looking for?" His eyes
darted around the room, lighting on the overturned
cereal boxes, empty pizza containers, the host of dirty
dishes. The place smelled like overcooked spaghetti
sauce. He noticed a tomato-colored spill on the stove
that ran down into one of the burners.

"What a slob," he muttered. The kids must have had to fend for themselves after the departure of their mother, he decided.

He opened the refrigerator and found ketchup, an empty mayonnaise jar, and a chicken drumstick, in the butter compartment, unwrapped and sporting an impressive growth of mold. No milk. No juice. No fresh meat, vegetables, or fruit.

Ray looked through the drawers, found mismatched silverware and tools: screwdrivers, a hammer, a broken tape measure . . . most of the other cabinets were empty. In the pantry was a sack of potatoes with vines growing out of it, and a torn sack of flour. It was a wonder the kids hadn't starved to death.

Leaving the kitchen, he went to the bathroom. It stunk of urine and excrement. The sink had a rust ring and the drain was pink with mold. The bathtub was worse, the toilet stopped up. Pitiful conditions, he thought, trying not to breathe through his nose. In the medicine cabinet he found a single worn toothbrush and a mostly used tube of Crest. There was also a comb that was missing half its teeth.

He returned to Ronnie's bedroom, muttering, "What am I looking for?" The answer was: an epiphany. This was the point at which he would either find something which opened the case up or he would admit that he had met a wall—at least, for the moment—and hang it up. There was still the footage due in at five, he reminded himself. But unless it showed a museum patron holding a sign stating "I'm the killer" . . .

Ray looked in the closet. Ronnie's wardrobe was not exactly sophisticated. The man owned three pairs of jeans, all of which had seen better days, and two flannel shirts. There was a stack of clumsily folded T-shirts on the floor. Next to that was a pile of dirty laundry. Ray went to the bed and checked under the pillows, wondering if Billy Bob or Lewis had done that already. Or had the mayor been so paranoid in his desire to keep the thing quiet that a search of the house had yet to be conducted? He considered calling in, but decided against it. If he got Betty, she would get on him for failing to heed the captain's order. Lewis would be at festival. So would Billy Bob. That left Fowler and Brinkley. Fowler was by the book and wouldn't be a help. Brinkley had come on too late to have the skinny and was scared to death he might catch it for assisting Ray.

He checked under the bed and found several pairs of dirty underwear and a rifle. Apparently the mayor had won out and no search had been made. Otherwise the gun would have been confiscated. He removed his jacket and used it to pull the rifle out. It was a Remington .30/06. He bent and saw another gun: a revolver. He retrieved it in the same fashion. A Colt .44. Neither smelled like it had been fired recently. Both were loaded.

Ray shuddered. If Ronnie hadn't been so drunk when he and Billy Bob had stormed in that morning, he could have simply rolled out of bed, taken up one of the weapons, and . . .

Using his jacket like a glove, he unloaded both guns and shoved them back to their hiding places. Putting the ammo in his pocket, he stood up. What had Ronnie been wearing yesterday? When they caught him, he was without apparel. And if he had been as drunk as he said he was, he would have discarded his clothes on the floor. In fact, from the looks of his house, he probably did that whether he had been drinking or not. But the floor in Ronnie's bedroom was clean. Too clean.

He went back to the closet and stared down at the pile of laundry. It had been smashed into the space so that the door could close. Why would a slob do that? A slob would leave the clothes strewn about and wouldn't bother closing the closet door. Unless . . . had he been trying to impress the two ladies? Doubtful. Not if he was sloppy drunk. Besides, the "ladies" didn't seem like the type who cared about a man's housekeeping skills. Only his wallet. Which was another thing that was missing. Had Billy Bob gotten Ronnie's wallet?

Ray crouched and lifted up a shirt, then a pair of pants. The pockets of the pants were empty. He laid them aside. There were children's clothes mixed into the heap. And towels. And a blanket that was wet with something sticky. Near the bottom was another pair of pants. He picked them out and stuck his hand in the back pocket. Voilà! A wallet. It had Ronnie's driver's license, which, Ray noticed, was expired, a VISA card, also expired, and a twenty dollar bill. The money from his encounter with Roth at the Clark?

It had to have been Roth, he felt certain. How many other Hispanic males with an interest in antiquities were roaming around Barrow?

Ray tried the other pockets and found a set of keys, a small, rusty knife, two dimes and a nickel. Replacing the pants, he started to scoot the pile back into the closet when he heard his shoe click on something. He reached down and felt under the clothing until his fingers found a hard, thin rectangle of plastic. A credit card. He pulled it out and blinked at it. Not a credit card—a pass to the Dance of the Whale exhibit.

A pass to the exhibit. Yes, it was Roth asking the questions. He had probably given Ronnie the pass with the $20. It seemed like a dumb move, except that Roth had been confident. Too confident. He had picked Ronnie out as a sucker, gotten the info he needed, paid him off—cheaply, at that—and later, framed him for murder. All without worrying over the pass. Who could link all of this to Roth, anyway? It was pretty slick and he was very cocky. And with the mayor hurrying things along . . .

Ray put the card and the cash into his pocket, wadded the laundry back into the closet and shut the door. As he made his way to the front door, he thought again of the children. No matter how it had all gone down, they had been here, hungry, cold, waiting for their father to come home. And when he had, he was drunk and in the company of a couple of hookers. What a life. Ray silently vowed never to do that to his own kids. He had no intention of failing them like that, but he had a nagging suspicion that it was in his blood. His own father had resembled Ronnie in many ways. Maybe it was a good thing he had died when Ray was little. That way he didn't have time to "teach" him as many things by example as Ronnie was teaching his kids. Ray felt guilty for thinking this. Guilty and strangely thankful.

He slid under the police tape and went out to the Blazer. Roth was involved. Ray knew that much. The rest . . . how it pieced together was still a mystery. But sooner or later, it would begin to come together. Hopefully sooner.

Starting the car, he left Browerville and drove back to Barrow. He passed the festival site again and went on to the station. Parking in front, he went in the main door. If the captain saw him, fine. He was about ready to share his findings anyway.

He marched down the corridor and found Brinkley hunched over a typewriter, pecking away at a form.

"I need to see him again."

"Ray . . ." he complained in a whine.

"Gimme the keys, I'll let myself in."

"You know that's against policy."

"Then get up and walk me down," Ray said rather tersely. He was starting to feel like a one man show, doing all the work for the entire department. Of course, part of that was by choice.

Brinkley got up wearily, grabbed the key ring off the desk and led him down the hall toward lock-up.

"The captain's here."

"That's okay."

"He'll know somebody's in lockup."

"Good."

"Ray, he's going to be upset."

"Don't worry. I'll make sure he knows it was my idea."

Brinkley didn't seem to take comfort in this. He opened the first door, then the second, then led Ray to Ronnie's cell. After pulling the bars back, he muttered, "Call me when you're ready."

"What now?" Ronnie asked.

Ray waited until Brinkley was gone. When the echo of the door had faded, he said, "Tell me about the pass."

➤ TWENTY-SIX ◄

"WHAT PASS?"

"To Dance of the Whale."

Ronnie squinted at him. "To what?"

"The museum exhibit."

"I don't know what you're talking about."

Ray flashed him the pass card. "You've never seen this?"

"No."

"Think, Ronnie. Did the tanik give it to you, along with the twenty?"

Ronnie shook his head.

"You're positive?"

"Pretty much."

"How do you suppose it got into the closet of your bedroom?"

"You got me."

As Ronnie sat sad-eyed and forlorn on the cot, Ray's mind worked to answer his own question. If it wasn't Ronnie's, a big "if," since the guy had been drunk and wouldn't remember if he'd won the lottery, whose was it? Did it belong to one of the women?

"You met your lady friends at the Clark?" Ray asked.

"Yeah."

"Working women don't usually hang out there."

"These weren't just working women. They were . . . classy."

Ray almost laughed. Classy women wouldn't be caught dead with Ronnie. Unless . . . "And they picked you up? Not the other way around?"

"Yeah. I was just sitting there and they came over and started getting friendly with me, asked me if I wanted to party."

"How much did they charge for this party?"

"Uh . . . I don't remember."

"Did you have cash on you?"

"Just the twenty bucks the guy gave me."

"Then how'd you pay them?"

"I . . . don't remember."

Ray swore under his breath and muttered, "What a surprise."

"All I remember is they were hot! A couple of brick houses."

Ray closed his eyes and tried to recall what the brick houses had looked like. One was tall and blond. The other was a redhead, a little shorter, a little younger too. Both were much too attractive, even after a hard night with Ronnie, to have fallen for him.

A scenario materialized: Roth had sent the ladies to set Ronnie up. They had gone home with him, maybe gotten him even more drunk, then, after he passed out, they went over and took Aana's ring. That would explain the sudden attraction of two "brick houses" to a greasy-haired, out-of-work local who was bombed

out of his mind. And that would also account for the
pass card. One of the women could have left it behind
when they were cleaning things up and placing the
evidence out where it would be easily found: the
bloody knife, the boots, the finger . . .

However, none of the above explained the murder.
Why not simply steal the ring? Why kill Aana? Unless
Aana had struggled and fought them for the ring. That
didn't seem likely. She was ninety-something. And
besides, she'd already been knocked down and possibly out by Ronnie.

Ray hailed Brinkley. A moment later the sounds of
locks clicking echoed through the corridor.

"Are you thinking maybe they did it?" Ronnie
asked.

"Who did what?" Ray asked.

"That it was a frame and those ladies killed your
aunt?"

Ray shrugged and followed Brinkley out.

"That's what it was, wasn't it?" Ronnie called. "A
frame? I was framed?"

As they left the lockup, Brinkley laughed. "What an
imagination on that guy. Framed . . . who'd believe
that line of bull?"

Ray didn't say anything. He was trying to decide
whether Ronnie was smart enough to commit a cun-
ning murder, one with the look of a frame. No. It was
too risky. And far too complex. Ronnie was a simple
man and had he killed Aana, he would have hidden the
weapon and the finger, buried them or tossed them in a
Dumpster, and then run like a rabbit. Even an intoxi-
cated fool would have invested a little time and effort
in escape and secrecy.

"I need to see the files on the ladies we arrested this morning," Ray said.

"You're on your own there, buddy," Brinkley said. "You know where the files are and you can dig into them at your own risk. According to that memo, under no circumstances are we to . . ."

"Yeah, yeah, I know. Thanks for the help."

"No problem. Watch yourself, Ray."

"I will." Ray continued to the file room and found Betty bent over an open door at one of the cabinets. She had the phone clamped between her shoulder and her ear and was flipping through file folders.

Ray was tempted to greet her, but knew that he would get an admonishing glare, a shake of the head and, after she got off the phone, a chewing out. So he carefully went to the cabinet containing the newest arrests and quietly opened it.

As Betty continued her conversation and search through the drawer, Ray leafed quickly through the arrests made by the Barrow Police Department in the last forty-eight hours. There weren't many: a disturbing the peace/alcohol possession, a couple of rowdies who had gotten into a brawl at festival, a drunk and disorderly, and a murder one. He pulled Ronnie's file and started back through the others. The women had to be in there somewhere. Unless Betty had taken to filing female perps somewhere else. When he had been through the new arrests two more times and failed to find the reports, he closed the door and tried the next one down.

He was paging through the folder of recent vehicular citations when he heard a noise behind him that

sounded rather like a bull caribou clearing its throat.
He froze.

"Raymond Attla . . ."

He turned around and smiled at Betty. She still had
the drawer open and was still clutching the phone. Into
the receiver she grunted, "I'll call you back." She
scowled at him before scolding, "What are you doing
here?"

"I missed you, Betty. I couldn't wait until Monday
to see you."

"Very funny. What are you looking for?"

"Uh . . ."

"Let me guess. The file on Ronnie?"

He smiled, embarrassed, and held it up. "Already
got that."

She snatched it away from him. "You know better
than that. You do understand that you are this far away
from being suspended, don't you?" She held up her
fingers.

"I'm gonna talk to the captain," he assured her.

"Good."

"But first, I need the files on the two ladies."

"What ladies?"

"The ones we busted with Ronnie."

"The hookers?"

He nodded.

"Why?"

"I just need to see them."

"*Need?* What you need to do is go home, Ray."
Before he could object, she said, "I heard about it this
morning."

"What about it?"

"How you lost it."

"I didn't lose it!"

"That's not like you, Ray."

"I didn't lose it!"

She gave him a concerned, motherly look. "What's going on?"

"I'm trying to put this case in the closed file."

"I mean with you. What's the matter?"

"Nothing."

"You've never beaten up a prisoner."

"I've never found my aunt's finger floating in a glass of water next to a man's bed," Ray shot back, feeling the anger of the incident return. "Besides, I didn't beat him up."

"Okay, roughed him up. Whatever word you want to use, it's unprofessional."

Ray didn't have a comeback for this. She was right. He had acted unprofessionally. She was also perceptive enough to realize that it was more than just finding a dead relative. Something else was bothering him.

"I don't know what happened," he finally admitted. "I just . . ." He shook his head.

"What do you need?"

"I don't know. Therapy? A long vacation?"

"I mean for the case."

"You'll help me?"

"Of course. When have I ever not helped you?" She frowned at him.

"I need the files on the ladies and a few minutes to read them over before I have a powwow with the captain."

Betty went to the same file cabinet he had been

rifling through and opened the top drawer. "They'd be in the new arrest file."

"I already checked there."

"You gotta know where to look."

"Oh, is that it?"

"Let's see . . ." She sniffed and went through the file again. "They're in here somewhere." After another time through, she pulled a handful of files and set it on the table. Shuffling through them, she muttered, "Or at least, they were. Hmm . . ."

"Told you."

She finally gave up and stuffed the folders back into the cabinet. "Maybe the captain has them." She started out the door, then turned and gestured for Ray to follow. Back at her desk she sat down at the computer terminal. "Should be on here, too." She typed for a moment, then, "What . . . ?"

Ray leaned over and examined the form she had up on the screen. It had that day's date and the time matched the early morning arrest. The charge was prostitution. The name in the suspect slot read: Wilma Flintstone. The square for a photo was blank. So was the fingerprint section.

"Is that some sort of joke?" Ray asked. He scanned down the form and saw that the address was Bedrock, the next of kin, Fred.

"If it is," Betty said, clicking in a key sequence, "the joke is on us." Another form appeared, this one belonging to Jane Jetson.

"What's going on?" Ray asked.

"Somebody must have hacked in, except . . ." She double-clicked on something called Fortress. "We've got a new security program running that . . ." She swore as a message box appeared with the message: *A breach has been detected!* "Now, how in the world . . . that's impossible."

"What's impossible?" a voice behind them asked.

Ray glanced over his shoulder and saw the captain standing there with crossed arms and a grim expression.

"The fact that Officer Attla is in the station?" the captain asked, "after he was ordered to go home and not show his face until Monday? Or the fact that I may just have to fire his butt right here on the spot?"

"Good afternoon, sir," Ray greeted timidly.

"My office," he grunted, turning on his heels.

"Oh, honey . . ." Betty lamented.

Ray sighed and trailed after him. When he was inside the office, the captain ordered, "Shut the door." Ray complied. "Have a seat." Ray did. The two men looked at each other. Ray began to calculate the budget adjustments they would have to make in order to survive on Margaret's salary.

"So?" the captain prodded, his face noncommittal.

"Uh . . . first, I want you to know that Betty and Brinkley had nothing to do with this. Also, I . . ."

"Skip it. Tell me what you've got so far."

"What I've got?"

"The case, Attla. Tell me about the case."

"Am I on the case?"

"As far as I can tell you are."

"And you're not going to can me for going against orders?"

"That depends. Tell me what you've got."

"Okay. Let's see . . ." Ray launched into an explanation, trying to cover all of the material and doing some brainstorming along the way: the note at Aana's that had obviously been written by someone else, the absence of her ring, the ring at the museum that bore a striking resemblance, Ronnie's account of the evening, the pass Ray had found under Ronnie's dirty laundry, the Hispanic tourist who had solicited information from Ronnie, the women who had picked him up, how they had gotten out on bail and subsequently disappeared, along with their files.

When Ray finished, the captain pursed his lips and rose. He paced the room for a minute before asking, "Can you tie any of this together?"

"Only with suppositions."

"Fine. Let's hear it."

"Right now I see it like this: Ronnie heads to Aana's to spook her but it gets out of hand. He strikes her, she falls, he freaks out and runs away. Later, somebody comes along and takes the ring."

"For the exhibit."

"Maybe. Yeah. I guess."

"So the murderer is connected to the Roth Foundation."

"Maybe."

"What about the reporter lady who was killed today?"

"She was a producer. And she had shot footage of the museum exhibit the day before. We think that whoever broke into her room and killed her, did it for that footage."

"*We?*"

"Uh . . . long story, sir."

The captain frowned at him. "According to Lewis,

they got the footage. Which means we've got bupkis, right?"

"They got footage, but not the museum footage. It was the wrong canister."

"Where's the right one?"

"It's supposed to be in on the five o'clock plane."

The captain nodded and glanced at the clock. "You think the murderer will be there to meet it?"

"That depends."

"On what?"

"On whether or not they realize they got the wrong film."

"We'll stake it out."

Ray was shaking his head. "We have to do this thing just right or he won't show. In fact . . ."

"What?"

"He may already be out of town. They could have hopped a flight without bothering to view the footage."

The captain paced some more. "You know Hodish is breathing down my neck on this."

"I know."

"He likes Ronnie as the perp. It's neat and tidy."

"But Ronnie couldn't have done the film producer," Ray pointed out. "He was in lock-up."

The captain paced back and forth like a caged animal. "If it isn't Ronnie . . ." He swore softly. "How are we supposed to keep this quiet?"

"We might not be able to."

"We *have* to. Going public isn't an option."

"If the Roth Foundation is involved, then that puts Paul Roth at the top of the list of suspects. If he didn't do the jobs, he probably ordered them."

"Geez . . ." The captain rolled his eyes. "Wouldn't that just be peachy? We arrest one of Hodish's pals at the peak of the biggest celebration of the year, with the eyes of the world on us?"

"Even if the guy is guilty?"

"*Especially* if the guy is guilty. Didn't you hear about Roth's contribution to the mayor's re-election campaign? If Roth is dirty, that'll throw mud on Hodish. Nobody likes him anyway. I still don't know how he made it into office."

"Vote tampering," Ray surmised.

"I wouldn't put it past him," the captain said, allowing a slight smile. "But if Roth goes down, Hodish will take a big hit. There's no way he'll make a second term."

"That's not all bad," Ray said.

"Except that he'll be out for blood for the rest of this term. He'll have my head on a pole."

"If it comes to that, he'll also have my resignation, along with most of the rest of the force on his desk."

"I appreciate the support, Attla, but I'd rather avoid that eventuality."

"Ditto." Ray stood up. "I've got some other leads to track down."

"Good. But remember the golden rule: quiet and quick. We need to put this thing to bed, and no matter who the evidence points to, we have to do it quietly. I want you to check with me before any arrests are made. Got that?"

"Yes, sir."

"No public spectacles. No showmanship. No heroism. Let's just do it and be done."

"Yes, sir." Ray started out of the office.

"Where are you headed first?" the captain wondered.

"The Embers."

"The Embers?" the captain called after him. "What does a strip club have to do with any of this?"

Good question, Ray thought as he hurried down the hall, pretending not to hear. Maybe nothing. But he was about to find out.

►► TWENTY-SEVEN ◄◄

RAY GOT INTO his Blazer and drove the six blocks to the Embers. It was between the station and the airport and he didn't want to come back for his car later when it was time to go after the documentary film reel. He also had the feeling he would be at the Embers for a while. Getting straight answers out of Chic Slim was never easy.

Pulling up on the street, Ray parked directly in front of the club. He was still amazed that it existed at all. Somehow, the council had seen fit to approve a strip joint in a town that allowed no alcohol and was strict in its policies against prostitution. Actually, the council had been heavily influenced in this decision by the mayor. It was only last year, under Hodish's copious supervision that this addition to the community had been added.

In Ray's mind, Mayor Hodish was responsible for many of the troubles now plaguing Barrow. His vision for The People seemed to be to fully immerse them in American culture and transform the sleepy whaling town into a miniature Anchorage. Population growth was one of his top priorities and to that end, he was in favor of any and all entertainment that drew tourists and, hopefully, transplants. This year's overblown Nalukataq was a prime example. So was the Embers. Formerly a movie theater, it had been purchased by a chain based in Seattle, remodeled, and made into "a private club for gentlemen of quality and sophistication." Or so the sign on the building claimed. Directly under it was a reader board with the words: "cold drinks, hot women."

As Ray made the corner and pulled into the empty dirt parking area, he caught a glimpse of something in his rearview mirror. A white sedan. He tried to make out the driver as it rolled past but there was too much glare on the windows. Was it the sedan from Browerville? No. Couldn't be. He dismissed it as coincidence.

Ray got out and frowned at the collection of framed photos of scantily clad women shabbily attached to the side of the building next to the entrance. Yes, he thought to himself cynically, this addition to the community did much to promote growth and health and well being. Just inside the door, he found an array of photos of what appeared to be the same women, minus their tassels, feathers, and Spandex costumes. The entryway stank of cigarettes.

The interior was quiet and dark, the stage empty. Too early, Ray decided. Men didn't come clamoring for titillation until evening. In another couple of hours the place would be jumping. Or, bumping and grinding, as it were.

He followed a dim trail of light into the back hall and down to Chic's office. Chic was behind his desk, a cigar clamped between his teeth, working a tabletop calculator. Ray watched him for a moment, wondering how the guy ever got the nickname Chic Slim. There was nothing Chic or Slim about him. He was a couple of hundred pounds overweight and his hair looked as though it had been cut with a weedwhacker. His real name was Lucius Bennedict and if you wanted to tick him off, you simply had to remind him of this.

"Say Lucius," Ray said. He was feeling ornery and also fairly certain that this man was involved in at least one if not both of the day's murders.

Chic looked up with an expression of rage. "Who the . . . ? Oh . . ." He relaxed a little and the anger turned to scorn. "What is it this time, *Officer*?" He made the last word sound like an insult.

"Just thought I'd drop by and say happy festival."

"What's happy about it?" he grumbled.

"We've been blessed by the great spirit of the bowhead."

"Bowhead, shmohead. You see this place?" He gestured at the main room. "It's a tomb."

"I'm sure business will pick up later."

"It's Saturday. We open early, at two. Usually the place is packed by now. But with this stinking festival . . ." He swore, defaming the bowhead and all those who chose to celebrate it. "Back home, when we get a holiday, we kick butt. But here . . . gotta get alcohol legalized."

"This isn't Seattle," Ray told him. "And getting the council to go wet won't happen."

"Give it time. They'll see the benefits."

"Sure they will," Ray mocked. "Let's see . . . alcohol is addictive, destructive, it ruins lives, leads to violence and promiscuity, breaks up marriages, plays a major role in domestic abuse, fosters unemployment and slothfulness, kills people on the roads, promotes liver disease, accelerates the rate of crime, knocks off brain cells . . . I can't believe we don't jump at the chance."

"What are you, Baptist?" Chic said, laughing. "Demon drink . . ."

Ray had to bite his tongue to keep from jumping all over Chic. While he and Grandfather differed on a good many things, Ray was a hundred percent in agreement with him when it came to the ill effects of liquor on The People. He knew firsthand what it could do to a man, a son, a family.

"I need to talk to you about your girls."

"You want me to set you up, Officer?" he teased. "I got some new honeys that would set your hair on fire."

"I'm looking for a blonde and a redhead . . ."

"A double dose, huh?" He whistled. "That'll cost you. Private dances are fifty bucks for five minutes. Two girls for ninety."

"What a deal," Ray said.

"We aim to please."

"I'm looking for two specific girls." He described each of them as best he could: good-looking, shapely, average height, long legs . . .

"We got lots to fit that description. What are their names?"

"I'm not sure."

"Well, then I don't know how I can help you."

"You've got shots of all the girls, don't you?"

"Pictures? Sure. But they're confidential."

"I need to see them."

"It'll cost you."

"It's part of a police investigation."

"Fine. Then go get yourself a search warrant. Of course, by the time you get back . . ."

"The pictures won't be here," Ray finished for him.

Chic grinned at him.

"How much?"

He glanced down at his calculator, thinking. "Two hundred."

"I'll go get the warrant," Ray said, turning.

"One hundred," Chic tried.

Ray glared at him. "Forty, and I won't take you to the station for questioning."

"You can't do that. I didn't *do* nothing."

"I can do that and you know it. Forty bucks, or we take a trip downtown."

Chic cursed and scowled. "Okay."

Ray pulled out his wallet and removed two twenties. It was all the cash he had, which is the main reason he had held fast at $40.

After taking the bills, Chic bent and pulled a drawer on his desk. It was packed with eight-by-ten black-and-white photos. He hefted the stack out and slapped them onto the desk. "Enjoy yourself." He went back to his calculator. "But don't get attached to any of them."

Ray picked up the stack and went back into the main room. He found a light switch and sat down at one of the tables. Each photo had a full-length shot of a young woman wearing only a G-string. On the back, written in Magic Marker was a name, an age, and a date. Their date of hire, Ray guessed. He leafed quickly through, amazed at the number of girls that were supposedly 18. Many of them were underage, he suspected, with fake names: Mimi Dogood, Honey Sweet, Scarlet Letter . . .

He continued through them, setting the discards in the chair next to him. They were all too young, except for a couple of forty-something women with admirable figures who were too old. A couple had obviously been hired for comic relief: a tremendously obese woman in desperate need of dental work, a tiny, tiny girl with breasts the size of basketballs . . . what a way to make a living, Ray thought.

When he reached the end without finding a familiar face, he gathered up the photos and took them back to Chic.

"Well . . . ?" Chic asked without looking up from his number crunching. "Find anything that strikes your fancy?"

"I saw a lot of teenagers."

"They're a big draw. Men like 'em young."

"Some of them are a little too young, I'd say."

Chic lifted his right hand. "We never hire under eighteen. Swear."

"Mmm-hmm . . ."

"And it's tough recruiting, I tell you. Even though we pay top dollar, I have a hard time getting ladies up from Outside."

"There's a surprise," Ray said. "Who wouldn't want to come a thousand miles north to the edge of civilization to wiggle and strut for a bunch of drunks?"

"Now, now . . ."

"What about your working girls?"

Chic pretended not to understand this. "My what?"

"The ones who do outcall?"

"I'm not following you."

"Parties. Escort." When Chic made a face that implied confusion, Ray added, "Hookers."

"We're on the up and up," he claimed. "No fraternization between our employees and our patrons."

Ray knew this to be an outright lie. "Listen, I don't have time for this. Now you can either cooperate, and I can cut you a modicum of slack, or I can make this into a vendetta and do everything in my power to shut you down and send you packing. And to tell you the truth, I'd enjoy that."

Chic thought for a moment. "How much is a modicum?"

Ray took hold of the edge of the desk and leaned forward. "I'm serious."

"Okay, okay. Don't go postal on me, officer." He took a deep breath. "We do have a few ladies who do private affairs." Chic replaced the stack of photos in the drawer, opened another and produced a folder. "Very sophisticated. Very swank. Nothing cheap or tawdry."

Ray laughed at this, unable to believe that Chic Slim knew the meaning of the words.

"Here we go." He opened the folder and presented it to Ray. It was a gaudy one-page brochure produced on a computer. At the top was the logo of the Embers and in fancy letters: "Private Gold." Under this was a short description of the services offered which employed phrases like "ready to please" and "to fulfill your secret desires" to get around the seedy truth. The rest of the page was made up of photos with flirty, *Playboy*-like blurbs written in first person. All of the ladies shared a love of the outdoors, adventure, candlelight dinners, and were anxious to kindle a romance with a man who knew how to satisfy a woman. None of the faces matched Ronnie's companions.

"Is that all of them?" Ray asked, feeling rather discouraged. He had fully expected to find the girls under Chic's care.

"That's it." He raised his right hand again. "Swear. You've seen my entire staff."

Ray tried describing the two women again. "Ring any bells?"

"They sound like dancer material. But . . . nope. I don't know them."

"Anybody else running a prosti . . . I mean 'private affair' operation up here?" He hadn't heard about any, but then, he wasn't Chic Slim.

"Better not be," Chic said. "We got a monopoly thanks to . . ." His voice trailed off.

"Thanks to who?"

"You-know-who."

Ray did. Chic was referring to Mayor Hodish. "You're not holding out on me, are you, *Lucius?*"

"No," he said through clenched teeth. "And don't call me that."

"Call you what? *Lucius?*"

"I'm warning you."

"And I'm warning you." Ray leaned in again and took hold of Chic's ugly plaid tie. He was fairly sure that if Chic made a move, he would leap the desk and close his hands around the man's fat neck until he passed out on the floor. Which meant that the captain was right, along with Billy Bob, Betty, and most of all, Margaret. He was on the edge, perilously close to being out of control. "If you know something . . ."

"I don't," Chic said hoarsely, trying to swallow.

After a long, disturbingly satisfying pause, Ray released him. Chic coughed and rubbed his neck.

"Happy Nalukataq," Ray grunted, walking out of the office.

This temper thing was getting scary, he decided as he returned to his car. Too much coffee, not enough sleep, the frustration of this case . . . he hoped it was something along those lines. Something minor. But he had the sinking feeling that it was bigger than that. What if he was about to have a meltdown? What if his entire being was on the verge of a volcanic eruption of anger, repressed or otherwise?

He started the car and pulled onto the street, making an effort to file this away for later. Right now he had to think. It was a little early to head to the terminal for the film, but he didn't have anywhere else to be.

He drove slowly, in the general direction of the airport, trying to sort out what he had learned. Not much. Chic apparently wasn't running the ladies who had picked up Ronnie. Which meant what? That they were Roth's people? Maybe. Or maybe Chic hadn't shown him his entire employee roster.

If the ladies had been Roth's, and if they had stolen Aana's ring, and if they had murdered her in the process, and if they had framed Ronnie . . . it was a long string of ifs, Ray decided. All conjecture. Nothing hard.

He was about to start down the airport road when he noticed a car a block behind him. A white sedan. *The* white sedan? What the . . . ?

He made a sudden right turn, accelerated, made a left, a right, another right, ran a stoplight, turned back onto the street he had just been on. Having made a big circle, he pulled to the side of the road in front of a gas station and watched his rearview mirror. Ten seconds passed. Fifteen. Finally the sedan appeared. It drove along and then swerved to the curb and stopped.

Ray picked up the radio. "Dispatch, this is Patrol 1, come back."

There was a surge of static, then, "Patrol 1, dispatch. Is it my imagination, or have I talked to you more today than when you're on duty?"

Ray ignored this. "Betty, I need you to run a plate for me." He got a pair of binoculars out of the glove box and looked at the license of the sedan via the rearview mirror. After reading the numbers to her, he asked, "Got that?"

"You betcha. I'll get right on it."

"Thanks. If the captain asks, tell him I'll be at the airport taking care of the matter we discussed."

"You need backup?"

"Not yet. All I'm doing is meeting a plane. Piece of cake."

TWENTY-EIGHT

RAY REPLACED THE mike and sat watching the sedan for a moment. Why would someone care where he went and what he was up to?

He shifted into first and pulled away from the curb. A block behind him, the sedan hesitated, then casually did the same, as though the driver just happened to be traveling in the same direction.

Ray was thinking that if he could persuade Billy Bob or Lewis to give him a hand, one of them could pull in behind this guy and they could sandwich him and see what he was up to, when it dawned on him: Justin! He had forgotten all about meeting him to talk over the activities at the museum.

Ray twisted the wheel of the Blazer and made a sharp U-turn in the middle of the street. That was the good thing about this old Chevy, he thought to himself smugly. It leaked oil, drank gas, and didn't have a very good heater. But the wheel base was short and you could turn it on a dime.

He hit the pedal and raced toward the sedan. Taken by surprise, the driver simply continued along nonchalantly. Ray waved as the two vehicles passed each other, taking note of the man at the wheel. He had dark hair and was wearing sunglasses. This struck Ray as odd since the sun was shrouded by a thick layer of low clouds. He glanced at the side mirror and saw the sedan pull into the lot of a convenience store. The man parked, making a pretense of doing a little shopping.

Ray went on, convinced that he hadn't seen the last of the car. When he arrived at the ice cream place, he saw Justin sitting out front on a bench, the video camera in his lap. Ray parked and got out.

"Sorry, I'm late." He glanced at his watch, then gestured at the interior of the parlor. "Buy you a sundae?"

Justin smiled and followed him in.

"How'd it go?"

"Okay. I got it all on tape."

"Good."

Ray ordered Justin a large hot fudge.

"You wanna see it?"

"Sure," Ray said.

Justin fiddled with the buttons and then set the unit on the table in front of Ray.

Ray looked into the viewfinder but saw only static. "I don't see anything."

"It's coming."

On cue, a scene appeared: the exhibit room at the museum. The camera was aimed at the collection of rings, the lens out to its widest view. Mrs. Hucheck was standing off to one side, smiling, obviously delighted at all the attention her museum was drawing. Paul Roth was near the center of the frame, next to a short, portly gentleman who had the look of an English scholar. The two men were talking, nodding, discussing something.

"There's no sound," Ray complained.

"Sure there is." Justin produced a Walkman from his pocket and plugged the headphones into the video camera. He handed them to Ray.

"But you can sign off on the policy, right?" Ray heard Roth saying.

"I really should itemize it and put a value on every . . ." the other man tried to explain.

"You've got an inventory right there," Roth interrupted, a little testily. "What more do you need?"

The other man, whom Ray assumed was the insurance appraiser, shook his head. "At the very least, I must examine a piece from each of the various displays."

"Fine. All I'm saying is that *I* want to choose which pieces."

"That's very irregular, Mr. Roth. Standard protocol is . . ."

"I don't care about standard protocol. I care about my exhibit. That should make your company happy, right? Now if you aren't interested in insuring us . . ."

The examiner sagged a little at this threat. "It's not that we don't want your business . . ."

"You could have fooled me." They both stood their ground for a moment. "Listen," Roth finally said, "just let me pick the pieces and I can have you on your way."

"I don't know . . ."

"My chief concern is that you might not realize which piece in each section is worth the most, therefore devaluing the exhibit."

"Mr. Roth, I appraise these sorts of things for a living. It's my job. I've been doing it for over twenty years, and . . ."

Roth turned away, shaking his head, and suddenly spotted the camera. "Is that thing on?"

"I'm taping the appraisal for the Discovery Channel," Justin's voice said.

"Who gave you permission to do that?" Roth glared at the camera. "I want to see that tape before you leave."

"Yes, sir."

"In fact . . ." Roth took a step toward the camera, but stopped when the insurance man said, "I have a plane to catch, Mr. Roth. We can either do this now, or we can do it when you get to Seattle, which will mean you won't be insured for the trip."

"I took off before he could see the video," Justin told Ray proudly. The kid was hunched across the table peering past Ray, into the viewfinder. "This part's boring," he said, reaching to hit the fast-forward button.

Ray watched as the picture moved jerkily and quickly: Roth went to one of the glass cases, put on a pair of gloves, unlocked the case, carefully removed a beautiful pot with whale markings. The appraiser, also in gloves now, took the pot and went to a table that had been set up over to one side. He adjusted a lamp and put a magnifying device in one eye. After studying the artifact briefly, at least, it seemed brief in fast-forward, he returned it to Roth who put the item back into the case and locked it shut. They continued this procedure, selecting one or two pieces from each display until they reached the rings. As Roth unlocked that case, Justin hit play. Roth paused and surveyed the collection, as though unsure which to choose. He picked up one, then put it back in favor of another.

"That's Aana's," Justin said.

"The one that *looks* like Aana's," Ray corrected.

"It's hers all right."

Roth carefully turned the ring over to the appraiser who bent to examine it under the intense light of the lamp. He frowned, twisted it in his fingers, squinted through the eyepieces. Finally, he raised up, nodding, and gave it back.

Justin hit fast-forward again and the two figures went into high speed, Roth stepping from display to display and the appraiser following him, giving each selection a short, critical look. After the final piece, the appraiser took his eyepiece out and the two men shook hands.

"That's about it," Justin said, hitting stop. "I cut out right after that, before that guy could take the tape."

Ray sat staring at the darkened viewfinder. "Nice work, Justin."

"Really? I did okay?"

"You did great. You'd make one heck of a cop."

"I've been thinking about that, Uncle Ray. I just might want to do that."

Ray laughed, amused and frightened that he might be sincere. Law enforcement was not exactly an easy, safe, or lucrative field. While there was always a need for good men, Ray cringed at the thought of his nephew following in his line of work. "You just stay focused on school. And your running. You're still planning on college, aren't you?"

"Yep. I'm hoping for UW, or maybe USC. Depends on how I do at State."

"I've seen you run. You're awesome. You'll do great."

"Thanks," Justin said, obviously pleased.

"I gotta go." Ray stood up. "Hang on to the camera and the tape for me, okay?"

"Sure. But aren't we going over to the café to meet Dr. Bradshaw?"

Ray looked at his watch. It was going on 4:30. "Uh . . . you go on ahead. Fill her in on what you've got there. I've one more errand to run."

"Can I go with you?"

"No." Ray shook his head. If the someone who had killed Jean Carter had noticed their mistake in taking the wrong reel and were still after the right one, it might be dangerous. He didn't want any civilians, especially kids, anywhere near the pickup zone.

Ray walked Justin to the door and waited until the boy had disappeared around the corner before heading to his truck. He got in, started it up, and pulled into the still empty street. Festival would go on for a while longer, depending on how much stamina the dancers had. Once it came to a close, there would be a traffic jam to end all traffic jams with tourists heading for hotels, restaurants and the airport. After which time, the case might never be solved.

As he drove along, trying to decide where to stake out the air freight area, he remembered the ceremony he was slated to attend at 5:30. Chances were, he wouldn't make it. If he got the footage and it proved inflammatory, to someone or other, he would be busy tracking that person down. If it didn't prove incriminating or didn't come in, he would head back to the station and start in on the plethora of reports he would be required to fill out in order to record what had transpired since that morning. And if someone showed up to snatch the film reel, he would take up chase and certainly wouldn't risk losing them or failing to make the arrest so that he could attend some stupid award ceremony.

He glanced at his mirror but saw no trace of the white sedan. That was a relief. He chalked up the earlier sightings to an a overly active imagination.

The whole thing with the mayor was ridiculous: giving out commendations for doing one's job. Ray had done nothing heroic or noteworthy. What was Hodish thinking? That it would look good for the cameras, get more exposure for Barrow, more exposure for him. Maybe he was planning to make a run at Congress or even the Governor's office and the excessive festival, along with this put-on award deal, was his way of kicking off the campaign and getting his name out there. Maybe that was why he was involved with the Dance of the Whale exhibit as well. That way he could evidence his deep love for The People, as well as his desire to promote all things Alaskan. Politics was such a joke.

Ray pulled into the airport lot and drove around to the side where a man in a booth guarded a fenced area leading to the hangers and runways. Ray opened his window and flashed his badge from habit.

"Hey, Jack."

"Ray! What's up, man?"

"Not much. They're making you work festival, huh?"

Jack nodded glumly.

"Overtime?"

"And a half," Jack groaned. "But still . . ."

"I know. I'm on too."

"Didn't used to be this way," Jack complained. "Used to be they shut the whole place down."

"Times change."

"Not always for the better." He activated the arm and it went up in a series of jerks.

"Take it easy," Ray said as he drove through.

"You too."

Ray pulled the Blazer over next to the air freight hanger and slipped it between a UPS truck and a FedEx van. No reason to advertise his presence. He got out and looked around. All was quiet. There were no planes taxiing, no planes at the terminal gates, a row of bush planes sitting pilotless and still over to one side. Today was not a day to be out flying. At least, not if you were Inupiat.

He got out and waved at a baggage handler who was leaning against the edge of a food services truck, smoking. The man waved back, unconcerned about who Ray was and why he was traipsing around in a secure area.

Carts and vehicles were parked at odd angles inside the baggage hanger. A dozen or so boxes and haggard-looking pieces of luggage had been lined up against one wall. On the opposite wall was a small counter with a sign: air freight.

He walked to the counter and saw a button with a note: ring for service. Ray pushed the button and heard a buzzer sound in the distance. He waited a moment and pushed it again. After a third time, a man came out of a door marked "Employees Only." He was wearing coveralls and a cap that said "Barrow Bears," a defunct semi-pro basketball team. He stuffed part of a sandwich in his mouth and put on a pair of work gloves as he strode across the hanger toward Ray.

"What can I do for you?" he asked, without looking at Ray.

"I'm waiting on a reel of film."

The man stepped behind the counter and produced a 20-ounce bottle of Mountain Dew. After sipping from it, he asked, "What flight?"

"The five o'clock."

"What number is it?"

"I don't know. Is there more than one due in at five?"

The man looked up at him, his eyebrows lowered. "What freight service?"

"I'm not sure."

He sighed. "Want to tell me how you got back here in the first place?"

Ray showed him his ID.

"So it's Officer, is it?"

Ray nodded.

"Which means you're a public servant, right?"

"Yep."

The man pulled a clipboard with a tall stack of invoices from under the counter, spun them around and pushed them at Ray.

"Which means I trust you." He took another sip of his drink and started back across the hanger.

"Where are you going?" Ray asked.

"To finish my lunch. Look through the paperwork and see if you find what you're looking for. Just leave it when you're done."

The man removed his gloves and disappeared through the employee door.

Ray took the clipboard and began paging through it, not sure he would recognize the film paperwork if he saw it. Would it be addressed to the Discovery Channel? Or to Jean Carter? Or the cameraman, Jeff Adams? They had been freelance, hadn't they? Did they have a company name?

He continued through the collection of shipping documents: electronics gear, dry goods, several slips for the U.S. Postal Service, several more for UPS and

FedEx, auto parts, plumbing parts, furniture . . . as Ray paged through the stack, he wondered if there were any passengers on the plane. It looked like enough freight to fill a C-130 to the gills: clothing, pharmaceuticals, fuel, beef, cleaning products . . . of course, everything had to be flown up. Everything from toilet paper to cords of wood. The only things native to Barrow were ice, snow, dirt, and whales. And The People, who hadn't always been there. He asked himself, for the one hundredth time, what had possessed his ancestors to settle on the North Slope of Alaska.

He stopped and flipped back to the previous page to reexamine a sheet that listed "celluloid" as the contents of the package. Celluloid? As in film? It was addressed to JC Productions, Inc. *Jean Carter* Productions? His eyes drifted down to the "comments" section at the bottom. In chicken scratch that put most doctors' to shame it said something about "35mm stock." Ray also made out the word "dailies." That had to be it.

He removed the sheet, folded it, and put it into the pocket of his jacket. According to his watch, it was 4:57. It wouldn't be long now. He would meet the plane, accept the package, take it back to the hotel and look the footage over with Adams. Hopefully that would tell him something useful. Something case-breaking. If not, he would give up on it, at least for now, go home, follow the captain's initial instructions, and stay away from police work until Monday.

He walked to the tarmac. There was no sign of the plane yet. Crossing his arms, he leaned against the side of the hanger and gazed south, waiting.

ANAQAMI

(EVENING)

*With the leaving of light
and sky and day,
comes an evil darkness
that even the tuungak fear.*

GRANDFATHER ATTLA

➤➤ TWENTY-NINE ➤➤

RAY HAD BEEN standing there for nearly ten minutes when a voice behind him said, "She's running late." He turned and saw the freight manager crossing to his counter. He was smoking, adjusting his coveralls as though they no longer quite fit him.

"How late?" Ray asked.

"'Bout fifteen minutes." He picked up the clipboard. "Picked up a tailwind, or she would have been real late. Left Anchorage forty minutes behind schedule." He blew smoke. "You find what you were after?"

"Yeah. Thanks." There was still nothing to see in the southern sky. The flat, treeless earth seemed to stretch into eternity. He checked his watch impatiently.

"Too bad about the Sonics," the man said, studying the clipboard.

"Yeah," Ray grunted. He didn't follow basketball that closely, but knew that many of those who did, rooted for the Seattle Sonics. They were the closest thing to a home team.

"They've been having trouble ever since they traded Kemp way back in . . . what was it? Ninety-seven?"

Ray nodded without looking back. His eyes drifted to the parking area beyond the fence. There was the white sedan. He could see a dark shape in the driver's seat. Why the heck was this guy tailing him?

"Don't know what they were thinking when they got rid of Kemp . . ." the man continued.

Ray glanced to the left and saw a familiar Volvo parked just a few rows away from the sedan. It was occupied by two shadows: Melissa and Justin. Apparently they had grown weary of waiting at the café and come looking for him.

He sighed at their relentless desire to help and at the man in the sedan and was about to walk out there and confront all three of them, when the freight manager called, "There she is."

Ray peered south and for a long moment didn't see anything. Then the lights of the plane winked at him.

The manager put on a pair of gloves and went to a baggage train. Climbing into the lead car, he started the engine.

"Can I go out there with you?" Ray asked.

The man shook his head. "Against FCC rules. But I'll be bringing everything in here to sort and prep for the delivery guys."

Ray watched him zip out onto the tarmac, the trailing cars making a sharp curve behind him. He drove to a spot that had been marked with yellow dots and circles. After jolting to a stop, he put on a pair of ear protectors, leaned back and lit a fresh cigarette.

As the plane approached, drifting toward the ground with outstretched wheels, Ray kept an eye on the man in the sedan. Was he after the footage, too? Or was he after Ray? Maybe it was the killer from the hotel waiting for an opportunity to do the same to him. Except . . . Ray hadn't done or seen anything that might make him a threat to anyone. Had he? Unless he was getting close to something without knowing it.

The plane touched down and shot past in a whoosh of hot air and engine noise. It was a 737, not a cargo plane, and Ray could just make out the outline of faces in the windows. He wondered who would be coming to Barrow at the tail end of festival. Probably oil workers or businesspeople who weren't concerned with ceremony and tradition.

The plane slowed at the end of the runway and then performed a cumbersome turn, rolling back toward the gate. Ray stood trying to keep an eye on the airliner, the freight man, the white sedan, and Melissa's Volvo all at once, and it made him anxious.

As the plane lumbered to the gate, a man with a pair of glowing sticks appeared and waved it in. There were no other service vehicles to greet it, no fuel truck, no food services truck, just the freight man smoking in his little car. Apparently the plane would be staying overnight in Barrow.

The pilot made tiny adjustments, turning slightly, rolling forward, positioning the plane within reach of the exit arm. The engines changed pitch and began to decelerate. The man with the light sticks went to assist the freight man who was unhooking a hatch on the bottom of the fuselage. After the conveyer belt had been extended, one of them disappeared inside the hatch. A moment later the belt was running and boxes, luggage and bundles of parcels were descending from the plane.

This would take forever, Ray thought, silently willing them to hurry up. The hour of down time had sapped what little energy he had and he was now ready to call it a day. And what a day it had been.

He was relieved to see that the man in the sedan was just sitting there. So were Justin and Melissa. He didn't care if they all wanted to follow him home tonight and stake out his house. Just as long as they let him take a shower, eat dinner and go to bed.

The freight man returned with his carts full. He made a quick circle in the hanger, unhooked his train, and raced over to hook up another empty set of cars. When he got back to the plane, he and his partner continued the unloading process. No wonder it took so long to get your baggage, Ray thought, watching them. They were in no hurry and didn't seem to be putting much effort into the job. Both were smoking, both using only one hand to hoist things, whenever possible. At this rate, it would take them half the night. Good thing the plane was laying over.

He could see people walking along inside the terminal, heading for the baggage claim area and felt like telling them to take their time, maybe stop at the little fast food place and order a burger. There was no rush.

After the freight man had come back with another set of full cars and replaced it with the third and last set of empties, Ray saw another cargo vehicle rolling out to the plane. It came from the other side of the terminal and wasn't pulling any carts. The driver was wearing an Airborne Express jacket. He parked and got out to talk with the freight manager. Ray didn't know what was going on, but he had a bad feeling in his gut.

He started walking out to the plane, but before he was a quarter of the way there, the Airborne Express man took one of the boxes off the baggage cart, got back into his own vehicle, and zipped away. Ray began to run.

"Who was that?" he yelled when he was close enough to be heard over the noise of the conveyer belt.

The freight man just looked at him.

"Who was that?!"

"Airborne Express driver," he answered.

"Did he show you ID?"

"No. He showed me a claim slip."

"For what?"

"You're not supposed to be out here."

"FAA would have a cow," the man at the top of the conveyer belt said.

"What was the shipping claim for?"

"Package to JC Productions, whatever that is."

Ray swore.

"What's the matter?"

He turned and sprinted back to his Blazer. The cart driven by the Airborne Express man was already out of sight. Ray jumped in, started the truck and hit the gas. As his rear tires spun and screeched, he realized that his small audience—the man in the sedan, Melissa and Justin—must be wondering what in the world he was doing. He was wondering the same thing.

The shipping claim . . . the man who killed Carter had stolen it from her room. Why hadn't that occurred to him? And now, by simply impersonating a delivery man, he had the film.

Ray cursed again and drove faster, racing along the tarmac to the far side of the terminal. He slowed as he approached a closed gate. There! Going over the fence! The Airborne Express man. He watched as the man hopped to the far side, ran to an ATV and bounded away across the parking area.

Shifting into reverse, Ray reached for the radio. The mike came to him trailing a severed cord. "What the . . . ?" Someone had cut the line. While he was standing there waiting on the plane, someone had been sabotaging his radio. It was like he was sleepwalking through this thing, letting things happen, reacting with the speed of a zombie.

He stopped fifty yards from the gate and shifted into gear. As he accelerated toward the gate, he wondered if the department would cover the damage he was about to do to airport property. The gate exploded open on impact and the Blazer leapt through. Ray glanced in his mirror and saw the gate hanging crookedly from two bent poles.

After traversing the lot, he reached the street and hit the brakes. There was no sign of the ATV. He looked left, toward the west. There was no place to hide out there. Only a fool would head that way. To the right was town and the security of buildings and people. He turned right.

Of course, an ATV didn't have to stick to pavement or even gravel roads, he reminded himself. It could tear off across the tundra. Maybe the driver had gone west, toward Wainwright. He slowed, panning the surrounding countryside.

Out of habit, he reached for his radio again, then tossed the cut mike on the seat. Cell phone, he thought. He dug it out of his pocket, dialed and was putting it up to his ear before he realized that it was dead. Not even enough power to signal low battery. Perfect. The Airborne Express man wasn't responsible for that. It was his own fault, for forgetting to charge it.

Rolling into Barrow, he decided that it was hopeless. He would have to go by the station, organize a search, and then go out looking for the ATV, which by that time could have gone just about anywhere.

He checked his mirrors and saw that the sedan was a quarter mile back, followed closely by Melissa's Volvo. Nothing like a parade.

Parking in front of the station, he was about to get out when he saw something between the buildings: a speck of white out on the Browerville Road, beyond the festival grounds. He hurriedly got the binoculars out of the glove box and managed to catch a glimpse of a figure in white on an ATV, just before it passed behind a building.

A white parka. One of the whalers headed home from festival? Or . . .

Ray jammed the gearshift forward and pulled away from the curb in a squeal of rubber. There were plenty of ATVs in town. Almost as many of them as there were snow machines. And only a fool would drive along in the open like that after stealing something.

Still, an ATV bearing a man in a white . . . the man from the hotel? Maybe he thought that by shedding the Airborne Express jacket he would go unnoticed. It was worth looking into.

Ray raced through the empty streets and was doing nearly seventy on the Browerville Road before the doubts began to flood his mind. It had to be a member of one of the whaling crews. Surely the Airborne impostor had hidden somewhere in town, changed clothes and was either watching the daily reel or had disposed of it by now.

What was it about that film that was so damning?

Ray slowed and looked down the hillside at Browerville. Where the heck was the white parka? Had he pulled into one of the garages? This was futile, Ray decided. And he was handling it very poorly. Wait until the captain found out that he had managed to let someone pilfer the film right from under his nose. Piece of cake, my eye.

He sat idling for a moment, thinking back over his choices and wondering where things had gotten so screwed up. Whoever and whatever was turning Barrow into a killing ground was doing so quite successfully, with little in the way of resistance from Officer Ray Attla.

He turned the wheel and started to make a U-turn. That's when he saw movement on the opposite side of the road, down on the beach: the ATV. It was scooting along parallel to the road, still heading north.

Ray shifted into four-wheel-drive and went straight off the road. He turned onto the beach and began following the ATV, staying well behind it, hoping not to be spotted. It seemed to work. The ATV continued on until it reached the point. Then the driver parked next to a solitary umiak. Ray slowed and pulled into some tall grass growing next to the beach.

Hopping out, he reached into his jacket for his gun, then sighed. No radio. No gun. No phone. No backup. Maybe it was time to look for a new line of work.

Staying low, he began to scamper closer to the

umiak. The man in the parka was distracted, busy hooking the boat to a snow machine. Which meant that he was a whaler, Ray thought, creeping his way forward. Except whaling season was over. That was the purpose of Nalukataq: to celebrate the end of the season. So what was this guy up to?

The man started the snow machine and slowly began dragging the boat across the gravel toward the closest floes. An excellent way to ruin a perfectly good umiak, Ray thought. A whaler would know better. A whaler would also know better than to be out on the floes in spring when the ice was thin and could give way without warning.

Using the umiak for cover, Ray trotted after the man, not sure what he would do if he caught him. What if he was armed? Did he still have the film? Was it even the same person? What if this guy was heading out to one of the abandoned camps to retrieve something? But why take the umiak? Maybe he did know how dangerous the ice was and was dragging the boat along just in case the ice gave way and he found himself trapped in the Beaufort. Not a bad idea, really.

The man in the ATV paused when he reached the ice and carefully pulled the boat up onto it. Ray was right behind him now, thinking about either making a dash at the driver or calling out to him. Something. Why not identify himself, alert the man that he was under suspicion and demand that he stop. Because if it was the Airborne Express man, he would bolt, that was why.

Ray stood hunched behind the umiak, waiting to see what the white parka would do next.

"Hang on!"

Ray flinched at this, startled and momentarily confused. That man knew he was back there? What was going on?

Suddenly the engine of the snow machine revved and the umiak jerked forward. Ray caught hold of the side and his boots began skidding across the ice.

A sense of déjà vu swept over him. This was his dream. Or at least, part of it. Lewis wasn't around. There was no dog in the boat. But he was hanging on as a snow machine accelerated over the floes. His grip tightened as he recalled the rest of the dream: being flung from the boat, sliding helplessly over the ice, going into the water.

The snow machine raced farther and farther out onto the floes. Ray's face stung with the rooster tail of snow being thrown up by the vehicle's traction belt. His arms were shaking, the muscles threatening to cramp. Over the whine of the engine, he could hear the ice cracking around them. This was madness.

He considered letting go but knew that could be disastrous. If he didn't fulfill the dream and wind up in the water, he would still have to walk back to the beach. A long walk over uncertain ice. And if this man knew he was there, which he obviously did, what would prevent him from circling back and running Ray down with the snow machine? This was a bad situation, he decided, trying not to panic. And with every yard forward into the Arctic Ocean, it got worse.

Glancing back, he found that he could no longer see land. The jutting, white/blue peaks of the floes were a barrier between them and Barrow. It was at that moment that he realized he had been set up. The man in the white parka had wanted Ray to follow him. He had purposefully let Ray see him out on the Browerville Road. He had led Ray along and was now taking him to one of the most isolated, desolate, treacherous locales on earth. To kill him. With a bullet, an ice pick, a whaling knife, or by simply leaving him to die of hypothermia. It didn't really matter which method was employed. Any way he looked at it, Ray knew he was a dead man.

⇒ THIRTY ⇐

THE SNOW MACHINE driver kept the throttle wide open for what seemed to Ray like an hour but couldn't have been more than five or ten minutes. They were within view of the remnants of an abandoned whaling camp when the engine finally changed pitch and they began to slow. The driver slid to a stop just fifty feet from an open lead of water.

Ray clutched the umiak. If the ice gave way, he thought, he wanted to be as close to this boat as possible. Survival in these waters was measured in seconds.

The driver dismounted and crunched his way back to Ray. "Let's go," he grunted from beneath the hood of the parka.

"Where?" Ray asked, unwilling to budge.

The white parka produced a pistol.

Ray reluctantly released his grip and followed the gesture of the barrel toward the open lead. Chop was rising to lap at the edge of the ice and Ray could actually feel a slight movement under the floe.

When they arrived at the water, the film canister came flying at him. Ray caught it.

"In," the man ordered.

"You gotta be kidding."

Before Ray could object, he had been turned, shoved forward, and was falling. In the next instant: darkness and cold. A cold so penetrating that he wondered if he might already be dead. His head ached and his limbs throbbed. He couldn't feel his hands or feet. His thoughts were slow and his efforts to swim clumsy and powerless.

Somehow, he managed to break the surface. He saw the man walking back to the snow machine.

Ray went under again and in the numbing, painful black, he saw faces: Margaret, Keera, Freddie, Grandfather, Billy Bob, Lewis, Betty, the captain, his father, his mother . . . they swirled around him and he heard laughter. Not mocking but happy and lighthearted. He suddenly recalled a thousand occasions, important and trivial, that had drawn the laughter.

With memories assaulting him, he chided himself for having been so stupid. The whole thing was a setup, his cold-impaired brain told him. A setup. He had walked right into it. Just like Ronnie had. Ronnie was a drunk, a loser, not very bright. What was Ray's excuse? Was he really that ignorant? Why hadn't his training, or at least his instinct, kicked in and enabled him to see this coming? Why had he blundered into it like a fool?

He made one last attempt at treading water and came within sight of the surface. But it was too far away, a world away, lightyears away. And he was tired. So tired and so cold and he was dying so why did it matter nothing mattered except the darkness closing in closing in.

Trust the great tuungak. *You have been chosen to walk in the way of light. The way of light will lead you.*

He looked and saw a snowy owl settling on a branch directly above him. "The way of light will lead you."

"Help me!" Ray pleaded.

"Trust the great tuungak." It fluttered its great wings and lifted off, rising, rising into a sky of hard-shining stars.

Ray felt a void in himself, a loss. The owl had taken part of his heart. He wanted to go with it. "Take me with you!"

The owl circled and seemed to hover directly over him. "Not yet. Look for the light." Suddenly the owl was Aana Clearwater.

She smiled and then drifted away, into the darkness between stars and Ray was alone. He wanted to go. He wanted to follow her.

And then the light came. And Ray felt himself rising into it. The light was bright and warm and beautiful.

➤➤ THIRTY-ONE ➤➤

"GRAB HIS OTHER ARM!"

"I've got it."

"We need a blanket."

"Get him over here, away from the water."

Ray heard his teeth chattering, then saw Melissa's face. Next to her was Justin. Next to Justin was a man who looked strangely familiar.

"Ray! Ray?" Melissa was shaking him, rubbing his hands and arms. Justin had taken off Ray's boots and was rubbing his feet. He could feel none of this, was not particularly concerned with his condition, but was intent upon placing the man. It finally dawned on him: the café. The man had been sitting at the bar. And he had been the guy driving the white sedan. A surge of panic rose in his chest but he was too stiff to act on it.

"He . . ." was all Ray could manage. He couldn't point or accuse, and he couldn't warn Melissa and Justin. "He . . ." Looking down, he realized that he was still clutching the film canister in one hand.

They wrapped him in a blanket and carried him to a

makeshift tent left behind by the whalers. Ray watched, his mind oddly alert, his body oddly without feeling as they started a fire. As the flames warmed the interior of the tent and thawed out his skin and appendages, in crept the pain.

He moaned and Melissa consoled, "It's okay. That just means we got to you in time. The scary thing would be if it didn't hurt."

As Ray grit his teeth and tensed his muscles against it, she explained, "Another few seconds and you would have had permanent frostbite damage. Another minute and . . ." She shook her head.

"Thanks," Ray said. He was trembling severely.

"You have a little hypothermia, but otherwise, you're good to go."

"I . . . don't . . . feel . . . good to . . . go . . ." he stammered.

She told Justin, "See if you can find something for him to wear in one of the other tents."

Justin left and the man from the sedan asked, "How is he?"

"He'll make it."

"He followed . . . me," Ray said, glaring at the man.

"I know," Melissa said. "That's how we found you."

The man offered his hand. "Roger Luck, FBI."

Luck, Ray thought, doing his best to shake hands. What a prophetic name. "Why'd you . . . follow . . . me?"

"We knew you were getting close to them."

"Close . . . to . . . who?" Ray stuttered, pulling the blanket tightly about him.

"The Roth Foundation." Luck unscrewed a thermos and poured Ray a cup of steaming coffee.

Ray warmed his hands in the steam, then gulped some, burning his throat.

"Slow down," Luck cautioned.

"Why is the FBI . . . after Roth?"

"Insurance fraud," Luck answered.

"That's not really a Fed thing, is it?" Ray asked.

"Not usually. But in this case, yes. We believe they've been putting together these museum exhibits just to collect the insurance."

Ray sipped the coffee, slowly feeling as though he might live.

"They sponsored one down in New Mexico. A big Navajo thing. Supposedly worth six million dollars. About two weeks after the insurance forms were signed, the museum where it was showing burned to the ground. There was some evidence of arson, but nothing to pin it to Roth."

"So the Dance of the Whale exhibit is a fraud?" Ray asked.

"Maybe. We think they're about to pull the same scam. It was insured as of today. It moves to Seattle tomorrow. My guess is that something bad will happen to it between here and there."

"And it's payday for Roth," Ray said.

"Exactly. Except, it wasn't so easy this time. Things backfired on them when the insurance man showed up early."

"And they didn't have it ready," Ray thought aloud. "Some of the artifacts are fake, right?"

Luck nodded. "Others are stolen. I doubt Roth got any of the stuff legitimately."

Justin came in carrying a bundle of clothing. He

handed it to Ray: a pair of stained coveralls that stunk of fish. "It was all I could find."

Melissa left as Ray, with the help of Luck and Justin, clumsily removed his wet clothing and put on the coveralls. As he transferred his wallet and keys, he found the charm: the frowning woman.

"Aana's charm," Justin said. "Maybe that's what kept you from drowning."

"Yeah, maybe." Ray turned it over in his hand. The repair job was shabby and the charm had begun to break in two again. Ray blinked at it.

"What's the matter?"

"Nothing," he grunted. Actually, he was wondering why a killer would bother to glue a broken charm back together. To avoid bringing bad luck on himself. Except . . . if Roth killed Aana . . . he wouldn't care about an old superstition, would he? And if Ronnie had done it while sloppy drunk, he certainly wouldn't have scared up some glue to mend it. That left . . . who?

"Any warmer?" Luck asked, looking him over.

"No, but this is very chic," Ray answered, his sense of humor returning. The sleeves were too short, as were the pantlegs. He looked like a streetperson with no sense of taste. Ray put his soggy socks and boots back on and shivered.

"Let's get you back to town," Luck said.

They left the tent and Luck led Ray to a pair of snow machines. Melissa was already seated on one.

"Climb on," she encouraged.

"Where's the film?"

She patted the seat compartment.

Ray got on, threading his arms around her waist. If he hadn't been so cold, this rather intimate position would have embarrassed him. As it was, however, he didn't care if he had to ride back naked, just as long as the trip was quick and there were dry clothes and a warm bed waiting for him.

"Here." She slid out of her coat.

"That's okay. I'm fine," Ray tried to object.

"No, you're not." She draped it around him and buttoned it up. Then she gave him her mittens and helped him pull them over his hands. "Hang on."

Ray gripped her waist as they started off. Justin was driving the other machine with the FBI agent riding behind.

"What happened to the man in the parka?" Ray asked over the whine of the engine.

"He took off," she said over her shoulder.

"Was it the same man from the hotel room?"

"I don't know. I didn't see his face."

"Which one? The snow machine driver or the man who killed Jean Carter?"

"Either."

They drove along for several minutes, the wind from their movement causing Ray's cheeks to burn. He had begun to shiver again and had lost feeling in his fingers when Melissa suddenly stopped. They were in view of land, but still a ways from reaching it.

"Wha's . . . a . . . mad-er," Ray slurred through frozen lips. He was clinging to Melissa as though she were a hot water bottle.

Justin had stopped too and they were all looking off to the left, at a lead of water.

"He must have broken through," Melissa said, dismounting.

Ray followed on feet that felt like stumps. "Who?"

Then he saw the snow machine hanging off the edge of the ice, its front end and skis partially submerged.

Luck and Justin reached the lead first. "Stay back!" Justin cautioned the FBI man. "This is sikuliaq."

"It's what?" Luck wondered.

"Thin ice. Only a kinnaQ would drive on it."

Ray and Melissa came up behind them and peered into the water. But there was nothing to see.

"Got any . . . rope?" Ray asked, teeth clattering.

Melissa lifted the seat of the snow machine and found a small coil. She had just taken it out when the ice cracked loudly and the abandoned snow machine slid into the water.

"Get back!" Justin shouted.

As the snow machine disappeared, a large chunk of ice bobbed to the surface. It took Ray a moment to realize that it wasn't ice, but a slick, wet white parka. With a body attached to it.

"Make a chain," he said.

Justin laid down on the ice, ready to try and retrieve the body. "I'm in front," Ray said. When all three of them glared at him, he said, "I'm already wet." He moved in front of Justin and Melissa. Luck got in back. Each of them grasped the feet of the next. Ray reached out over the water. "A little further." The chain inched forward. "Another foot."

"Another foot and you'll be in there with him," Melissa said.

They slid forward and Ray strained to get hold of the parka. He touched it with his mitten but couldn't grip it.

"Let's leave him for a recovery crew," Luck said.

"I'm almost . . ." Ray finally snagged the hood.

.

"Reel me in!" As they did, the hood gave, pulling away from the man's head, revealing long blond hair.

They pulled the body onto the ice and a woman's face looked at up at them, eyes open, skin slightly blue.

"She was with Ronnie," Ray said.

Melissa bent over the woman. "She's got a faint pulse."

"You're kidding," Luck said.

Working to resuscitate the woman, Melissa directed Luck wrap her in his jacket.

"She killed Aana," Ray thought aloud. "And Jean Carter."

"And she almost killed you," Justin said.

The woman suddenly coughed and convulsed.

"We've got to warm her up," Melissa said.

"I . . . I . . ." the woman whispered.

"Shh," Melissa said.

Justin took his coat off and draped it over her. "Let's put her on one of the snow machines."

"We'll have to leave someone out here," Luck said.

"Leave me. I can walk in," Ray said, not entirely sure that he could.

"No. I'll walk," Luck volunteered.

"I . . . I . . . didn't . . ." the woman pleaded. She looked like a mummy found preserved in ice. "I didn't . . . kill . . ."

Melissa looked at Ray.

"I . . . didn't . . . kill . . ." She began to choke, then abruptly stopped.

Melissa felt for a pulse. Swearing, she began chest compressions. Luck began to assist her.

Ray watched, thinking that the woman's death would be a travesty, as any premature death was, but it also meant they were losing a witness. If she was telling the truth . . . if she hadn't killed anyone . . . why lie when you knew you were on your death bed? On the other hand, if she was responsible . . . they were losing not only the murderer, but the link to Roth.

Two minutes later, Melissa gave up and waved Luck off. "She's gone."

Luck cursed and Justin immediately began to recite an Inupiaq prayer. All four of them bowed their heads in reverence. When Justin finished, they stood there for a moment, staring down at the woman.

"Let's get you home," Melissa said to Ray. They went back to their machines and sped across the final span of ice.

Ray's mind raced: if the woman had seduced Ronnie in order to get Aana's ring, but hadn't killed Aana . . . could there have been three people involved? Ronnie shows up to scare her, knocks her down, then this woman arrives and takes the ring—cutting it off because . . . because why? Maybe it wouldn't come off. Ray couldn't get his own wedding band off without soap, water and a great deal of effort. Maybe when Ronnie hurt Aana, he panicked and left the knife behind. The woman showed up, found Aana already unconscious, was in a hurry to get the ring, simply cut the finger off. But then . . . what? Someone else came along? Someone superstitious. A member of The People who didn't abide leaving an Elder to suffer, who couldn't leave a charm broken for fear of angering the tuungak.

Say it had been a Native. That left several thousand suspects, a number of whom would be leaving for their villages this evening when festival ended.

When they reached the beach and had cut off the

engines, Melissa got the film canister out and gave Justin her keys. "You drive my car. I'll drive Ray's Blazer."

"I can drive," Ray complained. "Besides, he's not old enough. He doesn't have a license."

"You gonna give him a ticket, officer?" Luck asked.

Justin grinned and got into Melissa's car. They began the trip back to Barrow, Melissa in the lead, Justin moving along cautiously behind her and Luck bringing up the rear. The heater in the Blazer was roaring at full blast and Ray actually began to warm up.

Soon they could see the Nalukataq area. Ray checked his watch: 5:19. If they hurried, he could make the award ceremony. He had no intention of doing that however.

As they approached the festival grounds, Ray looked up at a flag waving in the breeze. It bore a primitive-looking whale image and, like the other flags posted around town, was intended to ward off evil spirits, which was in accordance with tradition, as well as draw in the tourists—which was *not* according to tradition.

How was it possible to be faithful to the heritage of The People and sell it down the river at the same time? he wondered. Ray blinked at the whale image as the flag went by the window. "Of course!"

"You okay?" Melissa asked.

He looked over at her. "I can't believe it took me this long."

"What?"

"I know."

"You know what?"

"I know who did it."

THIRTY-TWO

"Who?"

Ray opened his mouth to explain, but realized he couldn't. It was all circumstance and assumption. But he knew he was right.

"Stop up here at the festival grounds."

"Why?"

"I need to talk to someone."

"You need to go home. Or maybe to the ER. You could have a little frostbite and still be hypothermic."

"I've had frostbite before," he said, watching the gathering at the festival. "Hypothermia, too."

"That doesn't mean you can leave them untreated."

"This shouldn't take long."

"Here," she handed the radio mike to him. "Call for backup."

Ray pointed out to her that the cord had been cut.

"White parka did that. I think."

"Maybe she killed Aana."

"No."

"Jean Carter then. I saw her."

"No. You saw someone in a white parka." He gestured for her to pull over. "Whoever killed Aana did it out of respect."

"Respect?"

"She was unconscious, maybe bleeding from her missing finger, right?"

"Yeah, but . . ."

"It was the eve of Nalukataq, sort of like the eve of the Sabbath to the Jews. She was killed to put her out of her misery. Then her body was covered so it wouldn't be found until after festival, thereby circumventing the taboos."

"And keeping it hidden."

"That too. The frame-up of Ronnie was plan B, just in case."

"What about Jean Carter?"

"That was to get this," he said, patting the canister with his mitten. Ray popped the door open and got out stiffly. He was warmer now, but his legs were weak and his head was pounding. He shuffled across the parking area.

"You're not going to tell me who it is, are you?" Melissa said. She was like a faithful dog and just wouldn't give up or go away. Ray appreciated this. He needed the support, both physically and emotionally.

"I have to be sure."

"I thought you said you were sure."

"I'm mostly sure. Ninety percent sure. If this was *Who Wants to Be a Millionaire,* I'd take a chance and guess. But it's not, so . . ."

They waded through the throng at the blanket toss, where a child of about eight was being flung high into the air. Ray shook his head at the recklessness. They skirted the edge of the picnic area and went to the booths.

"Where are we going?" Melissa asked.

"You'll see."

Ray walked up to the Dance of the Whale booth, thankful that he didn't have to go any further. He didn't have many more steps in him today.

"Well, Officer Attla," Roth greeted pleasantly. The smile disappeared as he looked past Ray.

Ray glanced back and saw Justin and Luck coming.

"Busted," Ray said, grinning.

"I don't know what you're talking about."

Ray looked down at the attendant in the whale mask. He reached across and undid the velcro chin strap. When he removed it, long red hair spilled out. "I almost didn't recognize you."

The woman glared up at him, then twisted her head at Roth.

"What do you want, Officer?" Roth asked, no longer cordial.

"How about the truth?"

Roth just glared at him.

"We can do it here, very orderly. Or we can go downtown and I'll turn you over to my buddies, who, I should say, don't take very kindly to having a partner of theirs drowned. Or nearly drowned."

When Roth didn't say anything, Ray added, "That's attempted murder, you know."

"I demand to have my lawyer present," Roth said flatly.

"Lawyer, my eye," Luck said. "Let me have him for five minutes, Officer Attla. I'll convince him to cooperate."

"That's police brutality," Roth said, without conviction.

"I'm not with the police," Luck said in what sounded like a threat.

Roth glanced around, as though looking for a means of escape.

"You killed Aana Clearwater to get her ring, didn't you?" Ray accused.

"He did it?" Melissa said.

Ray warned her off with his eyes.

"No," Roth denied.

"And you killed Jean Carter, the Discovery Channel producer. To get her film."

"No!"

"Because it implicates you in an insurance fraud scheme."

Roth licked his lips nervously. "That's ridiculous."

"Is it?"

"You can't prove a thing."

"Wanna bet?" Ray reached into his coat and produced the film canister. He had no idea if it was even watchable now that it had been submerged in seawater or if it would implicate anyone. But it was worth a shot.

Roth glared at the canister.

Ray told the woman at the booth, "Bad news about your friend." He watched her expression change from worry to shock. "She didn't know how to tell the good ice from sikuliaq. That's why we advise taniks to stay clear of the floes."

Roth was shaking his head. "I didn't . . ."

"Let's see, two counts of murder, one count of attempted murder on a law enforcement officer . . ." Luck listed.

"One count of assault on a law enforcement officer," Ray tossed in, rubbing the back of his head.

"Numerous counts of theft, misrepresentation, fraud . . ."

Roth swore. "I didn't kill anyone."

"Then you ordered the killings, which is the same thing. You'll be in prison for the rest of your life," Luck promised.

"Or he could get death," Ray said. "The legislature is considering adding the death penalty up here," he bluffed. "If it passes, the law will be retroactive to 2000."

Luck nodded, playing along. "That would save a lot of taxpayer dollars."

"It's a waste to house violent criminals," Melissa joined in, "when you can dispose of them and be rid of the inconvenience."

"I didn't kill anyone!"

"Right . . ." Ray scoffed. He could tell that Roth was close to the breaking point. This surprised him. He had expected to have to interrogate him at the station for quite some time before he finally talked.

"I didn't kill anyone!" he repeated.

"Then who did?"

"I don't know."

"Bull," Ray grunted. He looked to Luck. "Got any cuffs on you?"

Luck pulled out a set.

"Wait until my partners get a hold of you," Ray threatened. "Especially when they find out I frostbit my toes. That'll really tick them off. Know why?"

Roth shook his head, eyes growing as Ray fiddled with the handcuffs.

"Because we hunt together a couple of times a year. We haven't missed a trip in six seasons. It's like a streak in baseball, something they want to keep alive.

But I probably won't be able to go anymore, because of my toes." Ray doubted that this would be the case. He had been frostbitten numerous times in the past and though the lasting effects were bothersome and the condition could be quite serious, he had yet to suffer so severely as to be disabled and kept from going about his usual activities. Roth, however, didn't know that. "Attempted murder on a fellow officer will put them in a foul mood," Ray continued. "But losing a hunting buddy . . ." He blew air to imply just how serious this was.

This seemed to push Roth over the top. "It wasn't supposed to happen this way."

"What wasn't?"

"We were just trying to make some money. No one was supposed to get hurt."

"Like I haven't heard that one before," Luck muttered.

Ray held up the film canister. It was dull with frost. "I guess when we have a look at this, we'll know more, huh?"

Roth cursed and sank to a chair. "It wasn't supposed to be like this. We didn't mean for anyone to get hurt."

"*We* who?" Ray asked tersely. He was growing a little impatient. Reaching across the table, he clinked one side of the cuffs onto Roth's wrist.

"Wait! I'll cooperate. But I want immunity!"

"Immunity?" Luck laughed. "You might get leniency, at best. Mr. Roth, you're looking at life in a federal pen . . ." He let the words hang. "Unless you decide to help us."

Roth glanced around in a panic. He swore again. "Okay . . ."

"You want to read him his rights?" Luck asked.

"He's your arrest," Ray said, stepping aside.

When Luck had read Roth the Miranda, he told him, "Now just sit there for a minute." The FBI agent pulled Ray aside. "You believe him, about not doing the murders?"

Ray nodded.

"Then who . . . ?"

"Let's ask Mr. Roth."

"If you won't give me immunity, you at least have to promise protection."

"You'll get it."

"I mean round the clock."

"I'm all over you," Luck assured. "I'll have you on a plane back to Seattle this evening."

This seemed to satisfy Roth.

"So who did it?" Luck asked.

After looking over at the woman, Roth begrudgingly began to talk.

➤➤ THIRTY-THREE ◀◀

IT MADE SENSE, Ray decided, listening to Roth's convoluted tale of a fraud scheme gone awry. And if Roth was actually telling the truth, which Ray sensed he was, it also emphasized the importance of carefully choosing your partners. Especially partners in crime.

When Roth had finished, Luck turned to Ray. "What do you think?"

"I think it fits."

Luck turned back to Roth. "Will you testify to that effect?"

"Depends on how much *leniency* you're talking about."

"I can't make a deal without consulting with the federal prosecutor."

Roth shrugged. He seemed to have recovered a little of his confidence and was ready to negotiate again.

"If you ordered the blonde to get rid of me . . ." Ray said.

"Like I told you, I had nothing to do with that. I didn't even know about it. The girls were hired to help us obtain additional artifacts."

"Via prostitution and physical violence?"

"No money exchanged hands," the woman said. "And I didn't hurt a soul."

"They were his idea," Roth complained. "He hired them from some outfit in L.A. So was the whole fiasco with the old lady . . ."

"My aunt . . ." Ray emphasized, glaring.

"Right. And the TV lady. And that business with you . . . all his idea."

"You had nothing to do with it?" Ray asked, skeptically. "You didn't even know what was going on?"

"No. I swear. All I was after was the insurance money. And when the examiner showed up today . . ." Roth cursed. "He nearly blew the whole deal."

"Newsflash," Ray said. "It is now officially blown."

Luck stepped around and finished cuffing Roth's arms behind his back. Then he cuffed the woman.

Melissa looked at Ray. "What now?"

"I guess we do what we have to do."

"It could get ugly."

"It already is ugly."

There was a pause in the relentless drumbeat. A moment later the crowd cheered and the entire mass of people began to drift toward the north end of the grounds, where a podium had been erected beneath a large banner that read: "Happy Nalukataq!"

"You need backup for these two?" Ray asked.

"I got 'em," Luck growled. "What about you?"

Ray scanned the street for Lewis or Billy Bob but didn't see either of them. "I'd appreciate it if you would call my station and have them send over a car."

"Okay." Luck began leading the two suspects through the crowd by their cuffs. A ripple of murmurs broke out at the sight and the sea of bodies parted before them.

"What if Roth's wrong?" Melissa asked. "Or what if he's lying?"

"What if he's not?"

There was a high-pitched whistle of a PA system being switched on and then a cheer went up. Ray looked to the podium and saw Mayor Hodish waving at the festival-goers.

"Come on." He began leading Melissa in that direction.

There was a thumping sound as the mayor tested the microphone, then he shouted, "Happy Nalukataq!" The onlookers returned the greeting with enthusiasm. The mayor stood there, grinning, pleased with the attention and waiting for the noise to die down. "It is my privilege to report that this year's festival has broken all records of attendance . . ." He paused, signaling that it was time to applaud. When the clapping fell off, he said, "And profits." More applause. "This is the first year that we have made money on the festival." The crowd was a little less appreciative of this.

"He commercialized a tradition of The People," Ray complained to Melissa. "Not exactly something to be proud of."

As they stood watching, Hodish blathered on about several other "firsts" that had occurred since he had been elected to office, taking credit for anything and everything that could possibly be construed as a positive development.

When he finally wound down and was reveling in the accolades of the attendees, Hodish switched gears. "At this point, I had planned to honor one of our fine law enforcement officers for his courage in the line of duty, however, I understand that he is unable to be with us today . . ." Suddenly Hodish spotted Ray and for a long moment the incurable windbag was speechless with shock.

Ray smiled at him.

"Uh . . . uh . . . well . . . uh . . . there he is, after all . . . Officer Attla . . . Officer Ray Attla." He put a false smile on and began to clap. The crowd mimicked him, turning to look at Ray.

"Come on up," the mayor said without much energy.

Ray looked at Melissa, then in back of him, hoping to see Lewis or Billy Bob inbound. Hands began to push him forward, several people shouted "Way to go Ray!" and he found himself approaching the podium.

Ray mounted the steps and nodded politely, quieted the crowd with a hand.

"Officer . . . uh . . . Attla . . ." Hodish stuttered, "is responsible for solving a particularly . . . uh . . . serious crime this morning."

The people grew quiet.

"It was his skill as a law officer that brought a swift arrest of the perpetrator."

Ray reached over and snatched the microphone from the mayor. "Thank you, Mayor Hodish," he said. "Unfortunately, that's not quite accurate. The truth is, I arrested the wrong man this morning." There was a collective gasp. "In fact, I've spent all day trying to make amends for that by finding the guilty party. And at long last, I am ready to put the matter to rest by saying . . ." He reached over and, with a smile, patted Hodish on the shoulder. "Mr. Mayor . . ." He paused, relishing the pained expression on the man's face. "You're under arrest."

The mayor tried to make light of it. "What a comedian!" he shouted. His eyes were pleading with Ray. "Not here," he whispered out of the side of his mouth.

Ray looked out and saw the cameras. There were four or five professional video crews, along with a host of hand-held consumer models, all trained at the podium. He traced the microphone cord with his eyes and saw that it snaked its way to a mixer board from which a half dozen more lines went into the crowd. The TV crews were picking up every word of this.

The mayor laughed boisterously again, fat cheeks flapping. A few members of the crowd joined him, but not many.

"Okay, I'll play along," Hodish said, smiling too much. "Under arrest for what?"

"Let's see . . . two counts of murder in the first degree, one count of assault, one count of attempted murder, not to mention insurance fraud . . ."

Hodish chuckled again, but no one chuckled with him. The eyes of the crowd simply stared. Snatching the microphone back, he stammered, "That's very funny, officer. Now . . . tell them you're joking. Please . . ."

Ray signaled for him to come closer, and as Hodish leaned in, he whispered, "You have the right to remain silent. If you give up the right to remain silent, anything you say can and will be used against you in a court of law . . ."

NUTAAQ QUAMMAQ
(NEW LIGHT)

*Death is a fluttering
of snowy wings,
a never-ending journey
toward the great, Almighty Kila;
keeper of all joy and light.*

GRANDFATHER ATTLA

➤➤ THIRTY-FOUR ◄◄

THE BEAT OF the drums was slow and abiding, the wail of the dancers rising and falling on the wind. The Elders sat in a long line at the front, facing the people. Above them the colorful "Happy Nalukataq" banner flapped and twisted in the wind.

When the music finally ceased, an old man rose stiffly and shuffled to the podium. "Da whale been good to us," he said in a thin, quiet voice.

"Yes!" "Aarigaa!" "AgviQ!" the crowd returned.

"I not know of better time to go to qilak dan Nalukataq. It sign dat tuungak pleased."

The crowd agreed again.

As the old man went on, switching back and forth from English to Inupiaq, Margaret whispered to Ray, "He's doing fine."

"I knew he would," Ray replied confidently. In actuality, he'd had his doubts. When Grandfather had been asked to give Aana's eulogy, Ray had expected him to turn it down. His voice wasn't much more than a whisper nowadays, and he had trouble standing for longer than a few minutes at a time. And then there was the forgetfulness. What if he blanked out in the middle of it? But the old man had agreed and was up there speaking without notes, without any written preparation whatsoever, giving an impassioned speech that honored both Aana and The People. Ray was very proud of him.

"What's he saying?" Melissa asked. She was on his right side, Margaret on his left and, as far as he knew, there were no negative feelings between the two women. Margaret trusted Ray and seemed comfortable with him having to work closely with a female professional. And while Ray found Melissa attractive, he had come to see her not as a potential threat to his marriage, but a friend and a trusted colleague.

"Uh . . . he's saying that Aana was wise and was a light bearer of The People."

Melissa nodded.

"A *torch* bearer," Margaret corrected.

"Same difference."

"Shh!" someone in back of them demanded.

When Grandfather wound down fifteen minutes later, the crowd stood and applauded, paying tribute to Grandfather, the Elders, and, most of all Hillary Clearwater.

The drums began again and the dancers leapt to their feet. It was a celebration of life, Ray decided, not a commemoration of death. The crowd converged on the dancers and a group of old women went to the picnic area and began to set food out on the tables.

"Is it over, Daddy?" Keera asked, pulling on Ray's arm.

"Sort of honey, the formal part. But they'll dance until dark." Ray looked down at Keera's face and saw in it an innocence that he could hardly identify with. This was her first funeral.

"Da-s!" Freddie suddenly shrieked. He began to clap and sway.

"Where did Aana go, Daddy?" Keera wondered. It was the third time she had asked this and Ray was growing a little weary of trying to explain. Apparently the last two attempts had failed.

"Aana is in Netsiliks," Margaret tried.

"Where's that?" Keera asked.

"Yeah," Melissa said. "Where *is* that?"

Margaret briefly described the Inupiat view of the afterlife: the idea that spirits lived on, some returning to earth, others going either to an intermediate netherworld reserved for skilled hunters and women with beautiful tatoos, or to the Land of the Crest-fallen where lazy men and untattooed women ate only butterflies. After appending her own, newly adopted Christian beliefs, she asked Keera, "Do you understand?"

Keera wrinkled up her nose. "So where is she?"

"In heaven, honey."

"Oh." Keera thought for a moment. "Then she can't sign my cast, can she?"

"No."

"Let's get some food," Ray suggested.

They were making their way to the line at the picnic area when someone hailed Ray.

"Looks like you're being paged," Melissa said, pointing at a huddle of men.

Ray groaned. "I'll catch up with you in a minute."

"You're off duty today, Ray," Margaret emphasized. "This is your aunt's funeral."

"I know." He walked over to the huddle and greeted the captain, Billy Bob, Lewis, and Brinkley.

"It was a nice ceremony," the captain said gravely. "Your grandfather's speech was . . . just right."

"Cept I could hardly make out a word," Billy Bob said. "Sounded perty, though."

"*Per-tee?*" Lewis said, making a face. "What's per-tee?"

Brinkley laughed.

"I wanted to express my condolences," the captain said.

"We're real sorry, Ray."

"Yeah," Brinkley grunted.

"You aana was fine la-dee."

"Thanks," Ray said.

"I also wanted to let you know," the captain continued, "we got a confession out of the mayor."

"He tell us da whole story," Lewis said.

"You were right on the money, Ray," Billy Bob said. "They set up old Ronnie."

" 'Member da woman who freezed, da popsicle lady?" Lewis asked. "She took da ring and da finger and frame Ronnie."

"Who sent her?" Ray asked.

"Da mayor says it was Roth," Lewis said with a grin. "Roth say it da mayor."

"But it was the mayor who came along behind and cleaned it up," the captain explained, "killed her and put the body in the shed. He said it was out of respect for Aana."

"Yeah, right," Ray grunted sarcastically. "And let me guess, he glued her charm together as a tribute."

"Naw," Billy Bob said, taking him seriously. "He

done that 'cause he was afraid of drawin' the bad luck of the tun-gek."

"Toon-guk," Ray corrected.

"That's what I said."

"The murder of the film producer was the mayor's idea. Part of the clean up," the captain continued.

"What was on that film reel that was so important?" Ray asked.

"Nuthin'," Billy Bob said. "But he was afraid it caught him and old Roth talkin' over what they was gonna do to fool the insurance man."

"The insurance examiner showed up early, by a week," the captain explained. "He was supposed to do the policy in Seattle. So when he came here, they had to improvise in order to fill a few of the holes they had in the exhibit. The way Roth tells it, three-quarters of the pieces are fake. The others are . . ."

"Stolen," Ray guessed. Thus far, his gut instinct and his assumptions had proven to be true. "And he ordered the woman to kill me, because . . . ?" He still hadn't figured out that part.

"You were a threat," the captain said. "The mayor thought that by taking you off the case and promising you a shiny medal, you'd be satisfied and leave it alone."

"He don't know you like we do," Billy Bob said, thumping Ray on the back.

"You lika lead sled dog," Lewis said.

"How's that?" Ray asked, a little embarrassed.

"You run and run, neva stop even to make yellow snow."

Brinkley found this hilarious.

"I'll just assume that was a compliment," Ray muttered.

" 'Course it was," Billy Bob said.

"We'll let you get back to your family," the captain said. "And Attla . . ." His voice suddenly recaptured its usual, slightly harsh, professional tone. "I don't want to see you in the office until next week."

"But sir, what about the reports . . . ?"

"Did I stutter?" he asked Billy Bob.

"No, sir. I don't believe that you did."

"Was I unclear?" he asked Lewis.

"You clear, sir."

"Brinkley, you have a problem hearing me?"

"No, sir."

"Captain," Ray whined, "what am I supposed to do for a week?"

"Take a vacation. Go to Anchorage. Sleep in. Repaint your house. Catch up on your reading. I don't care what you do, just do something other than police work. Got that?"

"Yes, sir."

Lewis whispered, "I got time coming. How 'bout we go hunt ugruk?"

Ray ignored him. "Thanks, captain."

"Good job, Attla. And I mean that."

He nodded, slightly embarrassed by this. The captain seldom doled out praise and when he did, it was the genuine article. As he returned to the picnic area, Ray decided that it was a true privilege to be given paid leave and he needed to make the most of it. The down time would allow him to rest, recharge, maybe even get back on track in terms of his emotional health. It might be just what the doctor ordered.

Margaret, the children, and Melissa were already inching along the food tables, loading their paper plates. Not wanting to cut in, Ray got in line behind a group of young men. They were dressed for dancing and had apparently just finished as they were huffing and puffing. It took him a moment to notice that Justin was among them. Next to him was a cute teenage girl—the infamous Julie he was always talking about, Ray assumed.

Justin blushed a little as he introduced his girlfriend.

"It's nice to finally meet you, Julie," Ray said.

"You, too," she said, smiling as a blush colored her cheeks.

"So you caught him," Justin said.

"Yeah. We caught him."

Justin shook his head sadly. "I can't believe it. Why would a leader do that?"

"I don't know," Ray said. "I guess power can make you kind of crazy sometimes."

"Make rill cra-zee."

Ray turned and saw Grandfather behind him.

"Nice job on the eulogy," Ray said.

"Uh?"

"Your talk," Ray said. "It was very good."

"Ah . . . tanku. But it not hard to talk 'bout some-body like Aana Clearwater. She good woman. I miss her."

"Me too," Justin said.

"We all will," Ray agreed.

"But she not gone," Grandfather said. "She just move her place. Go somewhere else. Jur-nee to better somewhere."

Ray and Justin both nodded.

"See!" Grandfather said. He pointed at the sea with a trembling finger. "Der she go."

Ray gazed out at the floes and saw exactly what he

expected to see: ice and a scattering of deep blue leads. He looked back at Grandfather. The old man truly was losing it, he decided. They would probably have to put him into a nursing home soon.

"She wait for dancing, then go," Grandfather said happily.

Ray sighed and smiled. "She always liked dancing," he humored.

"It *is* her," Justin said, his eyes wide, his arms drawing Julie closer to him.

Ray squinted at the floes again and was about to question the boy's sanity when he saw it: a snowy owl circling far out over the ice. It hovered, made a gliding turn, then dove for the sea.

Grandfather muttered a string of Inupiaq that, roughly translated, meant: "Farewell beloved. Go with the spirit of the whale."

"Yes," Justin said. "And may the tuungak carry you to the land of joy and light."

Ray waited, expecting to see the owl rise again. But the bird was gone. It had disappeared into the floes.

BIBLIOGRAPHY

Barrow, Alaska: "A True Story." Video. Touch Alaska: Barrow, AK, 1995.

Hess, Bill. "Gifts from the Whales." *Native Peoples*, October 1998, pp. 26–32.

Kidder, Lyn. *Barrow, Alaska, from A to Z!* Bonaparte Books: Anchorage, AK, 1995.

Langdon, Steve J. *The Native People of Alaska*. Greatland Graphics: Anchorage, AK, 1993.

McLean, Edna Ahgeak. *Abridged Inupiaq and English Dictionary*. Alaska Native Language Center, University of Alaska Press: Fairbanks, Alaska, 1995.

People of Snow and Ice. Time–Life Books: Alexandria, VA, 1994.

Rexford, Delbert. "Nalukataq! Sharing the Bowhead Whale." *The Open Lead*, August 1986, pp. 28–36.

Smelcer, John E. *The Raven and the Totem: Traditional Alaska Native Myths and Tales*. Salmon Run Books: Anchorage, AK, 1992.